A CLUE FOR THE PUZZLE LADY

BANTAM BOOKS

New York   Toronto

London   Sydney

Auckland

A CLUE FOR THE PUZZLE LADY

Parnell Hall

A CLUE FOR THE PUZZLE LADY
A Bantam Book / November 1999

BOOK DESIGN BY GLEN M. EDELSTEIN

Library of Congress Cataloging-in-Publication Data

Hall, Parnell.
A clue for the puzzle lady / Parnell Hall.
p.   cm.
ISBN 0-553-80096-5
I. Title.
PS3558.A37327   C68   1999
813′.54—dc21
99-38012
CIP

Published simultaneously in the United States and Canada

Bantam Books are published by Bantam Books, a division of Random House, Inc. Its
trademark, consisting of the words "Bantam Books" and the portrayal of a rooster,
is Registered in U.S. Patent and Trademark Office and in other countries. Marca
Registrada. Bantam Books, 1540 Broadway, New York, New York 10036.

PRINTED IN THE UNITED STATES OF AMERICA

BVG   10 9 8 7 6 5 4 3 2

For Stanley,
who loved a good puzzle.

A Puzzle from the Puzzle Lady

I am pleased to be able to include the following crossword puzzle, compliments of the Puzzle Lady. Miss Felton and I hope you enjoy it.

A word of caution: Since solving the puzzle will identify the killer, you should not do so until after reading the book. You would probably not be able to anyway, as several of the clues are based on a knowledge of the story.

The answers may be found in the back of the book.

A CLUE FOR THE PUZZLE LADY

by Miss Cora Felton

ACROSS

1 Sonny, or lead singer of rock group mentioned on CRUCIVERB-L
5 Minimal lot size on Cold Springs Road
9 Operated
12 Sherry to Cora
13 Ed Sullivan's really big ones?
15 Lounge or pony
16 Crime scene
18 Surprise attack
19 Open on the victim
20 A long time
21 A-frames, for instance
23 Deer
24 Very French
25 The 60s, e.g.
28 Foamy wave
32 Foe
33 Cereal
34 Soft drink
35 Early man
36 Fork end
37 Motel rental
38 Finish last
39 Skating locale
40 _____ off (repel)
41 Probable action of Barbara Burnside's car
43 Pined for or played college prank
44 Skin rash or small dwelling
45 John Dickson
46 Ebert milieu
49 Single
50 Expire
53 Type of code
54 Graveyard Killer
57 What this book should be
58 Keen
59 Put up
60 Type of training
61 Shade of color
62 Night light

DOWN

1 What Aaron wouldn't dare call Sherry
2 All right
3 Shoes worn by murder victim
4 Number of shots fired
5 Not at sea
6 Intone
7 Guns the engine
8 Answer to 14) A
9 Surface left by Kevin Roth
10 "I cannot tell _____"
11 Gets sleepy
14 Entrapping
15 Chief Harper's antagonist
17 Prepared
22 Wager
23 Murder weapon part
24 What Oscar winners seem obliged to do
25 What Billy Spires undoubtedly offered
26 Bestow
27 Stop
28 What Johnnie done to Frankie
29 Schwarzenegger role
30 Not dead
31 Narrow on one end, wide on the other
33 Salt water
36 None of your business
40 Lesions
42 Vigor's cohort
43 Fertilizer
45 Songwriter Leonard
46 Give a damn
47 Rages
48 Way to drink whiskey
49 Child's building set
50 Hamlet, for one
51 "Do not go gentle _____ that good night"
52 Garden for 35 across
55 Tipped to show respect
56 Forbid

© Parnell Hall 1997

A completed crossword puzzle grid (13 columns wide), filled in by hand:

1 B	2 O	3 N	4 O	■	5 A	6 C	7 R	8 E	■	■	9 R	10 A	11 N
12 A	K	I	N	■	13 S	H	E	W	14 S	■	15 P	O	L	O
16 B	A	K	E	17 R	H	A	V	E	N	■	18 R	A	I	D
19 E	Y	E	■	20 E	O	N	S	■	21 A	22 B	O	D	E	S
■	■	23 H	A	R	T	■	24 T	R	E	S	■			
25 D	26 E	27 C	A	D	E	■	28 W	H	I	T	E	C	A	29 P
32 E	N	E	M	Y	■	33 B	R	A	N	■	34 C	O	L	A
35 A	D	A	M	■	36 P	R	O	N	G	■	37 U	N	I	T
38 L	O	S	E	■	39 R	I	N	K	■	40 S	T	A	V	E
41 S	W	E	R	42 V	I	N	G	■	43 M	O	O	N	E	D
■	■	44 H	I	V	E	■	45 C	A	R	R	■			
46 C	47 I	48 N	E	M	A	■	49 L	O	N	E	■	50 D	51 I	52 E
53 A	R	E	A	■	54 T	55 H	E	H	U	S	56 B	A	N	D
57 R	E	A	D	■	58 E	A	G	E	R	■	59 A	N	T	E
60 E	S	T	■	■	61 T	O	N	E	■	62 N	E	O	N	

A CLUE FOR THE PUZZLE LADY

1

THE FIRST CLUE CAME WITH A CORPSE.

The body lay next to a gravestone in the Bakerhaven Cemetery.

Police Chief Dale Harper stood in the pouring rain and looked down at it with displeasure. What was a corpse doing in the cemetery? Chief Harper was not unaware of the humor in the question. A body in the cemetery—the press would have a field day. Chief Harper frowned and wiped the water off his face.

The body was that of a young girl in her late teens or early twenties. She was lying facedown with her head twisted to the side. Her left eye was open. Chief Harper wished he could close it. It was eight in the morning, he had barely had his coffee, and the sight of her made him queasy. What in the world was she doing there?

And why was she in the cemetery? If she'd only been on the other side of the fence, not a hundred yards away, she'd have been in the township of Clarksonville, and he wouldn't have gotten the call that dragged him away from the breakfast table before his toast had even popped, on a rainy Monday morning the last day in May.

But, no, this corpse fell under his jurisdiction. The good citizens of Bakerhaven would expect him, as chief of police, to do something about it. It was up to him to find out who killed her and why. At the moment, he didn't even know who she was.

"Never seen her before," the caretaker said.

It was the fourth or fifth time he'd said so. A shriveled little man with a somewhat belligerent nature, Fred Lloyd had found the body when he'd arrived for work this morning. He'd driven in the gate, and his headlights had picked up the girl's silhouette. He'd called the police station, the cop on duty had called the chief, and now Lloyd and Harper were standing together in the cemetery in a drenching rain.

"So you said." Chief Harper knew he should interview Mr. Lloyd, but at the moment he couldn't think of a thing to ask him. The guy had found the body, he'd never seen the girl before, and what else was there?

Chief Harper wasn't entirely up on procedure because murders just didn't *happen* in Bakerhaven, Connecticut. Waterbury or Danbury, sure, those were big cities, they had their share of crime. Bakerhaven was one of those small, quiet, respectable towns where nothing much happened. There had not been a murder in Bakerhaven in the year and a half that Dale Harper had been chief. So he was not entirely sure what to do.

One thing he knew was he couldn't touch the body until the medical examiner got there. The ambulance he'd called for had arrived, and the paramedics had confirmed what he already knew, that the girl was dead. But they couldn't take her away until the medical examiner saw her, and Barney Nathan, the notorious stick-in-the-mud who served that function, was undoubtedly taking his own sweet time finishing up *his* breakfast before venturing out on a morning like this to stand in the cemetery in the rain. The paramedics had gone back to the shelter of their ambulance. Chief Harper hunched his orange slicker up over his neck, wished he were somewhere else.

The phone bleeped.

Chief Harper reached under his slicker, fished out the cellular phone, flipped it open, said, "Hello?"

"Dale?"

Chief Harper sighed. His wife. "Yes, dear."

"You ran out on breakfast. Is everything all right?"

"I can't talk now. I'm out in the rain."

"Clara's upset. She doesn't want to go to school."

"I can't deal with that now."

"What shall I tell her?"

"Tell her to go to school."

"Dale."

"Ellen. I'm in the cemetery. A young girl is dead."

"Oh, my God. Who?"

"It's no one we know. I can't talk now. Tell Clara if she doesn't go to school she'll miss all the gossip. The phone's getting wet. I gotta go."

A car drove through the cemetery gate, stopped behind the police car. An umbrella popped out from the driver's door, mushroomed open. The trim figure of Barney Nathan emerged. Despite the early hour and the rain, Dr. Nathan was nattily dressed in a blue suit, white shirt, and red bow tie. He would have looked more in place on the dais of a medical convention than at the scene of a homicide.

If this was a homicide.

Dr. Nathan stepped carefully through the streams of water up to the two men. "What do we have here?"

"You tell me," Chief Harper said.

"You mean you haven't touched it yet?"

"Just to make sure she's dead. Aside from that, we've all been waiting for you."

If Dr. Nathan took that as a pointed remark, he didn't acknowledge it. He went over to the grave, bent down beside the body. Examined it with one hand, while holding the umbrella with the other. After a few moments he straightened up.

"Okay. Let's get her out of here."

"So what do you think?"

Dr. Nathan's smile was superior. "Much too soon to tell. I'll have to do a postmortem."

"Any idea when she died?"

"That's what I'll be trying to determine. Okay, that's all I need here. They can take her away."

"In other words, I can touch the body," Chief Harper said.

"With all due care. I still have to determine the cause of death."

"Yes, of course. I'd also like to know who she is."

Chief Harper rolled the body over.

The girl was wearing a cotton pullover and blue jeans. No shoes or socks. Harper felt in the hip pockets, looking for an ID, but they were empty. The right front pocket had some cash. Eight dollars in bills and some change. He put it back.

The left front pocket appeared empty, but proved to contain a folded piece of paper. Chief Harper slid it out in his cupped hand, and looked up to see Barney Nathan standing there watching him.

Which irritated him. Granted, Chief Harper had never liked the man, but it was more than that. Chief Harper had waited for the doctor, held everyone off, shown him the proper respect for his office. In return, Dr. Nathan had not given him the time of day, and was now looking over his shoulder, poking his nose into police business, as if insinuating he didn't trust him to do his job.

This particularly grated since Chief Harper wasn't all that confident about doing his job in the first place.

Which is why, instead of opening the paper, Chief Harper palmed it and casually slid it into his pants pocket as he straightened up.

"Okay, you can take her," he said.

"You find anything?" Dr. Nathan said.

"She's got no ID on her."

"That should make it more difficult." Dr. Nathan gestured to the two medics in the ambulance to bundle up the body.

"Where they taking her? The hospital?"

"No. My office. I have one of the rooms set up for autopsies."

"Uh huh," Chief Harper said. As he watched Barney Nathan walk off, he couldn't help wondering how much the good doctor charged the town for the service.

With the umbrella gone, Chief Harper was getting soaked. He gave way for the paramedics, nodded to the caretaker, and plodded through the mud over to his police cruiser. He hopped in the front seat, started the car, turned the heater up. He snuffled, found a tissue, blew his nose. It occurred to him it would be just his luck to catch a cold.

Dr. Nathan had already driven off. Watching him go, Chief Harper reached in his pocket, and pulled out the piece of paper he'd taken from the pocket of the girl.

He knew it was probably nothing. And he was not entirely sure why he had concealed it from the doctor. With low expectations, he unfolded the paper.

It was an ordinary piece of lined notebook paper.

Chief Harper looked at it and blinked.

On it was written in ballpoint pen:

4) D — LINE (5).

Chief Harper shook his head. Just his luck. A dead body in the graveyard wasn't enough. He had to get an enigmatic clue.

Chief Harper sighed, wondered what it meant.

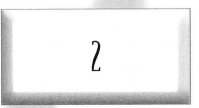

2

AFTER THE AMBULANCE LEFT, CHIEF HARPER TOOK A CRIME SCENE RIB-
bon out of the trunk of his police car and went back and cordoned off
the grave. He considered it a futile gesture and felt stupid doing it; still
it had to be done.

Chief Harper had no stakes on which to hang the ribbon, so he
wrapped it around the gravestones. It encircled nine of them, eight on
the perimeter, and one inside, the one where the girl had lain, the one
that was just a mud puddle now.

When he was done he got in his car and drove back to town.

Bakerhaven, Connecticut, was one of those small towns you could
drive right through and never see a store. Not that they weren't there,
they simply weren't conspicuous. Discreet, hand-painted signs were all
that distinguished the shops from the private homes. Of course, most of
the shops *were* private homes, with the proprietors living upstairs.

The stores on Main Street also tended to be of the more genteel
variety, such as the pharmacy and the bake shop. Anything as blatantly
commercial as the laundromat or the pizza parlor was carefully tucked
away down one of the side streets, and gas stations and supermarkets
were banished to the outskirts of town.

The houses looked remarkably similar. On the three blocks of Main
Street that were considered *downtown,* most were white with black

shutters, though some were white with green shutters, and one was actually pale yellow.

Many of the stores were antique shops, enough so that the sign *Antiquers Crossing* would have adorned a crosswalk, had it not been narrowly voted down by the selectmen.

The police station was white with black shutters, and not only could have passed for an antique shop, it had, in fact, once been one. Jackson Dooley, an elderly antiquer who had outlived his family and died without heirs, had left the building to the town with the provision that it be used by the police. Jackson Dooley felt beholden to the Bakerhaven police for coming to his aid at the time of a burglary. This was somewhat magnanimous on his part, for cracking the case had not been hard. Mr. Dooley, who happened to know the burglar, had been able to tell the police the thief's address. It had remained for them to drive out to the man's house and arrest him.

Chief Harper pulled up in front of the police station, which was located just across from the library and down the street from Cushman's Bake Shop. Judging from the number of cars parked outside, Cushman's was doing a brisk business in spite of the rain, and in spite of the fact that the proprietor, Mary Cushman, couldn't bake a lick—it was common knowledge her pastries were trucked in every morning from New York City.

Chief Harper was tempted to stop in for a muffin—after all, he'd missed breakfast. But people would want to know why he was there. That was the trouble with living in a small town. Everyone knew he ate breakfast at home. Not that that was big news, but he was the police chief, and everyone knew what he did. If he showed up at the bake shop, people would want to know why. And he didn't want to tell them.

Chief Harper killed the motor. He got out of the car, dashed up the two steps to the police station, and pushed open the door.

Dan Finley was at his desk. The young, eager officer who'd called him away from breakfast sprang up when he came in. "Did you see her? Is it true?"

Chief Harper hung his wet slicker on a hook and wiped his forehead on his sleeve. "Yeah, it's true. A young girl's dead. Barney Nathan's cutting her up now."

"Who is it?"

"I don't know. That's the first order of business. Grab a camera, get over to the doc's, get a picture. Then get copies made. We'll have to circulate 'em. Try to get an ID."

"She didn't have one?"

"None at all."

"Anything give us a hint? Like a letter sweater? Some indication where she went to school?"

"No."

Chief Harper grabbed a hand towel from the bathroom, dried his hair.

"What does the doc say?"

"Says she's dead. Acts like he's doing us a favor just telling us that much."

"And that's it?"

"That's it. She looked to me like she might have been hit over the head, but then I'm not a doctor."

"Any chance it was accidental?"

"Not much. If it was an accident, what was she doing there? And where were her shoes?"

"Shoes?"

"The girl was barefoot. She was wearing jeans and shirt, but no shoes or socks. Who's going to go running around a cemetery at night with no shoes or socks?"

"Any witnesses?"

Chief Harper shook his head. "We'll have to canvass for them. Not that I expect much. You call Sam?"

"He's on his way. Or at least he will be. I woke him up."

"Good. We're gonna need him."

"We got anything to go on? Anything at all?"

Chief Harper frowned. "Actually, yes. But it doesn't help."

"What's that?"

"Glad you reminded me." Chief Harper reached in his pants pocket and pulled out the folded paper. Luckily, it was still relatively dry.

"What's that?" Dan Finley said.

"This was in her pocket. Aside from a little cash, it was the only thing on her. I was hoping for a lead. Instead I get this."

Dan Finley unfolded the paper. Read, *"Four d line five?"*

"Yeah. Great, huh?"

"What do you think it means?"

"I have no idea."

"Oh, yeah?" Dan Finley said. "Well, you know what it looks like to me?"

"What's that?"

Dan Finley's eyes were shining. He had freckles and sandy hair, and when his eyes lit up, it enhanced his boyish quality. "It looks like a crossword puzzle clue."

Chief Harper frowned. "How do you get that?"

"Easy. Four d stands for four down. That's the number of the clue."

"The number of the clue?"

"Don't you do crossword puzzles? That's how clues are numbered. Four down. Twelve across. Twenty-eight down. The number and the direction."

"So what's line five?"

"I don't know. Either four down intersects with line five, or the clue *is* line five."

"How could the clue be line five?"

"I don't know. Why don't you ask the woman on TV?"

"What?"

"You know. The woman in the ad. 'A good breakfast cereal is no puzzle. Take it from the Puzzle Lady.' You must have seen the ad."

"I've seen it. So?"

"She's here in town. Didn't you know that?"

"Oh, I suppose," Chief Harper said. He vaguely recalled his wife or daughter saying something to that effect.

"Yeah, well that's what I heard. Mickey Hempsted's wife, Sarah, saw her at the Country Kitchen playing bridge. You can't miss that face. Anyway, she'd be the one to ask."

"What's her name?"

"I don't know, but it will be in the paper."

"Huh?"

"She's got a column in the morning paper. Crossword puzzle column. Every day." Dan gestured to the newspaper on his desk. "Want me to look it up?"

"No, I want you to get over to the doc's, get to work on that ID. We're not going to get anywhere till we know who she was."

"Right. Now where did I see that camera . . ."

Dan rummaged through the drawers of his desk, came up with a Polaroid camera.

"I better check the battery and the film. Smile, Chief."

Before Chief Harper could protest, Dan raised the camera and the flash went off in his face.

"Seems to be working," Dan said. He pulled the picture from the camera, tossed it on his desk. "In about a minute you'll have yourself a nice picture. I'll go shoot the girl."

"Don't get the camera wet," Chief Harper said, but Dan had grabbed his slicker and was already out the door.

Chief Harper finished drying himself, and returned the towel to the bathroom. Hanging it on the rack, he happened to glance in the mirror. He frowned. The man looking back at him wasn't young, but he wasn't old either. The curly brown hair was not that gray, not that thin. Of course it always looked darker when it was wet. And, it occurred to him, he was old enough to notice that it was darker.

He looked at himself and sighed. Was this the face of a man about to embark on his first murder case? Yes, he told himself. It was a broad, solid, rugged face. At least he looked competent.

Chief Harper came out of the bathroom. The Polaroid picture Dan Finley had taken was lying on his desk. Harper sat at Dan's desk, picked up the picture and pulled off the negative.

So much for competent. His eyes were wide, his mouth was open, his head was tilted to one side, and his hand was up as if to ward off a blow.

He looked like a buffoon.

Yeah, that was more like it.

Chief Harper tossed the photo down on the desk, leaned back in the chair, and rubbed his head.

The phone rang. He scooped it up. "Bakerhaven police. Harper here."

"Dale. What's this about a murder?"

Chief Harper groaned. Henry Firth had heard about it already. The county prosecutor had opposed his hiring, had even gone before the selectmen to lobby against him.

Henry Firth would be eager to see him fail.

"A girl was found dead in the cemetery. So far that's all we know."

"What are you doing about it?"

"We're investigating it."

"I'm aware of that. *How* are you investigating it?"

"Barney's doing an autopsy now. We'll know more when we get the results. Right now we're trying to ID her and canvass for witnesses."

"That's not enough."

"I beg your pardon?"

"This is serious, Dale. This is a *murder*. It has to be solved."

"No kidding."

"I'll be right over. See what you've got."

"I won't be here. I'm going out."

"Out? Where?"

"To investigate a murder," Chief Harper replied, and hung up the phone.

Chief Harper put his head in his hands. He inhaled, exhaled twice. He felt as if the world were closing in on him. Okay, he had to go out. Investigate a murder. Go do something. Anything was better than dealing with Henry Firth.

His eyes lit on the newspaper. He picked it up and flipped through, looking for the crossword column.

It wasn't hard to find in a paper the size of the *Bakerhaven Gazette*. In less than a minute Chief Harper was looking at what was unmistakably the column of the woman he'd seen on TV.

The column was headlined: THE PUZZLE LADY. Underneath, was a picture of a rather robust, elderly woman, with curly white hair, steel-rimmed spectacles, twinkling eyes, rosy cheeks, and a smile that was just a little bit enigmatic and a little bit smug.

Under the picture was the name *Miss Cora Felton*.

The puzzle was your standard crossword puzzle. If Chief Harper had counted, he would have found it to be a fifteen-by-fifteen square. He merely registered the fact it was exactly what he had expected.

Except for the theme.

The puzzle was entitled *Lost Her Knitting*. In addition to the puzzle, there was a short anecdote that preceded it. The anecdote was about a woman who had lost her knitting. Chief Harper read it, failed to see the point.

Oh well, at least he had the woman's name.

He sighed, reached for the phone.

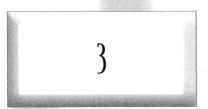

3

Before the phone rang, Sherry Carter was actually in a pretty good mood. She sat at the kitchen table, sipping her coffee and reading the crossword puzzle, and feeling quite content.

The move to Connecticut had worked out well. Sherry and her aunt had been able to find a modest but comfortable house at a rent that they could afford, living together wasn't all that bad, and they hadn't been there long enough to start going stir-crazy yet. In fact, they were only half unpacked, and were still living out of boxes. But Sherry didn't mind. Setting up her computer and modem had been enough to keep her happy.

She had also gotten a job. Sherry had answered an ad in the local paper for a substitute nursery school teacher. She had no experience, but it was a private school so no teaching certificate was required. And the kids loved her. When she went for the interview, the children wouldn't leave her alone. The woman who ran the school had hired her on the spot. So far she'd substituted twice, with great success.

Of course it wasn't steady work, but Sherry already had a job. She was working at it, when the phone rang.

Sherry Carter was proofreading the Puzzle Lady column before faxing it off to the 256 newspapers that carried it nationwide. It was a job she'd done for nearly two years, ever since the very first column.

At the moment, Sherry Carter was checking one of the four long clues. There were two horizontal and two vertical, all of them ten letters each. Sherry was checking 16 across. The answer was *sweepstake*. The clue was *TV month opposite give*. The *TV month* was *sweeps* month and *opposite give* was *take*.

It was, all things considered, a relatively easy clue. But then the Puzzle Lady's puzzles had not become widely popular by being difficult to solve. The puzzles were comfortably accessible enough to be enjoyed by the masses, while just challenging enough to be fun. *TV month opposite give* would do nicely. Though, it occurred to her, the Puzzle Lady would get letters from purists pointing out that sweepstakes should be plural.

Sherry Carter smiled. She leaned back in her chair, took a sip of coffee, felt at peace with the world.

The phone rang.

Sherry reached for it eagerly, hoping it was the nursery school asking her to come in. It was a little late for them to be calling, but there was still a chance.

"Hello?"

But there was no one there. Just the crackling open line. A moment later there was a click and then she got a dial tone.

Sherry hung up the phone and her smile faded.

The same thing had happened the night before. If it happened again she'd have to report it. Sherry wondered how long it would take to get repair service in a small town like this.

If it *was* a malfunction.

If it wasn't Dennis.

Sherry shuddered, instinctively rubbed her sore ribs, courtesy of her abusive ex-husband's last little visit. He'd ambushed her outside her apartment, been waiting behind a parked car. She'd known at once she was in trouble. His long, blond hair was matted and snarled, his leather jacket was torn, and there was a red welt on his chin. The typical pattern, par for the course. Having lost a fight at the pub, Dennis would redeem his manhood by winning one at home. But for once she got lucky. A passerby had called the police and a patrol car had gotten there before he could do much damage.

The bruises were almost gone.

It couldn't be him.

Could it?

Sherry told herself, no, rationally there was no way Dennis could know that she was here. The house and phone were not in her name; even if he knew what town she was in—which he didn't—there was no way he could get the number. It was a glitch in the phone line, plain and simple, happened all the time, and whoever it was would just call back.

She no sooner had that thought when the phone rang again. Only it didn't reassure her. Quite the opposite. What if it was Dennis?

That was a frightening enough prospect that Sherry was tempted to let the answering machine pick up. She told herself she was being silly, reached for the phone. In spite of herself, she expected to hear his voice.

But it wasn't for her.

"Cora Felton?"

Sherry heaved a sigh of relief. She hoped it wasn't audible over the phone. "Who's calling, please?"

"Is this the Puzzle Lady?"

"This is Sherry Carter. I'm Cora Felton's niece. May I help you?"

"No, I need to speak to her. Is she there?"

"I'm afraid she's sleeping, can I take a message?"

"Sleeping?"

"She works late. Can I take a message?"

"No, I'll come out. You live at 385 Cold Springs Road?"

"I beg your pardon?"

"Wake her up. I'll be right there."

"You most certainly will not. Leave us alone, or I'll call the police."

"I *am* the police."

"What?"

"Sorry. I should have made that clear. I'm Dale Harper, I'm the Bakerhaven chief of police. I need to speak to Miss Felton. It's a police matter. I'll be right over. Please wake her up."

Sherry Carter hung up the phone in mounting dread. The police? Cora was wanted by the police? What in the world had that woman done now?

Sherry rushed to the front window, looked out. The sky was dark and the rain was falling, but she could see the driveway clearly. The car was there, and, while it was parked across the driveway at something of an angle, it did not appear to be scratched. Her worst fears were groundless. So what was this all about?

Sherry hurried to the back hall. Pushed open the door on the right.

And there she was, sleeping soundly, the trademark enigmatic smile on her face, just as if nothing had happened.

Sherry grabbed her arm, shook her. "Aunt Cora!"

Cora Felton stirred, groaned, rolled over on her side, opened a bleary red eye. The odor of stale gin wafted up from the bed.

"Wake up, damn it!" Sherry said. "We've got trouble."

4

"Ow! Too hot!"

"Hold still."

"You're burning me."

"Aunt Cora."

"What's this thing on my head?"

"Leave that on."

"What is it?"

"A shower cap. Your hair has to be dry."

"Why?"

"Hold still."

In desperation Sherry Carter was trying to wake Cora Felton up by holding her under the shower. It was only half working. Cora was conscious but barely coherent. She was also rather heavy, and Sherry was having a hard time holding her up.

"Stop squirming."

"I'm not squirming."

"You're not helping. Aunt Cora, what did you do last night?"

"Do?"

"Yes, what did you do?"

"Didn't do anything."

"Then why do the police want you?"

"The police?"

"Yes. Why do the police want you?"

"Can't remember."

"You can't remember why the police want you?"

"No. Can you?"

"Aunt Cora—"

"Oh, that's too cold!"

"Aunt Cora. Did you have a run-in with the police last night?"

Cora sagged against Sherry's arm. "You know, someone was just asking me that."

"I was."

"Oh."

"Aunt Cora. Snap out of it. Think. What did you do last night?"

Cora Felton scowled. Cocked her head. Water ran down her cheek, cascaded off her chin. She took no notice. "Played some cards. Had some drinks. Met a man."

"What man?"

"Nice man. Reminded me of Frank. My third husband. Nice man, but married." Cora Felton nodded in agreement with herself. "So was Frank."

"Aunt Cora. Did anything happen with this man?"

"Nosy, nosy, nosy," Cora muttered. "Ow! Too hot!"

"Aunt Cora."

"Turn the water down. I'll talk, I'll talk. What do you want to know?"

"What happened with this man?"

"Probably nothing. Can't remember. Can I get out now?"

"Aunt Cora, listen to me. A policeman is coming. You have to pull yourself together."

The front doorbell chimed.

"Oh, my God. He's here."

"Who's here?" Cora Felton lost her balance and slumped against the side of the shower stall. She clung to the soap dish, blinked up at Sherry through the water, smiled and said, "Oops."

For a moment Sherry was tempted to simply give up and let the policeman have her. It was just for a moment, and yet she felt a pang of guilt. Sherry could never do that to her aunt, no matter how exasperating she was. For all her faults—and there were certainly many—Cora was a kind, warmhearted woman, and Sherry really loved her. Cora had always looked out for Sherry when she needed her most, like when her marriage had broken up, and Sherry would always look out for her.

Even when it wasn't easy.

"Aunt Cora, listen. A policeman's here. And he's looking for you. So here's what you do. You sit there, you keep your mouth shut, you listen to what he has to say. I'll do the talking. You just keep from falling off your chair."

Sherry turned off the water, yanked Cora out of the shower, grabbed a towel.

5

CHIEF HARPER STOOD IN THE BREEZEWAY DRIPPING WET AND WONDERED why they were taking so long to answer the bell. A red Toyota had been parked askew blocking the driveway, and he had been forced to pull in behind it and then sprint across the lawn to the kitchen door.

Which no one seemed to want to answer. There was of course a front door, but it was exposed to the rain, on the one hand, and not nearly as convenient, on the other. Chief Harper doubted if they actually used it. Still, it occurred to him maybe he should try that door. Instead, he pushed the kitchen bell again. He could hear it ring inside the house. So they had to know he was there, they were just making him wait. He shuffled his feet impatiently, looked around.

Three eighty-five Cold Springs Road was one of the prefabs built in the mid-50s, before the selectmen legislated against such structures. Other existing ordinances prohibited them from being built close together, required at least a one-acre lot. So the house, though modest, had no near neighbors. There was woods to either side, a meadow across the road. A wide front lawn. It probably looked nice when it wasn't raining.

Where *were* they?

After what seemed like forever, the door was opened by an attractive young woman with short, curly dark hair. She wore a yellow pullover, blue jeans, and running shoes. To Chief Harper she looked like a college student, though he realized she must be older. Or maybe he was just getting older.

"Sorry about that," the young woman said. "You're the police chief?"

"That's right," he said. "Chief Harper."

"I'm Sherry Carter. Miss Felton's niece. We spoke on the phone. Please come in."

Chief Harper did, found himself in a small anteway leading to the kitchen. He stood on the welcome mat, shuffled his muddy feet.

The young woman was all crisp efficiency. "Why don't you just take them off? Let me take your raincoat. Here's a towel."

Chief Harper surrendered his slicker, slipped off his shoes, dried himself on the towel. He followed the young woman through a well-stocked country kitchen with a central butcher block table, and a sparely furnished modern living room piled with boxes.

"You must forgive me, the place is a mess. But then we weren't expecting company," the young woman said.

She led him through a door into a small study.

Cora Felton sat in an overstuffed chair, a blanket pulled up under her chin. Poking out from beneath it was the top of her dressing gown. There was a box of tissues on the table next to her, and her eyes were red. Otherwise, she looked exactly like the woman who smiled out of the newspaper every morning.

"Miss Felton?" he said.

She winced slightly at the sound, then raised her eyes and smiled.

The young woman hovered over her solicitously, patted her shoulders. "Please do sit down," she told him, indicating a chair. "You'll forgive my aunt if she doesn't get up, but she has a cold. And what can we do for you?"

Chief Harper sat. "I'm Dale Harper," he said, somewhat apologetically. "The chief of police. I'm investigating a crime. I was hoping you could assist me with my inquiries."

Cora Felton blinked at him. If she'd understood him, he wouldn't have known it.

"I beg your pardon?" the young woman said.

"I'm sorry. I'd better explain. A girl was found murdered early this morning."

"Murdered?"

"Yes. In the cemetery. Next to one of the gravestones. The caretaker drove in this morning, and there she was."

"Who was she?"

Chief Harper frowned. He'd wanted to get the Puzzle Lady's reactions. He wondered if there was any tactful way to talk to her alone. "For the moment, we don't know," he said. "She's young, late teens, early twenties. Blonde, thin, attractive, appears to have been hit on the head. That's all we know at the present time."

"You want us to look at a picture?" the young woman asked. He recalled her name was Sherry something.

"I don't have a picture."

"Then why are you here?"

"I'm here, actually, to talk to the Puzzle Lady," he said rather pointedly. "As I told you on the phone. Miss Felton, I'm sorry to bother you, but I need your expert opinion."

Cora Felton looked at him. Her blue eyes were wide. It struck him as an owlish look. "Opinion?"

"Yes."

She blinked, seemed to give him her full concentration. "Opinion of what?"

"A clue."

"Clue?" she said.

She raised her hands from the arms of the chair, lurched sideways slightly, and caught herself. Her robe gaped open, and for a second he had the disconcerting impression she wasn't wearing anything under it.

"Yes, a clue. Found on the body."

She blinked again. "Body."

She seemed so confused, Chief Harper felt bad about overwhelming her with a murder. But he had a job to do. "See for yourself," he said. He reached in his shirt pocket, pulled out the slip of paper, and passed it over.

She unfolded it, pushed the glasses down on her nose, held it at arm's length, and squinted. *"Four d line five?"* she said.

"Yes. What do you make of that?"

She pushed the glasses back up and frowned. "Let me see, let me see, now. *Four d line five.*"

"You think *four d* means *four down?*" the younger woman said.

Chief Harper scowled at the interruption. "It might," he said. "If that was the case, Miss Felton, would that suggest anything to you?"

"I don't know." She cocked her head, furrowed her brow, seemed to consider. "Did you count four graves down from where she was lying?"

The younger woman stirred, opened her mouth, closed it again. Chief Harper noted her impatience, was relieved she hadn't interrupted again.

"That's a thought," he said. "I can't say that I did. What about *line five?*"

"Yes. *Line five.* That certainly is confusing."

"Let me see that," the young woman named Sherry said. She practically grabbed the paper out of the older woman's hand. "Oh. Five in *parentheses.* Of course."

"Why of course?" Chief Harper asked.

"Because it made no sense the other way. *Line five?*" She smiled apologetically. "I'm sorry. I proofread all the columns before they go out. So I'm used to recognizing crossword puzzle clues. *Line five* is not a standard crossword puzzle clue. On the other hand, what's written here, *line (5),* makes perfect sense. The five in parentheses would indicate the answer has five letters."

Chief Harper turned back to Miss Felton. "Is that right?"

"Yes, of course. Sherry is quite accurate when it comes to such matters."

"Tell me, is that why you're here," Sherry said, "because you figure this is a clue from a crossword puzzle?"

"That's certainly how it appears," Chief Harper answered. "If you take it all together, *four d line five.* If the five stands for five letters, that would make it look like a crossword clue, now wouldn't it?"

"I suppose," Cora Felton said.

"If you already know that, why are you here?" Sherry asked.

"No puzzle there," Chief Harper said. "I want you to solve it."

"Solve it?"

"Yes. What's the answer? What does it mean?"

Cora Felton opened her mouth, cocked her head. Her whole body seemed to follow, listed slowly to the left.

Her niece jumped in. She put her hands on Cora Felton's shoulders, seemed to push her upright. "I don't think you understand," she told Chief Harper. "There's a huge difference between creating puzzles and solving them."

"I would think if you were adept at that sort of thing . . ."

"Yes, of course. But this isn't a puzzle, it's a fragment. You know how you solve a crossword puzzle, Chief? With interlocking clues. Think of the word. *Crossword.* The words cross. They have common letters. That's how you can tell if your answer is right."

She pointed to the paper. "In this case, the clue is *line,* the answer is five letters. You know how many meanings there are of *line?* It's a noun, it's a verb. The line in the sand. A line of poetry. You line a drawer or a playing field. A dresser drawer you line with paper. A soccer field you line with lime. There's a line in front of a movie theater, a line in the middle of a highway. A clothesline, a line an actor says in a play, What's my line? There's dozens more. Any of which could yield an answer to that particular clue. The only way you could narrow it down would be if you had another word going across to check if the letters fit. To expect my aunt to solve this on the basis of one clue is totally unfair."

Chief Harper frowned. "All right, look. Let's not get off on the wrong foot here. No one's quoting anybody, no one's running to the media. You're not going to see headlines like PUZZLE LADY FINDS CLUE, or if that's what you're afraid of, CLUE STUMPS PUZZLE LADY. I'm here in the hope of getting any advice that will point me in the right direction. So, can you give me anything at all?"

Cora Felton considered. For a moment, Chief Harper had the impression she'd thought of something. But all she said was, "I'll have to work on it. Leave your number and I'll give you a call."

"Nothing immediately suggests itself to you?"

"Something suggests itself to me," Sherry put in. "This is not fun and games, Chief Harper. You're dealing with a killer here. I don't want you putting my aunt in danger."

"That was not my intention."

"Maybe not. But you've appealed to her for help, in the hope she might solve the crime. The killer might get that idea also."

"Not from me. I assure you, Miss Felton, I won't even mention you."

Cora Felton waved this off. "Oh, I'm sure we'll be safe. It's just having so little to go on. You will call us if you learn anything more?"

"But you will work on it?"

"Yes, of course. Was there anything else?"

"No, that's it," Chief Harper said. "Thanks for your time."

He left feeling vaguely unhappy about the whole visit. What was it about those two women? Whatever it was, Chief Harper couldn't shake the feeling he'd been had.

6

"Is he gone?"

"Yes."

"Thank God. I'm dying for a smoke."

"Aunt Cora."

"Relax. You said he's gone." Cora Felton fumbled a pack of cigarettes up from under her blanket, extracted one, lit it with her lighter. Took a deep drag. "Ah, that's better. What a headache."

"Yes," Sherry said, "what a headache. And all because of that damn TV ad."

"That TV ad pays for this house."

"You never should have done it."

"How could I turn it down?"

"You think that cop's here because of the newspaper column? No. That cop wouldn't do a crossword puzzle if his life depended on it. He's here because he saw you on TV."

"I need a Bloody Mary."

"Aunt Cora."

Cora Felton pushed the blanket to the floor, struggled to her feet. Her dressing gown fell open. She felt the draft and looked down. "Why am I naked?"

"You took a shower."

"I did?"

"Yes."

"Why?"

"It seemed a good idea at the time."

"If you say so," Cora said. "Well, time for brunch."

Cora plodded into the kitchen, dropping cigarette ash behind her. Jerked open a cabinet drawer, took out a bottle of vodka. Set it on the butcher block. Took out a glass, opened the freezer, dropped ice cubes in. Winced at the sound. "Ice cubes are *so* loud."

She opened the refrigerator, took out tomato juice, and mixed a Bloody Mary without the benefit of a shot glass. The vodka estimate was generous. She added Worcestershire, Tabasco sauce, and celery salt, stirred it around.

She took a huge sip, lowered the glass. "Ah, that's better," she said, and smiled a huge smile. She looked just like she did in the pictures, except with a red mustache.

And the fact her robe was hanging open.

"Must you?" Sherry said. "If that cop comes back—"

"We'll offer him a Bloody Mary. Though he probably doesn't drink on duty." Cora noticed her dressing gown and tried to tie it up, but couldn't holding the Bloody Mary. She had the belt in one hand, the drink in the other. She frowned at them as if they were a logic problem of annoying complexity.

Sherry solved it for her by taking the glass. Cora cinched up the robe, retrieved the drink, took a huge sip, and exhaled happily. She seemed to be getting her second wind. "Sherry, this is exciting."

"Aunt Cora."

"An actual murder. And we're in on it. I wish I felt better. If I'd known, I would have come home early."

"Really?"

"Sherry, we have to figure the clue."

"You've gotta be kidding."

"Don't be silly. This is a murder. A girl is dead. We have an obligation."

"*We* have an obligation?"

"Exactly. If it really is a crossword clue, then we have to solve it. Not that it necessarily is. I kind of like the four-graves-down idea."

"Aunt Cora."

"You pooh-pooh it just because it's mine. And line five? That fits right in. What if it's four graves down in the fifth row of graves?"

"Don't be silly."

"Why is that silly?"

"The five was in parentheses."

"So?"

"And if that's the answer, we're not needed," Sherry pointed out. "The police can solve that perfectly fine by themselves."

"True, true, you're undoubtedly right. So the clue is a line with five letters. If that's four down, we're going to need to see something else across. Which means we need to find another clue. Maybe we should go to the cemetery."

"Aunt Cora."

Cora Felton put up her hand. "Not now, not now. But if you say we can't work on this clue without help, then we need help."

Her cigarette defied the laws of gravity. Sherry picked up an ashtray, held it out, just as the ashes tumbled to the floor.

"Aunt Cora, try to understand something. The TV ad was a mistake. We're living with the mistake. There's nothing we can do about it, we have to make the best of it. But this. This is an absolute disaster. You start trying to solve a murder, and you know where your picture is going to wind up? On the cover of the *National Enquirer*. And the headline isn't going to be PUZZLE LADY SOLVES MURDER, it's going to be PUZZLE LADY EXPOSED. And that's only if we're lucky enough not to get PUZZLE LUSH or PUZZLE SLUT."

"Thanks a lot."

"And what's gonna happen then? How many papers do you think are gonna stand beside us? The Puzzle Lady image is wholesome. That's the sell. You tarnish that, you got nothing. They'll never forgive you. For destroying the image. It's as bad as Minnie cheating on Mickey Mouse."

"She did that?"

"You get the point?"

"Yes, I do. You're a stick-in-the-mud, you want me to butt out of a murder. Whaddya think your chances are?"

Sherry tried another tack. "All right. It's not just that. There's something else. I've been getting hang-ups."

"Hang-ups?"

"Yes. This morning and again last night. The telephone rings, I pick it up, the line's open but there's no one there."

"What do you mean, no one's there?"

"I say *hello* and no one answers. There's just the sound of the open line on the other end. Then I hear the phone hang up and I get a dial tone."

"Do you hear breathing?"

"I don't know."

"You don't know if you hear breathing?"

"Aunt Cora."

"Sherry, it's nothing. Phones do that all the time."

"Yeah. But I can't help thinking."

"What?"

"What if it's Dennis?"

Cora Felton shook her head. "Sherry, Sherry, Sherry. That's so stupid. How could Dennis know that we're here?"

Sherry pointed at her, nodded her head. "There, you see? That's the whole thing. Rationally, I know that he couldn't, that it's all in my head. You're in the newspapers and you're on TV, but it's nationwide, there's no way to know where you are. But now this. Murder in Baker-haven. It's local, it's specific. You get your name mentioned in connection with this, it's like telling Dennis we're here."

Cora Felton frowned, looked at her. "You're really upset about this, aren't you?"

"Can you blame me?"

"Of course not."

"So you see, we can't afford to help."

Cora Felton's eyes widened. "Oh, no, no. We can't afford not to."

"What?"

"Sherry. That cop is cooperating. As long as we help him, he'll help us. He said he wasn't gonna mention us."

"But someone else might. Particularly if they play up the puzzle angle."

"So tell him not to."

"Huh?"

"Tell him to withhold it." Cora took a big slug of Bloody Mary. "That's what the police do anyway, isn't it? Withhold an important fact only the killer would know. To weed out all the cranks confessing to the crime. Get him to withhold the puzzle clue, no one will get a lead to us. No one will even know we were there."

"Unless they see us tromping around the crime scene," Sherry pointed out. "You're not really going to do that."

"Sherry, darling." She patted her on the cheek. "I grew up on Agatha Christie. I spent my whole life reading murder mysteries. Let me tell you something. Crossword puzzles are nothing. This is the real thing. If you think I'm going to miss it, you must be crazy."

Cora Felton tossed back the last of the Bloody Mary. "Now then. Let's roll up our sleeves, put our heads together, and come up with some five-letter words for *line*."

7

CHIEF HARPER KEPT HIS KEYS OUT AS HE SPRINTED UP THE FRONT STEPS of the police station. He'd locked the station when he'd gone to see the Puzzle Lady, and he didn't feel like standing in the rain fumbling for his keys. But the door was already unlocked. He pushed it open and went inside to find Sam Brogan manning the desk. A cranky little man, with a thin black mustache and gleaming bald head, Sam pointed his finger and announced, "I hope you understand I'm on time and a half."

"It's a murder, Sam. We all gotta pitch in."

"And we all gotta be paid. I worked last night until one in the morning. I wasn't due back till five."

"It's a murder case. Didn't Dan fill you in?"

"Oh, sure. On the phone he says, Get in here, there's been a murder. When I ask him, he doesn't have time to talk, he'll fill me in when I get here. When I get here, he's gone. There's no one here. That's a fine way to run a police station, no one there."

"So, what's happening?"

"Henry Firth dropped by. You just missed him."

"What'd he want?"

"Wanted to know where you were."

"What'd you tell him?"

"Told him how should I know? Didn't seem to please him none.

Then he wanted to know all about this murder, and what could I tell him when I don't know a thing."

"I suppose you made that clear to him?"

"Absolutely. He got nothing out of me. For all I told him, we know absolutely nothing."

"Thanks for your support," Chief Harper said dryly.

The front door banged open and Dan came in, shaking the water off his orange slicker. "Oh, good, Sam's here. I got a picture of the girl, they're making copies now, we should be able to get an ID."

"What about the autopsy? How's that coming?"

"Slow," Dan said. He hung his raincoat on a hook. "You know the doc. Taking his own sweet time. Acted like I was really putting him out wanting to take a picture. Like I was holding him up, so if the autopsy wasn't done, it was all my fault."

"Yeah, I'm sure," Chief Harper said. "He give you any indication when he might be done?"

"None at all. If you want to call and ask, he'll tell you never if you don't stop interrupting him."

"Great."

The phone rang.

"Maybe that's him now."

"Yeah, complaining about me," Dan said. He set the camera on his desk, flopped down in the chair.

Sam scooped up the phone. "Bakerhaven police, Officer Brogan speaking." He listened, said, "Yeah, just a minute. Chief. Some woman for you."

Chief Harper took the phone. "Yeah. This is Chief Harper."

"Hi. This is Sherry Carter. Miss Felton's niece."

"Oh. Yes. Hello," Chief Harper said. "Have you got something?"

"In a way. You have to understand, this is just preliminary . . ."

"Yes, of course."

"Well, if we're right in our assumption, that four down is a five-letter word for *line,* then a likely solution would be *queue.*"

"I beg your pardon?"

"The word *queue. Q-u-e-u-e.* A British expression for a line of people. For instance, the line waiting to go into a theater. It's used as a noun and also as a verb. To queue up for something."

"You say it's British?"

"That's right."

"Not American?"

"I didn't say that. It's an English word, it's an American word. It's in use in both countries. But it's in *common* usage in England. In America it's rather rare."

"Are you sure?"

"You ever hear people talking about queuing up for tickets at Yankee Stadium?"

"Not that I recall. That's certainly interesting, Miss Carter. By any chance, did you get anything else?"

"Spiel."

"I beg your pardon?"

"As in handing you a *line*. The guy talks a good *line*. A salesman's *line*. A salesman's *line* can be a *spiel*. It's also what he's selling. His *line* of merchandise. In which case, *line* equals *goods*. Which happens to have five letters."

"That doesn't sound very promising."

"Of course not. Like I told you, there's nothing to go on. Until you narrow it down, there's too many choices. For instance, if it's a line of poetry, *line* could equal *verse*. Or if you were lining a drawer in a dresser, line could equal *cover*. Because you're covering the bottom of the drawer. See what I mean?"

"That doesn't help."

"No kidding. We need more information. Have you identified the dead girl?"

"Not yet. We're working on it. Not that it's likely to help."

"Anything would help. Right now we're totally in the dark. Anyway, we were thinking, maybe you could play down the crossword puzzle angle."

"Why?"

"For one thing, to weed out cranks. We need more clues. When we get them, it would be nice to know they came from the killer, and not some nut who read about it in the paper and thinks it's fun."

"Makes sense. I'm not sure it's possible, but I'll think about it. In the meantime, anything comes up, I'll let you know."

Chief Harper hung up the phone and stood up.

"What was that all about?" Sam Brogan wanted to know.

"She solve the clue?" Dan said.

"In a manner of speaking. She had several solutions. Her favorite is *queue.*"

"*Q?*"

Chief Harper filled Sam Brogan in, and went over Sherry Carter's explanation of the word.

"British," Sam said. "Would that mean the killer is an Englishman?"

"That would certainly narrow the field," Chief Harper said. "But it doesn't seem likely. And it's only one solution. Others were *verse, cover,* and *spiel.*"

"How do you get that?" Sam Brogan said.

"That's not important, because none of them are apt to be right. Most likely the whole thing's a waste of time. Sam, do me a favor. Hustle down to the photo shop, see if you can hurry 'em along. I need that ID picture."

Sam Brogan went out into the rain as Aaron Grant came in. The young reporter for the *Bakerhaven Gazette* had obviously gotten wind of the story. He spotted Dale Harper and Dan Finley, stopped, smiled, and spread his arms. "Well, well, well. The gang's all here. And Sam Brogan just went out. That's pretty much the entire Bakerhaven police force all in one spot. Tell me, what's the occasion?"

"You must know, or you wouldn't be here," Chief Harper said.

Aaron Grant snapped his big black umbrella closed, and shook it out. It had kept his slacks and sports shirt miraculously dry. "The rumor's out Dr. Nathan's got a live one." He pretended to wince. "Ouch, bad choice of words. My editor would take that right out. I mean a *dead* one. You know what I mean?"

"Who told you that?"

"Well, actually, the good doctor did, by slamming the door in my face. He might as well have hung up a sign, I'VE GOT A DEAD BODY. If Nathan's not going to comment, I wondered if you would."

"That doesn't answer my question," Chief Harper said. "What sent you running over to the doc's on a rainy morning like this?"

"Now you're asking me to name my sources, Chief?"

"Are you saying you were tipped off?"

"If I wasn't, why am I here?"

"That's what I'm asking you."

"Why ask if you already know?"

"I wasn't asking *if,* I was asking *who.*"

"That gets back to the sources issue."

"Is this sparring necessary?"

"You tell me."

Chief Harper frowned. Aaron Grant wasn't more than two years out of college. Harper had seen him grow up, found it hard not to think of him as a boy. "Well now," he said, "you're going to get it anyway, you might as well get it right. A girl was found early this morning in the cemetery. Dead. No identification on her. Barney Nathan's trying to determine how she was killed and when. So far that's all we know."

"Uh huh. And where's Sam Brogan going in such an all-fired hurry?"

"To check on the pictures."

Aaron Grant's eyes lit up. "You got pictures?"

"Just a photo for the ID. You'll get one."

"Now?"

"As soon as they're done. Sam went to check."

"Can I tell him you said to give me one?"

"Sure thing."

Aaron's eyes flicked to the door, then back. "You got anything else? Any other facts for me?"

"That's all I know. We got a dead girl. I could describe her, but you're gonna get the picture."

"Yeah, right."

Aaron Grant snatched up his umbrella, went out the door.

"Little twerp," Dan Finley said. "Why'd you give him a picture?"

"It got him out of here," Chief Harper said. "We've got enough problems without dealing with the press."

"That's for sure."

The phone rang.

Dan Finley scooped it up. "Bakerhaven police, Officer Finley speaking." He listened, covered the mouthpiece, cocked his head. "It's the TV people."

Chief Harper grimaced.

"Great."

8

CHIEF HARPER WASN'T GOOD ON CAMERA. NOT THAT HE'D HAD MUCH practice. In his short term as police chief he'd only been interviewed once, that time the young Pruett boy got caught in a well. He'd mumbled his way through that one, awkward, nervous, and uncomfortable, even though it was only the one local station. This time it was a half a dozen news crews, huddled under umbrellas on the police station front steps, shouting questions at him, sticking microphones in his face, and expecting to hear words of wisdom.

Chief Harper fiddled with his damp collar, cleared his throat. Became aware that rain was falling on his head. "All I can tell you is that early this morning a young girl was found dead in the Bakerhaven Cemetery. She has not yet been identified, and the cause of death has not yet been determined, but we are treating it as a potential homicide."

On the word *homicide,* a small but unmistakable stream of water ran down his forehead into his left eye, and a graphic identified him as POLICE CHIEF DALE HARPER.

On the TV screen, the picture cut to a newsman with a microphone standing in front of the police station where Chief Harper had stood. A graphic identified him as RICK REED, CHANNEL 8 NEWS.

"And there you have it," he said. The young man had a sardonic, mocking tone. "In the quiet, peaceful, respectable town of Bakerhaven, a shocking, brutal crime. The police have no information as to who the girl was, where she came from, why she was there, or how she was killed. In short, they haven't got a clue."

A picture of the dead girl filled the screen.

"This is the girl in question. If you know her, Channel 8 is asking you to please call the station."

The picture cut back to Rick Reed, who cocked his head, raised his eyebrows. His smile was almost a smirk. "The police could use your help."

Sherry Carter blinked at the television screen. "Oh, dear," she murmured.

"That was rather unkind," Cora said.

"This is the man we're counting on to help us?"

"He's doing a fine job so far. He didn't even mention us."

"He didn't mention *anything*. He sounds like he doesn't *know* anything."

"He probably doesn't," Cora said. "You gonna eat that cutlet?"

"I'm not hungry anymore."

"Then pass it over. It would be a shame to waste it."

Cora Felton and Sherry Carter were eating dinner on the coffee table in front of the TV. Sherry had prepared boneless chicken breasts with sliced mushrooms, a long-grain rice with pine nuts, and a salad vinaigrette. She was almost out of the balsamic vinegar she used to make the dressing, and had been wondering where she'd be able to get more outside of New York City before the newscast had driven it out of her head.

"I thought you were on a diet," Sherry said.

"I'm always on a diet. That doesn't mean I can't eat."

"Aunt Cora."

"You gonna eat that chicken or not?"

"I'm not."

"Then I am," Cora said. "It's really delicious."

She speared the remaining chicken breast, plopped it on her plate, began sawing it up. She popped a bite in her mouth, looked at her watch.

"Going out tonight?" Sherry asked.

"I'm playing bridge."

"In the bar?"

"In the restaurant."

"In the bar in the restaurant?"

"What's your point?"

The television had gone to commercial. A four-year-old boy sat at the kitchen table with a spoon and a bowl of cereal. He took a bite, made a horrible face, dropped the spoon, shoved the bowl away, and slumped down in his seat with his elbows on the table and his chin in his hands.

The smiling face of Cora Felton filled the screen.

"Are you puzzled about what to feed your children? Well, you shouldn't be. I love a good puzzle, but not when it comes to nutrition. Take it from the Puzzle Lady. A good breakfast cereal—"

Sherry picked up the remote control and switched the TV off.

"Hey!" Cora protested. "I resent that."

"Aunt Cora, look," Sherry said. "I don't know how to impress this on you, but there probably never was a more important time for discretion."

"Oh, pish tush," Cora said. "What, we're gonna hide in our house just because someone got killed? You'll pardon me, but that's not my lifestyle."

"No, your lifestyle is drinking and gambling."

"A penny a point. Just to keep it interesting."

"Don't con me. That's steep. And you're only playing bridge because you haven't found a poker game."

"That's true," Cora said, chewing the chicken. "It's tough looking so sweet and innocent. No one invites you to play cards."

The phone rang.

Sherry stiffened.

"Relax," Cora said. "I'll get it."

Cora got up, went to answer the wall phone in the kitchen. She came back a minute later, sat down, and began digging into the chicken.

"Well," she said, "you got your wish."

"How's that?"

"The bridge game's off."

"Oh?"

"That was Iris Cooper. The selectmen are calling a town meeting on account of the murder. So bridge is out."

"The players are going?"

"Well, Iris Cooper is. She's the first selectman."

"Uh huh. If bridge is off, why are you eating so fast?"

"I don't want to be late."

"You're going to the town meeting?"

"Sure. Aren't you?"

"No, I'm not. And you shouldn't either."

"Why not?"

"You know why not. This is not the time to call attention to ourselves."

"Don't be silly. Everyone's gonna be there. No one's gonna notice us."

"No one's gonna notice me because I won't be there."

"Sherry, how are you going to meet someone if you just hang out at home?"

"Aunt Cora, give me a break. Meeting someone is not a high priority right now."

"Well, it should be. Young girl like you."

Cora Felton shoved the last piece of chicken into her mouth, picked up her plate. She piled it on top of Sherry's, headed for the kitchen. Sherry followed her out.

"Aunt Cora, if you go running around the town meeting—"

"Running around? What do you mean, running around?" Cora dumped the plates in the sink. "Now, what do I wear?"

Sherry followed her into the bedroom, where she began pulling dresses out of the closet. "Wore it last night. Wore it last week." She held up a red satin dress. "Oh, Arthur hated this one."

"Arthur?"

"My second husband. He couldn't stand it."

"You've had it that long?"

"Well, I couldn't part with it. It has sentimental value." Cora dug into the closet, came out with a low-cut, silk leopard-skin-print sheath. "Ah, here we are. Perfect."

"Aunt Cora."

"Just kidding," Cora said. She patted Sherry on the shoulder. "You're really way too tense."

"Now stop right there." Sherry's voice had an edge to it. "I'm sorry, but that's the type of thing Dennis would say."

"I stand corrected. Sherry, pick out a dress. Let's go to the town meeting."

"No."

"Why not?"

Sherry rubbed her forehead, put up her hand. "Aunt Cora, look. I know we didn't come here to get away from Dennis."

"Right," Cora said. "But it's a bonus, and you'd hate to blow it."

"Yeah, but it's more than that." Sherry frowned, held up her hands, working it out. "No, I didn't come here to get away from him. I know it, and you know it. But Dennis doesn't know it. And if he finds me, he'll *think* I did. Wanna bet how he'll feel about that?"

"Point well taken." Cora smiled. "Sherry, sweetheart. You have my word. I'm not about to do something stupid." She hung the silk dress back in the closet, pulled out a conservative gray and black print, regarded it approvingly. She smiled again, patted Sherry on the cheek. "Relax. I promise you, no one will know I was there."

9

THE BAKERHAVEN TOWN HALL WAS A LARGE, TWO-STORY, WHITE, wood-framed building at the end of Main Street, just north of the village green, and sandwiched in between the county courthouse and the Congregational church. By the time Cora Felton got there, the parking lots of all three were full. She cruised around the green, but cars were parked solid on all four sides. Cora finally wound up parking in the driveway of the church. She was partially blocking a blue sedan, but there was nowhere else, the meeting was about to start, and she figured she'd be leaving first. Cora cut across the green, and joined the few stragglers going up the front steps.

The town hall was packed. The meeting room had a capacity of two hundred and fifty people, but there were probably closer to three hundred there, enough so that many had spilled out into the lobby. Cora Felton pushed her way in, looked around.

From all appearances, the Bakerhaven town hall had not changed in fifty years. On one wall was a list of all registered voters from 1928. On another was an oil portrait of one of the town's founding fathers. The painting bore no plaque, however, and Cora had a feeling even the selectmen would have been hard-pressed to say who he was.

Cora Felton elbowed her way into the meeting room, recognizing an occasional face to which she usually could not provide a name: the woman who ran the bake shop—presumably Mrs. Cushman, since it was Cushman's Bake Shop, though she did not know for sure; the librarian and her son, whose names she also did not know; a man she knew to be a policeman, though he was not in uniform now; an older man who *was* in uniform, though she might not have recognized him without it; and a number of women she'd seen in the bake shop, though she had no idea who they were or what they did.

Off to the side she spotted Chief Harper standing with a plumpish middle-aged woman and a teenage girl, obviously his wife and daughter. As she watched, the woman buttoned a button on his shirt. He was in uniform. His hair was slicked down. He looked decidedly uncomfortable.

Iris Cooper stood at a lectern in the front of the room. A tiny woman, impeccably dressed in a blue linen pantsuit, the first selectman took her job very seriously. She had, in Cora Felton's opinion, a snippy, dictatorial manner, although Cora was sure Iris merely considered herself efficient.

Iris was standing next to a little man with a thin mustache. Cora didn't know him, but he reminded her of a weasel. She could imagine him poking his nose in, insinuating, finding fault. As she watched he leaned into the microphone and said, "Could we have it quiet, please?"

He most certainly could. It wasn't as if there was a dead hush at the sound of his voice, still, all conversation rapidly petered out. Iris Cooper was able to take over and say, "Thank you very much. You're all aware of why we called this meeting. Because of the murder of a young girl. Everyone is of course shocked, there have been rumors flying around all day. We want to give the people of Bakerhaven the facts, because, distressing as the facts are, they are not nearly as upsetting as all of this unfounded speculation. We want to let people know what happened, and just what we're going to do about it. I'm going to ask our prosecutor, Henry Firth, to say a few words."

"Thank you, Iris," the weasely-looking man said. He managed to elbow her away from the lectern without appearing to do so. He leaned on it, spoke into the microphone. "Ladies and gentlemen," he said, and his nasal voice reverberated from the speakers. "This is a truly shocking crime. I have been fielding questions all day as to just what we are going to do about it. There has been a lot of speculation, and what everyone wants to know is, will the case be tried here, or will we seek a change of venue and move it to another court? Well, I can assure you, when the killer is caught, we will try the case right here in the county courthouse, and I will personally prosecute him or her to the fullest extent of the law."

This was met by a murmur of approval, both from the townspeople at large, and the selectmen.

"Now then," Firth went on. "With regard to the facts of the case and what's being done about it, I am going to turn the floor over to Chief Harper, so he can bring you up to date."

Chief Harper walked to the front of the room, smiled grimly at Henry Firth, then stepped up to the microphone. He ran his finger under his collar, cleared his throat.

"This is all we know. A young girl was found early this morning in the cemetery lying next to one of the graves. We are treating it as a potential homicide. The girl has not been identified and does not appear to be local. We put her picture on TV, so far no one's come forward."

Henry Firth weaseled his way to the microphone. "Let me ask you, Chief: How was this girl killed?"

"We don't know for certain. We're waiting on the autopsy report."

"Uh huh. And *when* was she killed?"

"Apparently some time last night."

"Apparently?"

"So it would appear. Again, I don't have the report."

"Uh huh," Henry Firth said. "So you can't tell when this young woman was killed or how she was killed?"

"Not at the present time."

"And do you have any leads?"

"We're asking anyone with any information to come forward."

"I'll take that as a no. Is there anything else you can tell us?"

"Yes. There's every reason to believe this is an isolated incident, and there's no reason to be alarmed."

"Really?" Henry Firth said. "I wish I shared your confidence." His narrow face brightened. "Ah, I see Barney Nathan has just joined us. Dr. Nathan, would you mind stepping up here a moment?"

Barney Nathan was suave and dapper in his red bow tie, just as if he hadn't been cutting up a young girl all day. He pushed his way through the crowd, joining the others at the lectern.

"Dr. Nathan," Henry Firth said, leaning into the mike. "Perhaps you could shed some light on this terrible tragedy. Thus far the police have not even been able to label it a homicide."

"Well, it certainly is," Dr. Nathan said. "The girl was killed by a blow to the back of the head which crushed her skull."

This was greeted by gasps and the rumble of voices.

"Is that so?" Henry Firth said. He smiled. "You'll forgive me, but I am a prosecutor. If I could play devil's advocate here, Doctor, how can you tell she didn't just fall and hit her head?"

Dr. Nathan was definite. "Couldn't have happened. She was killed by a single blow to the back of the head, delivered with considerable force. She was struck with a blunt object, small, hard, and round."

"Like a pipe?"

"Like the end of a pipe. Or the head of a hammer."

"Interesting." Henry Firth put on his most solemn, pious face. "For-give me, doctor, but had the young woman been raped?"

Dr. Nathan shook his head. "She had not. I can assure you there was no evidence that this was a sex crime."

"I see." Henry Firth nodded gravely. "And what can you tell us about the time of death?"

Dr. Nathan smiled. "If you watch a lot of TV, you get the impres-sion doctors can pinpoint the time of death down to a minute. That simply isn't so. I can tell you for certain she died last night between eight o'clock and midnight. Most likely around ten, but that's only most likely. She could have died anywhere within that time span."

"Well," Henry Firth said. "Thank you for clearing that up for us."

Henry Firth's smile was a smirk. Chief Harper frowned, shuffled his feet. His face was red.

Cora Felton shook her head. As far as she was concerned, that tableau told the whole story. She could imagine the doctor stalling his autopsy, failing to report his findings to the police, being unavailable on the phone, and then arriving at just the right moment to undercut the chief in front of the selectmen. The public humiliation of Chief Harper was so obvious it reeked to high heaven. She wondered if the towns-people took it at face value. Decided they probably did. In Cora Felton's opinion the town meeting was a washout. Time to play some bridge.

Cora scanned the room for players, saw none. She was just about to give up when she spotted Vicki Tanner standing in the back near the exit. The youngest member of their bridge group, Vicki had straight straw hair and a little ski-jump nose. She was dressed, as usual, in a simple cotton dress and wore no makeup. While she looked perfectly presentable, she was, in Cora's estimation, one of those women it would not take much to look quite striking.

Cora Felton began edging her way toward her. The town meeting was winding down. After the doctor's revelation, no one had much to say, at least nothing of importance. It occurred to Cora if she could line up Vicki Tanner, the two of them could buttonhole Iris Cooper when the meeting broke up, and then they would only need a fourth.

As Cora Felton approached Vicki Tanner, she noticed the man standing next to her. He was a handsome man, slim, with boyish good looks. He wore a blue, double-breasted three-piece pinstripe suit, which was probably intended to make him look older, but in her opinion made him look young.

Cora Felton's hopes sank. Vicki Tanner had mentioned her husband was a lawyer from New York. This was undoubtedly him, stopping in on his way home from work. The chances of getting a bridge game off the ground were rapidly fading.

Still, she gave it a shot.

"Hi, Vicki," she said. "Any chance of getting out of here and playing some bridge?"

Vicki turned, saw her, blushed, appeared flustered. Not that she had any reason to be. Vicki was shy, and often appeared flustered. "Oh," she said. "Oh, you startled me." She turned to her husband. "Honey, this is the woman I play bridge with."

Cora Felton smiled. "Hi," she said. "I'm Cora Felton. You must be the young lover Vicki's so afraid her husband will find out about."

Vicki blushed a deeper red, but her husband just smiled and said, "You're a very naughty woman, Miss Felton. But I'm pleased to meet you nonetheless. I'm Stuart Tanner. I'm Vicki's husband, as I'm sure you've guessed."

"Pleased to meet you," Cora Felton said, but she wasn't. Stuart Tanner's presence meant his wife was going home. Vicki stammered all over the place apologizing, but assured Cora Felton she had no intention of playing bridge that night.

Cora gave it up as a lost cause. The town meeting was giving her a headache. Bridge was not happening. Nothing new was being discussed. Tomorrow was soon enough to start snooping. Right now she needed a drink.

Cora Felton vacillated a second, wondering if she stayed if there was *anything* of importance she might learn. The fact Vicki Tanner had been standing so near the exit tipped the scale. It was so easy just to slip out. Cora took one last look around, then went out the door.

On the other side of the room, the officer in uniform, Sam Brogan, pushed his way through the crowd and nudged Aaron Grant. "That's her," he said.

The young reporter craned his neck. "Who?"

"The Puzzle Lady. The one I told you about."

"Oh? She's here?"

"Just went out."

"You mean she left?"

"Yeah."

"Why didn't you tell me?"

"I just saw her."

"When'd she leave?"

"Just now."

Aaron Grant pushed his way to the door. He got outside in time to see a car pull out of the parking lot of the Congregational church. He considered following, but he couldn't even be sure it was her. Aaron went back inside, made his way over to Sam Brogan.

"Catch her?" Sam asked.

"No, I didn't."

"Too bad."

"Yeah," Aaron said. He took out his notebook. "Tell me again about this puzzle clue?"

10

Tuesday morning was sunny and bright. The grass was still wet from the rain and dew, but the pavement was dry as Sherry Carter padded down the driveway in her bedroom slippers. One of the bonuses of living in the country was not having to get dressed to get the morning paper, and Sherry was still in her pajamas. She yawned, stretched, and noted with satisfaction that the red Toyota was not parked across the driveway. Sherry hadn't heard Cora come in, but apparently her aunt had been sober enough to put the car in the garage. Thank goodness for small favors.

As Sherry pulled the *Bakerhaven Gazette* out of the green metal delivery box, a milk truck went by. The driver smiled and waved, and Sherry waved back. A city girl, she'd forgotten about milk trucks, was surprised to discover they still existed. It occurred to her she could get her milk delivered. She wondered if she ever would.

Sherry smiled to herself as she unrolled the paper, flipped it open to the front page.

The headline was GIRL MURDERED!!! Underneath the headline was a picture of the dead girl, the same picture that had been on television. The same one the police had been showing people yesterday. To absolutely no avail, apparently.

Sherry walked slowly back up the driveway reading the account of the case. She flipped the paper over to read the bottom half of the front page, and stopped dead.

Smiling up at her was the face of Cora Felton. The headline over the picture read CROSSWORD CLUE???

One of the more bizarre aspects of the Bakerhaven murder is a clue found on the body of the victim. The clue, 4) D – LINE (5), is believed to be a clue from a crossword puzzle. For this reason, the police have consulted Miss Cora Felton, better known as the Puzzle Lady, for help in interpreting the clue. According to police sources, Miss Felton, who resides in Bakerhaven, has already been of help. She believes that 4) D stands for *four down*, like the number of a clue in a crossword puzzle. The clue itself would be *line*, and the (5) would indicate that the solution had five letters. Miss Felton has already come up with several possible solutions, the most likely of which is *queue*, a five-letter word for *line* in common British usage. However, it is way too early to speculate on what this might mean.

Sherry Carter looked up from the paper, blinking hard. She was having paranoid flashes of Dennis seeing the picture, Dennis reading the article, Dennis tracing the address.

Dennis coming to get her.

Sherry took deep breaths, calming herself. Told herself, no, it's nothing. It's a local paper. No one sees it but the people in Bakerhaven. Dennis had never heard of Bakerhaven. And no one in Bakerhaven had ever heard of Dennis. It's not a case of cause and effect. It's not a case of anything. It's unfortunate, but that's all. Nothing to panic about.

Sherry looked at the paper again. The article was by someone named Aaron Grant. Sherry wasn't sure, but she thought it was the name of the man who'd called for Cora Felton last night. Sherry could check it, she'd left her aunt a message. Not that it made much difference now.

Sherry shook her head. Why did Cora have to go to that town meeting? And why did she have to open her mouth? If Dennis got wind of this—

No. Sherry stopped herself. It's local, it's nothing, and Dennis doesn't know.

The phone rang.

Sherry froze in the driveway, stifled another panic attack. Told herself it wasn't Dennis. It was most likely the nursery school calling her to teach.

Which was just what she needed. Sherry hurried up the driveway, went inside, answered the kitchen phone.

"Cora Felton, please. It's Chief Harper."

Sherry didn't know whether to be relieved or alarmed. Which struck her funny. She smiled, in spite of herself.

"Oh, hi, Chief. This is Sherry Carter. Did you see the paper?"

"That's why I'm calling. Is your aunt there?"

"She's sleeping."

"Better wake her up. There may be repercussions and I'd like her prepared."

"This is awful. I didn't think she'd talk to the press."

"She may not have."

"Oh?"

"It might have been one of my men. That's not the point. The point is, what we do now."

"What do you mean?"

"There's news crews in town. If they pick up on this—"

"You think they will?"

"They might. If they do, it's important what she says. Go wake her up."

Sherry draped the phone over the back of a kitchen chair, hurried down the hall.

Her mind was reeling. News crews. Her worst nightmare. Maybe they were just local, but this was a murder, and Cora Felton was a celebrity, and if the New York stations should pick up on it . . . Sherry didn't even want to think about that. She had to wake up her aunt. Wake her up, sober her up, pound some sense into her head.

Cora Felton's room was dark. Sherry fumbled on the wall, found the light switch, flicked it on, and stood blinking at the bed.

Cora Felton was gone.

11

THE CRIME SCENE LOOKED DIFFERENT TODAY. YESTERDAY, IN THE POUR-
ing rain, Chief Harper could barely see a thing. Today, the sun was out,
the sky was crystal clear, and the whole Bakerhaven Cemetery
stretched out ahead of him, rows and rows of gravestones winding
around the side of the hill.

Chief Harper drove through the open gate and up the dirt road. He
could see the caretaker's truck in the far northwest corner of the cemetery, parked next to a small maintenance shed. He drove over, found
Fred Lloyd inside the shed working on a power mower. The caretaker
was lying on his back, tightening something with a small wrench.

"Lawn mower break down?" Chief Harper asked.

"All the time."

"Bad machine?"

"Just old." Fred Lloyd gave the bolt a final turn, rolled aside, and sat
up. "I told you, I don't know the girl. What do you want?"

"I just wanted to ask you some questions when it wasn't so wet."

"I was in yesterday. Gave a signed statement."

"I know. I read it. I still have some questions."

"Well, the answers are the same. I don't know her."

"I'm sure you don't. That's not what I was going to ask. Let's go back to the beginning. Yesterday morning you drove in here and saw the girl in your headlights."

"That's right. Otherwise I might have missed her in the rain."

"What time was that?"

"Seven-thirty in the morning."

"That's when you start work?"

"That's right."

"Why so early?"

"Some people like to come by the cemetery on their way to work."

"So?"

"So, I have to open up."

"What do you mean, open up?"

"The gate. I have to unlock the gate."

"The cemetery's locked at night?"

"Of course."

"And you unlock it every morning at seven-thirty?"

"That's right."

"What time do you lock it in the evening?"

"I don't."

"You don't?"

"No."

"Why not?"

"I'm not here. I go home at three."

"So who locks up at night?"

"Huey."

"Who's Huey?"

"The late shift. I'm the early shift, he's the late shift."

"So what time does Huey lock up?"

"Seven o'clock."

"Seven?"

"That's right. The place shuts down at seven."

"You know the procedure for locking up?"

"Yes, of course."

"But you don't do it."

"I've done it. When Huey's sick or out of town I've done double duty. Just like he's covered for me."

"But not last night."

"No. No, last night he was on. He'd have locked up at seven."

"And what is the procedure for locking up?"

"Make sure everybody's out. That's the main thing. You lock the gate with someone's car inside, there's hell to pay."

"Has that ever happened?"

"Sure. Southeast corner there's a couple of sections people pull off to the side and park, you wouldn't know they were there. I remember comin' to work one morning there's a Cadillac parked next to the gate. I mean, *inside* the gate."

"What did the driver say?"

"The driver wasn't there. He'd left the car and gone home. He said a lot when he showed up, though. Which wasn't fair. I hadn't locked him in. Plus the guy was blockin' me. And who said he had to leave his Caddie right in front of the gate so's I couldn't get my truck in, can you tell me that?"

"No, I can't," Chief Harper said. "But, aside from making sure everyone's out, what else can you tell me about locking up?"

"That's about it. You lock the shed here, make sure the mowers and the tools are away. And you lock the front gate with a chain and padlock."

"Where are the chain and padlock?"

"Chained to the gate. You think I wanna lug it around, maybe lose it, put it someplace Huey can't find? Beginning of the day, you lock the chain to the gate, at night you lock the gate shut."

"So, if someone wanted to get into the cemetery after seven o'clock at night . . . ?"

"They would climb over the fence. Not that hard to do. Happens all the time. It's mostly kids, teenagers who think it's cool to party in the cemetery. I'll come in the morning, find the beer cans and the cigarette butts. That's why, when I drove in and saw the girl lying there, my first thought was she'd had too much to drink."

"I see."

Fred Lloyd cocked his head. Looked at the chief narrowly. "You gonna ask me about condoms?"

"Condoms?"

"Yeah. Along with the beer cans and cigarettes, did I ever find condoms too?"

"Did you?"

"Can't say as I did."

Chief Harper frowned. "Then why did you bring it up?"

The caretaker shrugged. "Well, you're askin' everything else the reporter asked, I figured you'd ask that too."

"Reporter?"

"Yeah."

"You've had a reporter around asking questions?"

"Didn't I just say that?"

"You mean this morning?"

"Sure, this morning. Just before you. That's why it's so funny to hear you askin' the same thing."

"Was this Aaron Grant?"

"Who?"

"The reporter. Was it Aaron Grant? Young kid, early twenties."

"No, this was a woman."

"A woman?"

"Yeah. In fact, she may be still here. I didn't see her drive out."

"You told this woman just what you told me?"

"That's right."

"Anything else?"

"No. Just . . ."

"Just what?"

"Where the grave was. You know, where I found the girl. You didn't ask that 'cause you already know."

"I certainly do," Chief Harper said. "Why'd she have to ask? Couldn't she see the crime scene ribbon?"

The caretaker shook his head. "Isn't there."

"What?"

"Someone took it down. Kids, most likely. I got here this morning, ribbon's gone."

"Great," Harper said. He turned and strode off through the cemetery. It bothered him, the crime scene ribbon being gone. Not that it mattered, in terms of the investigation. It was just another example of no one taking his authority seriously.

He also wondered if he'd be able to recognize the grave without the ribbon around it.

He needn't have worried. The reporter was still there. She wore a broad-brimmed brown felt hat that obscured her hair and most of her face, and a pair of large sunglasses. She was kneeling down, examining the gravestone.

While she was doing so he walked up behind her and said, "May I help you?"

The woman gave a start, turned around and looked up. She recognized Chief Harper and smiled.

"Hello, Chief," she said. "Nice to see you."

Chief Harper blinked. The woman looked vaguely familiar, but with her hair tucked into her hat and her sunglasses on it was hard to tell.

He blinked again.

It was Cora Felton.

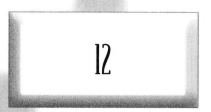

12

"WHAT ARE YOU DOING HERE?"

Cora Felton brushed the dirt from her hands as she got to her feet. "It's still a little muddy, isn't it? Of course, what would you expect with all that rain."

"Excuse me, but why are you here?"

"Well, I have to see for myself, don't I? You can't expect me to solve the crime without all the facts."

"I didn't ask you to solve the crime. I asked you to interpret a clue."

She smiled. "Which amounts to the same thing. In any case, you can't expect me to do anything without all the facts."

"I gave you the facts."

She put up her hand. "Oh, well, now I'm sure you think you did, Chief. But you must understand what you gave me was your interpretation of the facts. I need to see these things for myself."

"You don't need to see these things at all."

"No? Then tell me something, Chief. What's the name on this gravestone?"

"I have no idea."

"There you are. If you don't have the facts, how can I judge what you tell me? For your information, this is the grave of Emily Klemper, beloved wife of Jonathan Klemper, who died in nineteen fifty-eight.

Emily, not Jonathan. He died in nineteen fifty-four. His grave's over there."

"Then what were you looking for?"

"Huh?"

"You've already examined these gravestones. I mean, you must have if you know the husband's buried over there. Because you'd examine this one first. Find the name, and look for relatives. So, if you've already examined this gravestone, what were you looking for just now?"

"A clue."

"I figured that. Anything in particular?"

"I was hoping for something that would tie in with the clue we already have."

"The one on the front page of the morning paper?"

Cora Felton frowned. "Huh?"

"You didn't see the paper this morning?"

"I've been busy."

"So I see. For your information, your picture's on the front of the *Bakerhaven Gazette,* under the headline CROSSWORD CLUE."

"That's not good."

"No kidding."

"You get so much further with people if they don't know what you're after."

It took a moment for that to register. "I don't think you understand me, Miss Felton. The problem with the story is not that it will hamper your investigation, it's that it will put you in danger."

Cora Felton smiled. "I don't think I'm in any danger."

"Oh, no? You come snooping around the crime scene, first thing in the morning. The only person here is the caretaker, and he's busy working on a mower. Suppose the killer was lurking around?"

Cora Felton's eyes twinkled. "That's very interesting, Chief. The killer returns to the scene of the crime. You happen to read a lot of detective fiction?"

Chief Harper was not amused. "It's not funny," he said. "It's serious. If you're going to run around posing as a reporter—"

"I never said I was a reporter. If the caretaker got the wrong idea, that's hardly my fault."

"You're missing the point. You shouldn't be talking to the caretaker in the first place."

"I think you're missing the point, Chief. Have you examined this grave? Obviously not, if you don't know whose it is."

"What about it?"

"There was no clue in the name, but look at its position."

"Position?"

"Yes. Look where the road goes." She pointed to the dirt road that came up from the gate and bisected the cemetery. "See where the road forks left to go up to the caretaker's shed? At the same time it forks right to go over to the graves on the east side of the hill?"

"Yeah. So?"

She pointed. "Well, it's hard to see from here, but the road running east–west is right up there. And if you count down from the road— one, two, three, four." She spread her arms, smiled. "Well, this is the fourth gravestone in the row."

He looked at her. "Four down?"

"It's possible."

"What about *queue?*"

"It's possible too. There are a number of possibilities. It's too early to throw anything out yet. But here's the problem." She pointed again to the road coming up from the gate. "If you look at the road over there and count this way, well, this is the third row over. Which is wrong, if we take the message to mean the fourth grave in row five. This is actually the *fourth* grave in row *three.*"

"And what do you make of that?" Chief Harper said. And felt angry with himself for asking. He shouldn't be discussing this with the woman, he should be kicking her out of there and telling her never to come back.

"It would seem to indicate that our premise was wrong. That four down line five did not indicate the gravestone where the girl was found. That leaves two other possibilities."

"Two?"

"Yes. One, you take the premise that four down means four down from the road. Like I said before. If this is line three, then line five is two graves over. Which would make four down line five the grave just on the other side of her husband's." She consulted a small notebook in her hand. "Which happens to belong to a Morton Pressman, who died in nineteen forty-eight." She nodded. "The second possibility—and the one that I like better—is that four down means starting from this grave. So, if you'd like to count with me," she said, leading him along, "we go one, two, three, four down here, and then over two to line five. Which is the grave of Barbara Burnside, who died in eighty-four."

"Oh," Chief Harper said.

There was something in his voice.

Cora Felton looked at him. "What is it, Chief?"

"I knew Barbara Burnside. Went to school with her way back when. She died young. In an accident. Drove her car off the road. I was on duty at the time. Wasn't chief, of course, just a cop. I responded to the call. Was there when they pulled her out."

"An accident?" Cora Felton asked.

"Yes."

"Was there anything about it—"

"No, there wasn't," Chief Harper said. "It was Saturday night, she'd been at a party, and she'd been drinking. Had a fight with her boyfriend and went home. She was driving drunk and angry and way too fast. Just one of those things."

"So death was ruled accidental?"

"Death *was* accidental. Now, look. I know you'd like to make a mystery out of this. But I assure you, the dead girl has nothing to do with Barbara Burnside."

"Uh huh," Cora Felton said. She didn't sound particularly convinced.

"But that's not the point. The point is, you can't be doing this. Running around crime scenes, looking for clues. That's a matter for the police."

"Sure, Chief. I wouldn't want to step on your toes. Just let me know when you find the next clue."

"If there's another crossword puzzle clue, I assure you I'll ask you about it."

Cora Felton frowned. "Well, now. We were just discussing the fact it might not *be* a crossword puzzle clue. Suppose the puzzle did have to do with *graves* rather than *letters*. I would think you would want my help in figuring that out. Particularly since it's my premise to begin with."

Chief Harper thought that over. He didn't like it, but didn't feel like arguing. "If I find anything that supports that premise, I will let you know. In the meantime, Miss Felton, do you think you can handle the media?"

"I imagine I can do as well as you."

Chief Harper flushed. "I wasn't talking about stage presence. I understand you're comfortable on camera. I mean, do you think you can downplay the puzzle angle of this crime? On the theory that's the best way to foil the killer?"

"Yes, of course," Cora Felton replied. "That's all I wanted in the first place. Keep me in the loop, and I guarantee you I'll do my best to keep out of the spotlight." She shrugged. "Except . . ."

"Except what?"

Cora Felton smiled. "If I'm already on the front page of the paper, it's not going to be easy."

13

"SHERRY, RELAX. I TELL YOU, HE'S NOT AROUND."

"Are you sure?"

"Sure, I'm sure. The band's on tour. They're in Washington or Philadelphia or something."

"And Dennis is with them?"

"Of course he's with them. Where else would he be?"

Sherry was on the phone with Brenda Wallenstein, her roommate from college. Brenda was an artist with a loft in SoHo. Before Sherry and Dennis had split up, Brenda had let his band use it as a rehearsal hall.

"How do you know they're on tour?"

"They were through here last week. Debbie told me the itinerary."

"They're really working?"

"They've got gigs. Small-time, but paid."

"It's hard to think of anyone paying to see Dennis."

"You didn't always feel that way."

"Don't remind me."

"So how's small-town life treating you?"

"Great," Sherry said. "Couldn't be better. I'm getting annoying phone calls, there's been a murder, and a local cop wants to involve my aunt."

"How is Cora?"

"Cora's Cora. I love her, but at times I'd like to strangle her."

"And she's on the front page of today's paper?"

"Large as life. I nearly had a stroke."

"I'll bet. And this cop wants her to solve a murder?"

"No, he just wants her to interpret a crossword puzzle clue."

Brenda snorted. "That's a laugh."

"No kidding. The poor cop. He thought he was getting the Puzzle Lady. Instead he's unleashed a modern-day Miss Marple. You should have seen her eyes light up when she realized it was a murder. She's out there snooping now."

"Uh huh," Brenda said. "You still haven't answered my question."

"What question?"

"About small-town life."

"I thought I did."

"Don't be a goose. You met someone yet?"

"Brenda. I just got here."

"You been there long enough to get a job."

"I got lucky."

"Oh? I thought you hadn't been there long enough."

"I was talking about the job."

"I know you were. Haven't you met anyone?"

"I'm teaching nursery school."

"So?"

"So, the kids are young enough the parents are generally still together."

"That's cynical even for you. I wasn't suggesting you make a play for the kids' fathers. But, seriously, you met anyone yet? Or seen anything you liked?"

"Brenda, you're awful."

"So, shoot me. I'm a bad person. But I worry about you out in the sticks."

"I'm just fine."

"Oh, really? But you're afraid Dennis might be phoning you?"

"I admit it's a stretch. Still, I'm happy to hear he's not around."

"You're glad he's on tour and not strangling young girls?"

"She was hit with a blunt object." Sherry sighed. "What a mess. I just hope the police solve this soon and leave us alone."

The front doorbell rang.

"Uh-oh. I think that's him now."

"Who?"

"The cop. He called before, looking for Cora."

"I thought she wasn't there."

"She isn't."

"Then why would it be him?"

"He probably didn't believe me."

The doorbell rang again, long, insistent.

"Yeah, that's him."

"Oh? What's he like? Young?"

"He's middle-aged and married."

"Too bad."

"Brenda, behave yourself. I gotta go."

Sherry hung up the phone, hurried to the front door to let Chief Harper in.

Only it wasn't Chief Harper. It was a rather good-looking young man in tan slacks and a blue sports jacket. His shirt collar was unbuttoned, his tie was pulled down. His brown hair was wavy and carelessly combed, falling down on his forehead. He had a jaunty air.

"Hi," he said. "How's it goin'? Is the Puzzle Lady in?"

"Who are you?"

"I called last night. Remember? You told me Miss Felton wasn't in."

"That was you?"

"That's right."

"You're a reporter?"

"Yes, I am. I left my name and number. Did you give it to her?"

"I didn't see her."

"Oh?"

"She got in late. I'd gone to bed."

"And this morning?"

"I haven't seen her this morning."

"Is she here?"

"No, she's not."

"Did you leave my name and number where she would find it?"

"I have no idea."

"Oh?"

"It's on the message pad. If she looked on the pad, she would find it."

"Would she look on the pad?"

"I can think of one way to find out."

"Oh?"

"Go back to your office and sit at your desk. If the phone rings and it's her, you'll know she got the message."

He smiled, cocked his head, looked at her. She wore no makeup, and her hair was mussed. Her blue jeans had holes in the knees. Her red cotton pullover was loose, deemphasized her figure. And yet, he found her quite attractive.

Perhaps it was the fire in her eyes.

"That strikes me as somewhat hostile," he said.

"Oh, does it now?" Sherry Carter said. "Well, why would you get that impression?"

"Is there a problem?"

"Yes, there's a small problem. It's on the front page of the *Bakerhaven Gazette*. Though, I suppose that has nothing to do with you."

"Oh."

"Yeah. Oh. I take it you are what's-his-name who wrote the story?"

"Aaron Grant."

"Oh. Thanks for your byline. You ever think of checking your facts before going to press?"

"Yes, I do. That's why I tried to call Miss Felton last night. Too bad I wasn't able to reach her."

"So you just went right ahead."

He frowned, then smiled and shrugged. "Hey, pardon me, but what's the problem? The Puzzle Lady and I both write columns. We both want them printed. We both want them widely read. Are you telling me she doesn't *want* publicity?"

"There's good publicity and bad publicity."

"No, there isn't. All publicity is good publicity. You get your name out, it's good. You get your picture out, it's better. Now, nobody's gonna see my face, but they sure will see hers. And trust me, that can't hurt."

"And if the killer comes looking for her?"

"Give me a break. You must know that's not even a remote possibility. Not that I wouldn't love to play that angle up, but it's really a stretch."

"You'd love to play that up?"

"Yes, of course. What, you want me to lie and tell you what you want to hear? I would love a sensational angle like that. Not that I want to put her in any danger. But if she *were* in any danger, you think I wouldn't want to report it?"

"Am I supposed to find your candor refreshing?"

"Are you a writer too?"

"Why?"

"The number of people who use the word *candor* is somewhat limited."

"I don't think so."

"What?"

"I don't think a number can be limited. I think a group can be limited. I think a number of people can be few. I think a group of people could be limited, or simply small. But then, I'm not a reporter."

Aaron Grant found himself looking at her with interest. "What are you?"

"I'm a schoolteacher."

"Oh? Why aren't you in school?"

"I'm a substitute, actually. I only teach when they call me."

"I see," Aaron said. He cocked his head. "That's interesting. A teacher. You must be good with words."

Sherry frowned. "What's your point?"

"You must know a lot of them. Your vocabulary must be infinite."

"What is that, sarcasm? Irony?"

"No, just a simple statement of fact. Isn't your vocabulary infinite?"

"I'm sure *yours* is."

"No. I know only a limited number of words."

Sherry found herself blushing. "Oh, yes. A limited number. I should have known. You're very competitive, aren't you?"

"I'm a reporter. Getting the story first is my job."

"That's not what I mean, and you know it. You scored with *limited number*. You're right and I'm wrong. You also get credit for making your point subtly, instead of hitting me over the head with it. Now, you wanna take your aloof, arrogant, highly competitive— You got any other good adjectives for me?"

"How about handsome and charming?"

"That gives me conceited and smug."

"Not to mention supercilious."

"Supercilious?"

"I thought I told you not to mention that."

Sherry smiled in spite of herself. "All right, look. I know you have a job. But I don't think dragging us into the murder is a particularly good idea."

"Us?"

"Yes."

"I wasn't aware that I was dragging you into the murder. I thought we just met."

"You know what I mean."

"No, I don't. In what way am I dragging you into this?"

"I'm not going to tell you, because you'd write it."

"You mean there's something to write?"

"Absolutely not."

He grinned. "Then what is it that you won't tell me because I might write it, although it is nothing to write?"

"Off the record?"

He winced. "Oh, I hate that expression. It's like saying, here, let me show you something you want that you can't have."

"Then forget it."

"No, no, no. I didn't say that. It's just *off the record* is such a dangerous phrase if someone wants to abuse the privilege. They say, Off the record, and then tell you everything they don't want you to print. A lot of which you would have found out anyway. Are you then obligated not to print it? Even though you could have found it out from another source?"

"Boy, are you paranoid." Sherry shook her head. "What's the matter, are you afraid I'm going to say, Off the record, I'm the killer? And then you find yourself in an ethical quandary, like the hero in some godawful TV Movie of the Week."

"Quandary?"

"Don't start with me. You want something off the record or not?"

"Oh, absolutely."

"Okay, off the record: Cora Felton happens to be my aunt. Now, that is not particularly newsworthy, and has no bearing on this murder. And I would not like to read about it in tomorrow's paper."

"You're her niece? How about that."

"Can I trust you not to report that fact?"

"As long as it's irrelevant to the murder. If your relationship itself became newsworthy . . ."

"How could it?"

"I don't know. But if it did, that's another matter."

"And just who would determine that?"

"Circumstance would determine that."

"Circumstance is not a who."

"All right," he said. "I'm a who. And I will not abuse your confidence. Unless I have a reason even you would find hard to dispute."

"Can one dispute a reason?"

"I'm sure *you* can."

"Fine. You're not going to report the relationship. Now how about easing off the Puzzle Lady angle altogether?"

"That again would depend on circumstance."

"Such as?"

"Give me a break. If the clue turns out to mean something—"

"I would be very surprised. Look, we gave the police chief help because he asked for it. Not because we think there's anything to it. The idea that this is a crossword puzzle clue is Chief Harper's idea. Not ours. If you must know, Aunt Cora doesn't even think it's a crossword puzzle clue at all. She thinks a much more likely explanation is that it stands for the fourth grave down in line five."

Aaron Grant blinked. "What's that?"

"Count four graves down from where the girl was murdered. Then line five would be the grave in the fifth row."

"Are you serious?"

"No. That's the whole point. A theory like that has as much validity as the theory it's a crossword clue—i.e., none at all. Now, we can treat this as a crossword clue, and Aunt Cora can supply all kinds of solutions, like the ones you reported in your paper, but you and I both know it isn't. So why don't you cut us a little slack?"

Aaron Grant frowned. "I think I made myself perfectly clear. If I can give you a break, I will. But I still haven't met Miss Felton. If I could talk to her, get her reactions firsthand—no offense, but you have to go to the source—well, then, I might be in a position to do what you want."

"In short, you'd like us to cooperate, and you can't promise a thing."

"I'm glad you understand."

"I was being sarcastic."

"I know."

Sherry took a breath. "You're not amusing me."

"Not even a little?"

"In your dreams."

While Sherry and Aaron were talking the red Toyota pulled into the driveway and Cora Felton and Chief Harper got out.

Aaron Grant's grin was enormous. "Well, well, well," he said. "The gang's all here."

"Aunt Cora. Chief Harper," Sherry said. "What are you doing?"

"Dodging reporters," Cora replied happily. She spotted Aaron Grant. "And who might this be?"

"Funny you should ask," Chief Harper said sourly. "This is the reporter I told you about. The one who put you on page one."

"Sherry?" Cora Felton said.

Aaron Grant put up both hands. "I'm not going to pretend this isn't wonderful. I came out to see you, Miss Felton. I'm glad you're here. Your niece and I were just discussing how much of the puzzle angle I should print. But I must confess, the headline POLICE CHIEF DODGES REPORTERS is just so catchy that—"

"Very funny," Chief Harper said. "I'm not dodging reporters. The news crews showed up at the cemetery, and I didn't feel like giving them a quote."

"I don't blame you."

"And as for you, Aaron, I didn't know you were running the cross-word puzzle piece. I wish to hell you'd checked with me before you did."

"And why is that?"

"It's an angle I'd like to play down. As far as the public's concerned. If it really is a clue, I'd like to frustrate the killer by *not* publicizing it. You see what I mean?"

"It's a little late for that," Aaron Grant said.

"He means if there's another one," Sherry said.

"Another one?" Aaron Grant said. "Is there another one?"

"No, there isn't," Chief Harper said. "But if there was, we would keep it to ourselves. One, like I said, to frustrate the killer. And, two, to make sure it's a genuine clue, and not some nut copying what he read in the paper."

"Are you offering me a deal?" Aaron asked.

Chief Harper blinked. "What?"

"It sounds like you're offering me a deal. If I won't print the next crossword puzzle clue, you'll let me know what it is. Is that what I'm hearing here?"

Chief Harper opened his mouth to say, *No, it isn't,* but Cora Felton came in with, "It most certainly is." She crossed to Aaron Grant and looked him up and down, approvingly. "You seem like an intelligent and reasonable young man." She cocked her head at Sherry. "Handsome too. There's no reason why we shouldn't get along." She took Aaron by the arm. "Now, then, young man. Are you telling me if I share the next clue with you, you'll keep it out of print? And avoid mentioning me altogether?"

"Is that what you want?"

"It would be nice."

"Hey, hey, hey," Chief Harper interrupted. "What's going on here? Are you making a deal without me?"

"You can certainly make your own deal," Cora Felton told him. "There's no reason why this young man and I shouldn't have an understanding."

"I thought *we* had an understanding," Chief Harper said.

"We do. I'll assist you in any way possible, and try my best to avoid publicity." She smiled. "I'm trying to avoid it now."

"Yeah," Aaron Grant said. "And here I am, sitting on this wonderful story about you riding around in her car because you're dodging the press."

Chief Harper snorted in disgust. "This is getting out of hand. I'm sorry I ever asked about the damn clue. I'm beginning to think it isn't a crossword puzzle clue at all. Frankly, I need to get on with the case. Can I count on your cooperation in this matter? I'm talking to all of you. Can I count on all of you helping me out here?"

The cellular phone rang. Chief Harper reached in his jacket pocket, jerked it out. "Harper here." He listened a moment, said, "Okay, I'll be right there." He flipped the phone closed, stuck it back in his pocket. "Can you run me back to the cemetery?" he said to Cora Felton. "I gotta get my car."

"Certainly. Why?"

"This has been a lot of fun, but I gotta get back to work."

"Come on, what's up?" Aaron Grant asked. When Chief Harper hesitated, he added, "You got something else you're not giving out?"

"No, I guess not," Chief Harper said.

"So what is it?"

"They've ID'd the body."

14

THE LADIES DIDN'T GET MUCH BRIDGE PLAYED THAT NIGHT, EITHER.

"A runaway," Iris Cooper said. "Can you imagine that? All the way from the Midwest."

"Indiana," Vicki Tanner said. "That's what I heard. Muncie, Indiana."

"I thought it was Indianapolis." A large woman with a broad flat face, Lois Greely was Iris's bridge partner.

"No, it was Muncie. Where did you get Indianapolis?"

"I don't know."

"Well, I do," Iris Cooper said. "You made it up. You hear Indiana, the first thing you think is Indianapolis. It even sounds the same. So that's what you think. You even think you heard it."

"I *did* hear it." Lois Greely's voice was tinged with annoyance. A person of import, Lois was not used to having her opinion questioned, even by the first selectman. Lois and her husband Alan were well off by virtue of owning a most successful general store on the south side of town just over the covered bridge. The rickety, red, wooden, one-lane bridge—nicknamed McCreedy's Folly, after the farmer who had built it in 1845 to get his cows to pasture—was a major tourist attraction, and visitors to Bakerhaven tended to shop at the Greelys' store just for the sake of crossing it. "Of course, whoever told me could be wrong," Lois conceded grudgingly.

"Right," Iris said. "And they're the ones who think they heard it. Isn't that right, Cora?"

Cora Felton smiled patiently.

The women were playing bridge in the bar of the Country Kitchen, a popular, homey restaurant on the outskirts of town. At least they were supposed to be playing bridge. Only Cora Felton minded that they weren't. She sipped her drink, considered asking Lois to deal again. "I don't know about that, but I did hear it was Muncie."

"And she would know." Vicki Tanner said it triumphantly. "After all, she's cooperating with the police."

"Not anymore, I'm not," Cora said. "They asked me about one clue. It was really nothing. I'm sure they know that now."

"And the reporter who wrote the story," Lois said.

"The Grant boy," Iris said.

"That's the one," Lois said. "I thought he was still in school."

"No, I've seen him around," Vicki said. "Quite a handsome young man."

"Oh, you've seen him around?" Iris exclaimed. "Does your husband know that?"

"Oh, stop," Vicki said. "But he is good looking."

"Rather," Cora Felton agreed.

"Oh, so *you've* seen him?" Iris said.

"Of course she's seen him," Lois said. "He wrote the story."

"Actually, he wrote it without talking to me," Cora said. "I saw him today, told him he was all wet."

"What do you mean, all wet?" Iris asked. "Did you tell the police that or not?"

"Yes, I did. I also told them it was very unlikely. Which they believe. It's just the reporter who took it seriously."

"But what about the girl?" Lois demanded. "If they identified her, what's her name?"

"Dana Phillips," Vicki said.

"Are you sure?"

"Yes. Well, at least about the Dana. I think it was Phillips."

"And you think she's from Muncie," Lois said.

"I *know* she's from Muncie. And I know her name is Dana. She ran away from home some time last weekend."

"Her father identified the body," Cora told them. "The picture went nationwide this morning. He didn't see it, but someone else in Muncie did. This guy called the father, he called the network, and they faxed him the photo."

"The father has a photo fax?" Vicki said.

"Not a photo fax," Iris said. "A fax is a fax. It's like a Xerox. What goes in is what comes out."

Lois frowned. "Not in color. A fax won't give you color."

"You mean the man ID'd a black-and-white Xerox of his dead daughter?" Vicki said. "How awful."

"I doubt if that happened," Cora said. "It's not as if the man did this on his own. The Muncie police would be cooperating with our police and with the networks. I'm sure he saw a proper picture. At any rate, it's a positive ID."

"You know that for sure?" Iris said.

"I was there when Chief Harper got the call. Explaining why cross-word puzzles had nothing to do with it."

"It's a shame," Vicki murmured.

"A shame?"

"Oh, yeah, it's a tragedy and all that. But if there was a puzzle to be figured out. If there was something we could do."

"We?" Iris said.

"Well, no, *her,* of course. If Cora was working on something, she'd let us know, and we might have suggestions."

"Oh, now you're solving the case?" Iris asked Vicki.

"No, she's not," Cora said, "and neither am I. But that's no reason why we shouldn't think about it. Even if the crossword clue means nothing. Someone killed this girl for some reason."

"Obviously," Lois said.

"Yes, but it *isn't* obvious," Cora objected. "The girl was hit over the head with a blunt object and dumped in a graveyard. There were no signs of sexual assault. The girl was a runaway who didn't have any money, so robbery wouldn't be a motive. So why is she dead, and why is she here?"

"Here?"

"In Bakerhaven. You take a girl from the Midwest, what's her con-nection with Bakerhaven?"

"The police don't have one?"

"Obviously not. Her picture was on TV, nobody recognized her."

"Nobody *admitted* they recognized her," Vicki Tanner said.

"Good point," Cora said. "You can't take anything at face value because the killer's going to lie."

"Wait a minute, wait a minute," Lois protested. "Are you saying this murder is like a puzzle which you could figure out?"

"Why not?"

"A little presumptuous, don't you think?"

Cora Felton took another sip of her gin and tonic. It was her third or fourth drink, so she was inclined to be quarrelsome. "Not at all. I'm not saying I can solve this crime. I'm saying there's no reason we shouldn't try to think it out. If there's a rational solution, it's a puzzle just like any other. So why shouldn't we work on it?"

"Right," Vicki agreed. "Let's do it."

"You may not get a chance," Lois said.

"Huh?" Vicki said.

Lois pointed over her head.

Vicki turned in her chair and looked.

Her husband, Stuart Tanner, came walking up.

Vicki smiled. "Hi, dear."

Stuart put his arm around her, bent down, kissed her cheek, straightened up. "Hi, honey. I wasn't sure you'd be here."

"Why wouldn't I?" Vicki said.

"I thought we went over that. There's a killer on the loose, I don't want you coming home alone."

Vicki smiled. "Isn't he sweet? Annoying, but sweet. Honey, I'll be fine."

"Uh huh," Stuart said. He looked around the table. "Sorry to hold up your game. But it is upsetting. Having something like this happen. And then I'm away all day, and I don't know what's going on. Do they know who did it yet?"

"No," Vicki said. "But they ID'd the body."

"Really?"

"Yes," Lois said. "Some girl from the Midwest."

"Muncie, Indiana," Vicki contributed. "Her name's Dana something."

"Dana Phelps," Cora Felton said.

"That's it," Vicki said. "Not Phillips. Phelps."

Her husband's attention was on Cora Felton. "Weren't you in the paper this morning? Offering a theory of the crime?"

"Hardly," Cora Felton said. "You can chalk that up to an overzealous reporter."

"Uh huh," Stuart Tanner said. "I must say it concerns me that none of you seem to be taking this killing very seriously."

"Oh, we are," Cora Felton said. "But I know what you mean. I think if the girl had been local it would be different. But as it is, it seems very removed, both from reality and from us." She winced. "Boy, that sounded pompous and academic, didn't it? I think I need another drink. How about you, young man? You look like you could use a drink."

"As an attorney, I don't drink and drive. But tell me about the clue. How can you say it's all this reporter's doing? Didn't you tell the police about the clue?"

"It's a case of the chicken or the egg," Cora replied. "I didn't tell the police it's a clue, the police told me. At least they came and asked me. It was like, if this was a clue, what would it mean? Well, probably nothing. But they put my picture in the paper. Big deal. Tomorrow the news will all be about who this girl really was, and no one will care about the so-called clue. Now, if you're not going to buy me a drink, I guess I'll have to get one myself."

"I'll be glad to buy you a drink," Stuart said. "But really, Vicki. I'm just wondering when you're coming home."

"When we're done," Vicki told him. "It won't be that long. We're just playing a little slow."

"You want me to wait?"

"Don't be silly," Vicki said. "It could be another hour. I'll be fine."

"Are you sure?"

"Sure, I'm sure."

"Yeah," Iris said. "Give her a break. We're big girls, we can take care of ourselves."

Stuart Tanner didn't seem convinced, but he nodded. "Okay, honey, I'll see you at home."

As soon as he left, the women all started giggling about how cute and sweet and overprotective he was. All except Cora, whose reaction to Stuart Tanner was somewhat different. She was impressed by the fact he was the only one who seemed to take the killing seriously.

And she was aware of the fact he had managed to leave without buying her a drink.

15

WEDNESDAY MORNING AARON GRANT HAD A CUP OF COFFEE AT Cushman's Bake Shop, checked out the police station, where nothing new was happening, and drove to the *Bakerhaven Gazette*.

The newspaper occupied the bottom two floors of a three-story brick office building on Center Street just off of Main. Center Street actually ran east–west at the south end of town. It was not known whether the town fathers had named it Center Street in the same spirit in which a bald man might be nicknamed Curly, or whether they had originally intended it as the center street, only to watch the whole town grow up to the north instead. At any rate, the *Bakerhaven Gazette* was enough on the outskirts of town that parking was no problem. Aaron Grant pulled up next to the front door and went inside.

The presses on the ground floor were quiet. As the *Gazette* was a morning paper, the presses rolled at night. In the morning, the only activity was the delivery trucks, which by now were long gone. Aaron Grant went up the stairs to the second floor.

The press room was deserted too. Again, not unusual. The managing editor didn't get in until ten, and none of the reporters felt the need to show up before he did. In the morning the phones were manned by Mary Mason, a young Bakerhaven High grad earning money before going off to college. As the phones didn't ring that often, she was prone to long coffee breaks, and was probably on one now.

Aaron Grant went over to his desk to pick up the mail. That was one of the benefits of working in a small town. The newspaper got its mail first, as soon as it was sorted, and before it went out on the trucks. The post office was just around the corner, and the postmaster let Mary Mason pick it up.

She'd done so this morning. There were three letters on his desk. For Aaron Grant, three letters was a big day, since his columns weren't usually that controversial.

Aaron Grant ripped open the first letter. He read it and frowned. It was a fan letter of the simplest sort. The writer was merely writing to say how much she liked his column. No specifics were mentioned, no particular article referred to. From the content and the handwriting, the letter was probably the work of a high school girl. The letter was signed Jane.

The second letter was from Roger Rimley, whom Aaron Grant did not know, but could envision. A cranky old cuss, who was used to having things his own way. An apparent postgraduate of the school of shoot-the-messenger, Roger seemed to feel that the fault lay not with whoever had murdered the young girl, but rather with Aaron Grant for having reported it.

Aaron sighed, ripped open the third envelope. He pulled out the letter, unfolded it, and blinked.

There, typed on the sheet of paper, was: 14) A—SHEEP (3).

Aaron stared at the paper. Took a breath. Read it again. It was in every way, shape, and form identical to the crossword puzzle clue he had printed the day before. Only that clue had been in ballpoint pen. This clue was typed.

So was the address on the envelope. He noted now that there was no return address.

There was a postmark. The letter was postmarked this morning—June 2, A.M.—in Bakerhaven. All that meant was that was when the postmaster had run it through the canceling machine. When it had actually been mailed was something that would have to be determined.

By the police. That was the thought that came to mind. If this was an actual clue, it should be turned over to the police. Immediately. After all, Aaron Grant and the police had an agreement.

But, it occurred to Aaron, that agreement was the other way

around. If the police got another clue, Chief Harper had agreed to share it with him in return for him not printing it. Nothing was ever said about what would happen if *he* got another clue. That hadn't even been considered. Nor had he agreed not to publish any clue that he uncovered by himself.

So did he really have to give this to the police?

"What have you got there?"

Aaron Grant turned around with a guilty start.

Cora Felton stood smiling at him. Her eyes were twinkling. They were also slightly red, but Aaron Grant barely noticed, preoccupied with the fact that he had thrust the letter behind his back. That would never do. What an obvious, clumsy gesture. He brought it out, folded it up, set it on his desk. "What are you doing here?"

"I came to see you."

"Oh? Why? Not that I'm not flattered, but there was nothing in the paper this morning."

"Exactly," Cora Felton said.

"What?"

"There was nothing in the paper. Except yesterday's news about the identification. And you agreed to cooperate with the police and not publish everything, so I'm wondering if there's anything that you withheld."

"That was not the understanding."

"Oh?"

"I agreed not to publish the next clue if they let me in on it."

"Is that it?"

He stared at her. "What, are you psychic?"

"You mean it is?"

Aaron Grant looked at Cora Felton for a long moment, then picked up the phone and punched in a number. "Chief Harper? Aaron Grant. I'm down at the paper, I've got something I think you'll wanna see. . . . No, I think you'll wanna see it now. Because Cora Felton wants to see it too, and I thought you might like to see it first."

Aaron Grant listened, smiled, and hung up the phone. "Well, that settles that. Chief Harper will be right over. In the meantime, if you get so much as a glimpse of this, he promises to shoot me."

"That's an obvious bluff, and you'd be wise to call it," Cora Felton said, but Aaron Grant was having none of it, and when Chief Harper arrived three minutes later the letter was still on Aaron's desk.

"All right, what is it, and has she seen it?" he demanded.

"It's another clue, and if you're going to be like that, you can interpret it yourself," Cora Felton said. "At least, I *assume* it's another clue. This young gentleman is as secretive as he is handsome."

Aaron Grant found himself blushing. "It's a letter addressed to me. I'm afraid I opened it and handled it, because I had no way of knowing what it was."

"And what is it?" Chief Harper asked.

"It appears to be another crossword puzzle clue."

"You see," Cora Felton said. "Now, couldn't you have told me that?"

"One moment, please," Chief Harper said. He pointed. "You're telling me this folded piece of paper on your desk contains a crossword puzzle clue?"

"That's right."

"Just like the one on the body?"

"Yes. Except this one is typed."

"Typed?"

"Yes."

"You mean it's a letter?"

"That depends what you mean by a letter. Yes, it came in an envelope. An envelope addressed to me. The paper itself is not a letter. It's just a piece of paper with a clue typed on it."

"And what is the clue?"

"You want me to unfold the paper?"

"Probably not," Chief Harper said. He reached in his pocket, pulled out a pair of disposable rubber gloves. "I feel foolish about this, but there's no reason to take any chances." He pulled on the gloves and unfolded the piece of paper, aware of the fact Cora Felton was standing on tiptoes peering over his shoulder. *"Fourteen A sheep three?"* he read.

"Exactly like the other," Cora Felton said.

Chief Harper frowned. "Yes. And would you care to tell me what it means?"

"That's obvious," Aaron Grant said. *"Fourteen A* is fourteen across. Just like *four D* was four down. And the clue is a three-letter word for sheep."

"Which is?" Chief Harper said.

"Ewe," Cora told him.

Chief Harper felt the beginnings of a headache. "Me?"

"No, not you," Cora said. "Ewe. E-w-e. A three-letter word for a female sheep."

"Of course," Chief Harper said. "And how does it fit in with the other?"

"I beg your pardon?"

"That was what? Four down? And this is fourteen across. The first clue was *line*. One of the solutions was *queue*. That has an *e* in it. In fact, it has two *e*'s in it. So does *ewe*. So I'm wondering if they could have one in common. See what I mean? If this were a crossword puzzle, would the words cross?"

Cora Felton frowned. "It's possible. I'll have to play with it when I get home."

"You can't tell?"

She waved her hand impatiently. "There are many different ways to construct a crossword puzzle. I have to try to find one that fits."

"Uh huh," Chief Harper said. If he was pleased, you wouldn't have known it. He turned on Aaron Grant. "All right, what about you?"

"What about me?"

"Don't play dumb. We had a deal. Are you going to withhold this or not?"

"Your deal was if you told me anything I wouldn't reveal it."

"I am aware of what our deal was. I'm asking you a simple question. Can I count on you to hold this back?"

"Absolutely. Just keep me in the loop."

"Fine," Chief Harper said. He pulled a plastic evidence bag out of his pocket, unfolded it, stuck the letter in. "Where's the envelope?"

Aaron Grant pointed to it. Chief Harper added it to the bag.

"There," he said. "Now I can take these damn things off." He pulled off the thin rubber gloves. "You see the problem here," he said to Aaron Grant. "Yesterday you ran that story in the paper, all about the first clue. Now we get another. And I got no way of knowing whether it's a genuine clue, from the murderer himself, or whether this is some nut having a little fun with the police over what he read in the paper."

"I know."

"Do you? Good. Then you realize how important it is that you cooperate with me on this one, Aaron. You too, Miss Felton. I don't want word of this getting out."

Cora Felton's eyes went wide. "Me? You look at me? I will of course tell my niece, but she is the soul of discretion."

"I don't want you telling anyone."

"I understand. But I have to tell my niece. If I start working on the puzzle, she'll want to know what I'm doing. And if you think I could just say, sorry, I can't tell you, then you don't know my niece."

"Fine," Chief Harper said. He didn't sound like it was fine. "Do you suppose you could avoid telling anyone else?"

Cora Felton straightened herself up, harumphed, and gave him her most affronted glare. "You have my word."

"Uh huh," Chief Harper said.

He might have been slightly more reassured if it weren't for the faint trace of alcohol on her breath.

16

SHERRY CARTER COULDN'T STOP SMILING. THE CHILDREN HAD CHEERED the minute she walked in the door. They swarmed around her, laughing and shrieking and pulling at her dress.

"Tell us a story!"

"Do the numbers game!"

"Draw my picture!"

"Oh, you don't want me to do that," Sherry said.

The children squealed in protest. Sherry couldn't draw, but that didn't matter. The rough caricatures she did of the kids delighted them.

"What shall we start with?" Sherry said, tactfully deferring to the regular teacher she was partnered with. Fortunately, Mrs. Rhodes, with twenty years' experience, didn't seem jealous of Sherry's popularity with the kids. "Drawing sounds good," she said. "Why don't you start with that, and I'll catch up on my paperwork."

"Okay, let's start with drawing," Sherry told them, and the kids squealed again, and ran to set up the easel.

Sherry taught in a private nursery school in what had once been a private house. There were three classes divided by age—the twos, the threes, and the four/fives. Sherry was teaching the threes today. It was only the second time she'd taught them. The other time she'd substituted had been for the twos. Even so, she knew all twelve students by name, and even recalled their birthdays, which she'd asked them the first time she'd taught. This phenomenal feat did not impress her students as much as one might have thought. While it pleased them, being three years old, they accepted Sherry knowing their birthdays as a matter of course.

"Marcy Granover," Sherry said, pointing to a young girl with freckles, pigtails, and an enormous smile. "Who will be four years old on September twenty-fourth. Let's draw *your* picture."

Marcy Granover giggled and the class clapped and cheered.

Sherry marched to the easel, picked up the Magic Marker, and quickly sketched a girl with a small head and enormously out-of-proportion braids. She added a sprinkling of freckles, ears, eyes, and a mouth.

"There," she said. "All done."

"No! No! No!" the children screamed in protest.

Sherry appeared amazed. "No?"

"No!" they screamed again.

"Really?" Sherry said. "What did I forget?"

"The *nose!*" the children screamed.

Sherry turned to the picture, did a double take. "Oh, my goodness. I forgot the nose. Marcy, please. Would you help me out? Come up here and draw the nose."

Marcy jumped up, grabbed the Magic Marker, and added a long, pointed beak.

The children squealed in delight.

Sherry drew pictures of the whole class, always forgetting some feature the child would have to add. The children never tired of the game. Each time Sherry made her Ta-da! gesture and said, "All done," they all screamed, "No!" and told her what it was that she'd forgotten.

After drawing, Sherry did the numbers game. The game was simple. Sherry would arrange blocks on the floor, and the children would tell her whether it was odd or even. Sherry was pleased to find the children remembered the game from the first time she'd taught it.

"Odd or even?" Sherry asked, laying out five blocks in a pattern.

"Odd!" the children cried.

"Who wants to tell me why?"

At least half of them raised their hands.

"How about the boy who was born on July eighth? That would be . . . *you,* Matt Wilson. Why is the number five odd?"

Matt Wilson was a chubby boy with a very serious face. He bent down, pushed two of the blocks together, pushed two more together, then stood up and pointed to the remaining block. "Hasn't got a friend."

"That's right," Sherry said.

The children clapped and cheered.

Matt Wilson beamed.

"Do another. Do another."

After the numbers game, the children had juice and cookies. They sat at little tables, happily munching, while Sherry and Mrs. Rhodes went around helping them pour the pitchers of juice. When they'd all been served, Mrs. Rhodes went back to her paperwork, but Sherry stood and watched them eat, a misty look in her eye.

It was times like this when Sherry wished she'd gotten her teacher's certificate, so she'd have been eligible to teach full time in the public school. She loved teaching, but as a substitute the opportunities were few and far between. She'd been thrilled this morning when she'd gotten the call, enough that she'd felt a momentary pang of guilt. It was tough having to root for someone to be sick.

"Sherry," Mrs. Rhodes called.

Lost in thought, it took her a moment to respond to her name. "Yes."

"You have a visitor."

Sherry looked.

Cora Felton stood in the doorway.

Sherry's eyes widened in surprise. Cora'd never come to the nursery school. Sherry hurried to the door. "Aunt Cora. What are you doing here? Is something wrong?"

Cora shot a glance at Mrs. Rhodes, who was within earshot. "Can we go outside?"

"Not really. Why?"

"Please. I need your help."

"Why? What is it?"

Cora Felton looked at Sherry Carter in exasperation. She pulled her close, cupped her hand, and whispered in her ear, "We got another clue."

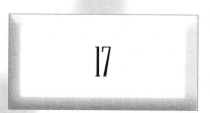

17

CHIEF HARPER HAD HIS HANDS FULL. HE HAD A POLICE OFFICER FROM Muncie, Indiana, on hold, he had news crews camped out on his doorstep, and he had an exasperated prosecutor at his desk.

"It's not enough," Henry Firth whined. "You're not doing enough."

"Just what more would you like me to be doing?"

"Are you kidding? I want you to find the killer. I'm the prosecutor. The people of Bakerhaven expect me to prosecute. But I can't prosecute this madman until you catch him."

"Surely the people understand that."

"Yes, but they don't care. They want something done."

"Fortunately, we are somewhat more reasonable," Chief Harper said dryly. "If you'll excuse me a minute." He pressed the button on his phone. "Officer Crocket? I'm sorry, you were saying . . . ?"

"We still haven't traced how she left town," the Muncie officer said. "Most likely on a bus, but Saturday night or Sunday morning, we have no idea. The last her parents saw her was Saturday afternoon. She didn't come home Saturday night, but they figured she was at her boyfriend's. She wasn't—at least according to him—but they didn't know that. That's where they thought she was. She wasn't allowed, by the way, but sometimes did.

"Anyway, according to him—Timothy Rice, the boyfriend—she came by that afternoon but didn't stay. According to him she was real upset over her grades. Her parents had been giving her a hard time about them. Her parents confirm that—not that they were giving her a hard time, but the fact she got bad grades. They'd had finals the week before, Timothy'd done well, but she'd nearly flunked. She'd been quite upset, but had given no indication she was on the point of running away."

"So he says."

"Right. What else could he say? I'm not taking it at face value, and I will talk to him again. Anyway, we're trying to trace the buses, but the drivers in question are out on their routes. I'm faxing the schedules so you can coordinate from that end."

"Thanks. Anything else?"

"No, but for what it's worth, from the reports I get this was not a particularly wild girl. She did poorly in school, had a fight with her parents, ran away from home. Getting killed in a cemetery in Connecticut doesn't compute."

"Okay, thanks. Let me know if you get anything else."

Chief Harper hung up the phone.

"So?" Henry Firth demanded.

"They're working on it. So far they've got nothing concrete."

"Another sign we need help," Henry said peevishly. When Chief Harper didn't respond, he said, "Any luck with that clue?"

Chief Harper frowned. "Henry. Just because Aaron Grant put something in the paper doesn't make it true."

"Was there a clue or wasn't there?"

"There was a paper in the girl's pocket. It doesn't have to be a clue. The woman in the article—the one who does crossword puzzles—doesn't even think it is. I'm playing it down, and I would advise you to do the same. Now, get out of here, Henry, and let me do my work."

Chief Harper watched Henry Firth go out the door. The prosecutor was a major pain in the neck. Always had been, always would be. Ordinarily, this was no big deal. But now . . .

Chief Harper got up from his desk, went to the door, opened it a crack, peered out.

Sure enough, there was Henry Firth in earnest conversation with the news crews, undoubtedly telling them everything he knew, and suggesting Chief Harper be taken off the case.

Chief Harper closed the door. He sat in his chair, leaned back, rubbed his head.

It was a good thing Henry Firth didn't know about the second clue.

18

Sherry Carter opened the front door hoping it was UPS with the new software she'd ordered for her computer. But, no, it was that annoying reporter in his preppy little outfits who probably thought he looked cool. Sherry had changed into cutoff shorts and a halter top, and didn't care how she looked, although she looked very good indeed. Aaron Grant smiled when he saw her.

Sherry wasn't impressed. "I'm sorry. She's not here."

"Yes, I know."

"Oh?"

"I came to see you."

"Why?"

"Maybe I like your looks."

"Oh, I doubt that."

"Why?"

"It's not politically correct. In fact, it's practically sexual harassment."

"Where do you draw the line?"

"Wherever I choose. That's the nice thing about sexual politics. Puts women in charge."

"Seems to me they always were."

"Did you come here just to spar?"

"No, I came to see you. Are you going to ask me in?"

"That depends on why you're here."

"Are we going to go around again?"

"I don't know."

"Fine," Aaron Grant said agreeably. "Can I assume you've spoken to your aunt about the new clue?"

"You can assume anything you like."

"Then I'll assume that. The new clue is a three-letter word for sheep. Cora says that would be *ewe*. I've agreed not to publish this information because I'm basically a nice guy. A very nice guy, since without it, all it leaves me for tomorrow is a rehash of my column today."

"Gee," Sherry said, "would that be the same nice guy who has a deal with the cops? Would that have anything to do with being nice?"

"I thought you didn't want to spar."

"I don't want to have this conversation at all. You're the one who's sparring."

"Well said. May I take that as an invitation to come in?"

"Oh, certainly," Sherry said. "I've done everything I can think of to encourage you."

Aaron Grant walked in the door, looked around. "Nice place you've got here."

Sherry flushed slightly. The living room was still a cluttered hodgepodge of unpacked boxes.

"I'm glad you like it," she said. "But we so seldom entertain. Am I being remiss as hostess? May I get you something? A cup of coffee? A soda? Some strychnine perhaps?"

Aaron Grant smiled. "Coffee would be fine. Thank you for asking."

Sherry shot him a look, turned, marched into the kitchen, with Aaron Grant trailing behind.

"Well, this is more like it." Aaron Grant looked around the kitchen, nodded approvingly. "Homey, functional. It's nice to see that you at least eat."

"You want this coffee or not?"

"Please."

Sherry took a mug with a black-and-white checkerboard design from the cupboard, filled it with the remnants from the Pyrex bottom of the drip coffeemaker. She stuck the mug in the microwave, zapped it on high for twenty seconds.

"Milk and sugar?"

"Please."

Sherry took the carton of milk from the refrigerator, set it on the butcher block table next to the sugar bowl.

The microwave beeped. Sherry took the coffee out, set it on the butcher block, added a spoon.

"Knock yourself out," she said.

Aaron Grant added milk, two heaping spoonfuls of sugar, and stirred it around. There was no saucer. Aaron finished stirring, looked around for a place to put the spoon. Sherry gave him a look that said Aren't men helpless, took the spoon, and put it in the sink.

"I didn't want to put it on the butcher block," Aaron said.

"What?"

"Thanks for the coffee." He took a sip. "Not bad for microwave brew. You're a woman of many talents."

"You're a man of none. Would you like to try again to tell me why you're here?"

"Sure," Aaron Grant said. He glanced around, spotted the computer through the opposite door. "Would that be your office?"

"You stay out of there," Sherry protested, but Aaron Grant was already in the door.

"And, yes, what do we have here? A crossword puzzle on the screen. And here's the word *queue*. Would that position be four down? And the word *ewe*. Would that be fourteen across?"

"Now, you look here—"

Aaron Grant spread his hands. "I am not printing any of this. Your aunt and I have a deal. The same deal I have with the cops. I'm giving her everything, she's giving me everything, nothing's going out. Now, if she's done some work on this, I need to know."

"Why?"

"Huh?"

"Why do you need to know? You just got through saying you're not going to print it. So why do you need to know at all? Just to satisfy your own curiosity?"

"Absolutely."

Sherry looked at him in disgust. "You can't admit that. That's selfish and unheroic."

"So what? You don't like me anyway."

"What's that got to do with it?"

"I don't know. It's your premise."

"My premise? What are you talking about?"

"Everything under the sun, it seems like." Aaron pointed at the computer screen. "To avoid talking about this. If your Aunt Cora started working on the clue I gave her, I want to know."

"Cora hasn't even been home."

"I didn't think so. You did this yourself, didn't you? You punched this up on the screen to see if it fit. You're a smart woman, you've learned enough from your aunt you figure you should be able to tell. So does it?"

"What?"

"Don't be dense. Does the word *ewe* fit? As fourteen across?"

"Yes and no."

Aaron Grant frowned. "Would you mind explaining that?"

She gave him a look, then turned to the screen.

On it was the grid of a crossword, a crosshatch of squares, with a few black squares and the words *queue* and *ewe*.

"Okay," Sherry said. "This is what I was working on before I was so rudely interrupted. This is a basic program for constructing crossword puzzles. What we have here is a fifteen-by-fifteen square, which is your fairly standard daily puzzle, which is why I started with it first. Fifteen squares across, fifteen squares down.

"This is what it looks like if we put *ewe* in as fourteen across and *queue* in as four down."

"How do you know that's where they go?"

"I don't. But some things you can infer." She pointed to the black square in the fourth box over. "Like this black square here. Four down is *queue*. So if this square wasn't a black square, it would mean *q* would be the fourth letter of one across. The number of words with *q* in the fourth position is somewhat limited."

"Ah. The old limited number."

"Right," Sherry said. "So, the more likely construction is what I have here. One across is a three-letter word. Then a black square. Then four across and four down are both words beginning with *q*."

"That makes sense. And the other black square in the top line?"

"Is a guess. As to where it goes. But there can only be one."

"Why?"

"Because *ewe* is fourteen across. Two black squares makes thirteen clues down in the first line, so *ewe* fits in there."

"What if there were three black squares?"

"Then fourteen across would move over one word and the *e* in *ewe* would intersect with the *u* in *queue*."

"But this way they both fit?"

"Yeah, but I don't like it."

"Why not?"

"The words don't intersect."

"Do they have to?"

"No," Sherry said. "But we have two clues, and there must be some connection. One's across and one's down, so the most likely connection is that they intersect. And both words have *e*'s in them. In fact, both words have two *e*'s in them, which makes an intersection likely."

"But they don't intersect," Aaron said.

"Right," Sherry said. "Unless we change the grid."

"Change it how?"

"I was about to try something smaller."

"Such as?"

"Twelve-by-twelve."

"Can you do that?"

"Sure."

Sherry pressed some keys, and the crossword puzzle vanished. She pressed some more, and a twelve-by-twelve grid appeared. Sherry and Aaron played around with the two words, but they couldn't get them to intersect.

"Eleven-by-eleven," Aaron Grant said.

"Huh?"

"Do eleven-by-eleven."

Sherry deleted the twelve-by-twelve, punched up an eleven-by-eleven grid.

"Now," Aaron said, "you've got three three-letter words across. That's nine words going down. In the second row you've got ten, eleven, twelve. In the third row across the first one is thirteen and the second one is fourteen. Go on. Fill it in. Doesn't it work?"

Sherry filled in the black squares, typed in *queue* and *ewe*.

1	2	3	■	4 Q	5	6	■	7	8	9
10			■	11 U			■	12		
13			■	14 E	W	E	■			
				U						
				E						
				■						

"That's it," Aaron Grant said. "That's it. We've done it."

"We've done what?" Sherry said. She swiveled her chair around to look at him. "We've found a way the words could conceivably fit. I hate to break it to you, but that was not a particularly difficult challenge. I knew there was a way they would, finding it was not that hard. Now that they do, would you mind telling me what they happen to mean? In terms of that poor young girl who's dead?"

"I have no idea."

"Neither have I. And Aunt Cora won't know either. Nobody could. This is a puzzle that doesn't make sense. And we don't even know if this last clue is a real clue at all, if it came from the same person."

"I know. That's my fault. I'm sorry. Even so."

"What?"

"If your aunt comes up with anything, will you let me know?"

"That's up to her."

"Right. Well, thanks for the coffee."

"Going so soon?"

"Sorry to disappoint you, but if I can't write about this, I gotta come up with something else."

"Fine. You do that. Just so it isn't crossword puzzles."

"I wouldn't dream of it."

"I'm sure you wouldn't. Trouble is, you already did."

"Yeah, I know," Aaron said. "I'm sorry about that. But don't worry. I'll fix it."

He smiled at her and ducked out the front door.

"Fix it?" Sherry stuck her head out the door, called, "What do you mean, fix it?"

But Aaron Grant was already climbing into his car. As she watched, he gunned the motor and drove off.

Sherry closed the door, leaned against it. Aaron Grant had to be one of the most exhausting men she had ever met.

She smiled, headed back to the computer.

19

WITHOUT THE CRIME SCENE RIBBON IT TOOK AARON GRANT A LITTLE while to find the grave. When he finally did, he saw that he had not been the first to do so. There were a lot of footprints in the soft earth. A lot of curious people had been by.

At least the TV crews were gone. Aaron hadn't seen them all day. With the passage of time, the story had lost its immediacy. If the girl had been raped it might have been another matter, but she hadn't. Now that she'd been identified, she was just a runaway unlucky enough to have been hit over the head. Tragic, of course, but not compelling. Not newsworthy. Not without something else.

Like the clue he'd promised not to use. How frustrating. The perfect story, and he couldn't write it. Of course a promise was a promise.

Or was it?

What was bothering Aaron Grant was whether he would actually withhold the story if he hadn't made a deal with the police. If it was only Cora Felton asking him to.

And her niece.

What was it about that girl? Uh-oh. The word *girl*. It occurred to him he'd better not even think it. Somehow she'd know. He shook his head.

What was it about her?

At any rate, he'd agreed to quash the crossword puzzle story, so that's what he was going to do.

Aaron Grant looked around. Okay, what was it she'd said? Four graves down from the body in the fifth row of graves. Carefully, Aaron Grant counted down, then counted over. He took out his notebook, wrote down the information on the stone.

Aaron Grant put his notebook back in his pocket, got in his car, left the cemetery, and drove back to the paper.

Bill Dodsworth popped out of his office when Aaron came in. The managing editor not only looked like a bulldog, he also always seemed to growl and bark. "There you are! You got somethin'? We need somethin'. Right now we got squat!"

"I'm chasing leads."

"*Leads?*" Dodsworth repeated. The editor had a sour expression even when pleased. "I don't need *leads*. I can't print *leads*. Give me something I can go with."

"I'm working on it," Aaron said.

He brushed Dodsworth off, continued through the pressroom, out the swinging door, down the hall, and into the morgue, where the back issues were kept. The morgue, a large, dark room with metal bins of papers, was foreign territory to Aaron Grant. In his short time at the *Gazette,* he'd had little cause to go there. Aaron hated research, preferred personal interviews.

Not this time. He switched on the lights, went to work.

Only he had no luck. All but the most recent newspapers were missing. Aaron couldn't find a thing earlier than 1990.

Aaron went back to the editor's office. "Where's the old papers?" he asked Bill Dodsworth.

"What?"

"The back issues. There's nothing in the morgue."

"Of course not. We're converting to microfilm. You ever pay attention at staff meetings? This is not something new. It's been going on for months."

"Where's the microfilm?"

"At the library."

"Oh?"

"Best place for it. We donated the papers, they donated the viewers."

"Who paid for the transfers?"

"Is that any of your business?"

"None at all," Aaron said.

He hopped in his car, drove to the library.

The Bakerhaven Library was a white, wood-frame building that a plaque on the front proudly proclaimed had been built in 1886. The wide wooden front porch was a favorite reading spot, and an old man sat on it now, reading the morning paper. In spite of himself, Aaron Grant couldn't help craning his neck to see if the man was reading his story, but the way the paper was folded, he had to be reading the sports.

Aaron Grant went up the steps and went in.

Edith Potter, the librarian, was at the front desk, typing card catalogue entries. She looked up when he came in. Her gray hair, as always, was pulled back into a bun. Her face appeared more lined than usual. It occurred to Aaron that this murder was getting to people.

"Aaron Grant," she said. "Oh, Aaron Grant. Isn't it awful?"

Aaron couldn't dispute that. He spent a few minutes convincing Edith he didn't know anything new about the case, then asked her where the microfilm was kept.

"Oh," she said. "Oh. You should ask Jimmy. He can help you with that."

"Jimmy?"

"My son Jimmy. He's home from school and he's been helping out. He'll be glad to show you."

"I'm sure I can do it myself."

Edith Potter smiled patiently. "Yes, but do ask him," she said. "He likes to be asked."

"Oh, yes," Aaron Grant said. He recalled that Jimmy Potter had always been a little slow. It wouldn't hurt to let him find the microfilm.

Edith Potter directed him to the back of the stacks where a tall, gawky boy was placing books on the shelves.

"Hi, Jimmy," Aaron said.

Jimmy Potter looked down from the ladder where he'd been working on the top shelf. "Huh? Oh, hi, Aaron. What's up?"

"You got time to help me with something?"

"Sure, Aaron. With what?"

"It's about the murder."

Jimmy nearly fell off the ladder and his face went white. "Don't know anything about that," he said.

"Of course not," Aaron said. He'd forgotten who he was dealing with, and felt a pang of guilt. "I know you don't. That's not what I meant. I just need help looking something up."

Jimmy exhaled. "Oh. Oh, that's different." He climbed down from the ladder. "Sure thing, Aaron. Anything I can do."

"You know where they keep the microfilm?"

"Sure do."

"How about for nineteen eighty-four?"

"I can find it. You want the whole year?"

"No. Just anything on the death of Barbara Burnside."

20

JIMMY POTTER WOULDN'T QUIT. AARON GRANT HAD TAKEN WHAT Jimmy'd found him, said it was enough, and gone back to the paper to write his story, but Jimmy had gotten such a kick out of doing research for him that he'd kept right at it. And sure enough, he'd managed to find a few more mentions of the Barbara Burnside accident.

Jimmy wanted to print them out for Aaron like he'd done with the others, but he knew he couldn't because Aaron had said he didn't need them, and if Aaron didn't need them, then his mother wouldn't want him wasting the paper. So, instead, Jimmy just made notes of where the articles were.

Unfortunately, organization was not Jimmy's strong suit. By the time he was done he had written the information everywhere. When he realized this, Jimmy Potter was upset. He knew he couldn't hand Aaron Grant a pile of little scraps of paper. Why hadn't he used a big sheet of paper to begin with? That would have been the smart thing to do. Only he hadn't had a big sheet of paper on him. He would have had to go back to the little office to get one. And he hadn't wanted to go back to the office. Not while he was in the middle of looking stuff up. He certainly wouldn't have wanted to do that.

Jimmy went back to the office now, got a big sheet of paper, and a sharpened pencil. He could have sat at the desk, but it was piled with the file cards he'd been helping his mother type. There was even one in the typewriter. He could have taken it out and typed the list, but he didn't want to. Too hard. Too many numbers.

He took the paper and pencil, went out and sat at the big oak table in the reading room, and began copying the list.

He got three entries made before his mind began to wander. That was his problem with school too. Why he had so much trouble with his homework. He could never stick with it for any length of time without beginning to daydream. And that was under normal circumstances, when there was nothing going on.

Not like now.

Jimmy Potter couldn't stop thinking about the girl. The dead girl. The girl in the cemetery. No, not Barbara Burnside. The other one. The one lying by the grave.

A young girl. Teenage. Like the one sitting at the other end of the table. The young girl in the Bakerhaven High sweater who was bent over a spiral notebook copying something out of a book. She'd be about the same age. Only this girl was alive and that one was dead.

Dead.

What a strange concept. The girl had been alive, every bit as alive as this one here. And now she was dead. One minute she was alive, the next she was dead.

It was so strange.

Jimmy looked at the girl across the table. Imagined her dead.

His mouth fell open. What a horrifying thought. But what an electrifying one too. His body tingled and he felt afraid. Why had he imagined this young girl dead?

And who was she?

The girl seemed vaguely familiar, but he couldn't quite place her. He'd gone to Bakerhaven High just last year, but she would have been behind him in school. Way behind. She didn't look old enough to be a senior. She was a sophomore or a junior. Maybe even a freshman. Which would make her an eighth grader last year.

So young.

A pretty girl, but so young.

It was hard to think of her dead.

Jimmy Potter's eyes were very wide.

The girl's pencil snapped. She frowned, looked up in annoyance.

Her face froze. She blinked, hastily looked back to her paper. Her heart was pounding.

He was looking at her.

He'd immediately averted his eyes, but in that split second, she had seen. The image was still there, like a photograph, before her. The look on his face as he'd been looking at her. She shivered just thinking of it.

Her homework was no longer an option. Her pencil was broken, she wasn't going to sharpen it, or even look for a new one. She'd found what she was looking for. She didn't have to copy it, she could remember it and write it down when she got home.

Clara Harper shoved her notebook and pencil into her backpack, snatched it up, and hurried out the door.

21

"DADDY, HE'S WEIRD."

"Who is?"

"That boy. I tell you, he's really creepy."

Chief Harper wasn't surprised. His daughter was at the age to find boys creepy. "Uh huh."

"Da-ad! Are you listening to me?"

He actually wasn't. He was trying to watch the ball game on TV. Not easy to do with a teenage daughter. "Of course I'm listening to you."

"No, you're not. You don't even know who I'm talking about."

"Some creepy boy."

"Da-ad! I'm talking about Jimmy Potter. The librarian's son."

"Oh."

"Oh? Is that all you have to say? Oh?"

"Jimmy isn't weird. He's just a little slow."

"He's creepy. He's got this strange way of looking at you." Clara shuddered. "So, what if it's him?"

"Huh?"

"What if he's the one?"

Chief Harper was somewhat preoccupied by the fact the Yankees, trailing three to two, had runners on first and third with one out. Still, that statement registered. "The one? What do you mean, the one?"

"You know. The killer."

"Oh, for goodness sakes."

"Da-ad! *Someone* did it. Why couldn't it be him?"

Chief Harper smiled. "And what makes you think it is?"

"You should see the way he looks at me."

"Maybe he likes you."

"Da-ad!"

"Clara, you have school tomorrow. Did you do your homework?"

"And that's another thing," Clara said. "Why is he here? I thought he went off to college."

"He must have got out."

"I'm still in school."

"Some colleges get out early."

"That's not fair."

"Maybe not. But you're right about one thing. *You* still have school. Did you do your homework?"

"But don't you see?" Clara said. "He's away at school. He comes home, and, bang!, right away this girl gets killed."

"I don't think it's cause and effect."

"Dad!"

Chief Harper was vaguely aware of the fact that there were now two outs and the Yankee runners were still on first and third. "I hear you. He's on my list of suspects. He won't get away. Now, did you do your homework?"

Clara gave him a look and stomped off.

Chief Harper settled back in his chair to enjoy the game.

The Yankees managed to load the bases before Sam Brogan phoned in a missing persons report.

22

SHERRY CARTER SCOOPED UP THE PHONE. "HELLO?"

"Sherry? Hi, it's Aaron Grant."

"Oh. Hi. I didn't know we were on a first name basis."

"I'm sorry. You want me to call you Miss Carter?"

"I don't want you to call me at all."

"I'm not calling you. I'm calling your aunt."

"Oh, is that right? Am I supposed to be crushed?"

"No, you're supposed to call her to the phone."

"She's asleep," Sherry said.

From the kitchen came an exclamation and the sound of breaking glass.

"Really? Then perhaps I should let you get back to your party."

"Why did you call?"

"Huh?"

"Why are you calling my aunt now, this time of night?"

"To ask her a question."

"I assumed that. What were you going to ask her?"

"Why do you want to know?"

"Don't be that way. If it has anything to do with what we were working on, I'd be interested to hear it."

"It doesn't, directly."

"So what is it?"

Before Aaron could answer, Cora Felton came into the room carrying a tall gin and tonic. Her hair was mussed and her glasses were slightly askew. There was perspiration on her brow.

"Sherry, I must be getting old," she said, in a slightly too loud voice. "I just broke a glass. Oh, you're on the phone. Who is it?"

"Is that her?" Aaron Grant asked. "Put her on."

Sherry frowned, looked at her aunt. Cora Felton had gotten home, changed out of her clothes, and put on what Sherry referred to as her Wicked Witch of the West dress, a long, loose, flowing, black, pullover shift that had seen better days. Stained, tattered, ripped, and freckled with cigarette burns, it was her favorite dress, the one she always wore lounging around at home. To the many battle scars, Sherry noted, had now been added the stain of whatever was in the glass Aunt Cora had just broken.

Holding the phone, Sherry became aware of the fact she had not answered Aaron Grant, particularly when he said, "Hello? You still there?"

Her face began to redden. "Sorry. Aunt Cora isn't available at the moment."

"Sherry. Don't be a nudge. Of course I am. Who is that?"

"Sounds to me like she's available," Aaron Grant said. "Can't she come to the phone?"

"She's just getting ready for bed, and—"

"I'm doing nothing of the kind. Sherry, give me the phone."

Aaron listened to the phone being surrendered. Moments later he heard Cora Felton's voice, slightly slurred, say, "Hello?"

"Miss Felton, this is Aaron Grant. Sorry to bother you, but something has come up. Were you playing cards at the Country Kitchen tonight?"

Cora Felton guffawed. "You're not going to put *that* in the paper, are you?"

"No, I'm not. One of the card players was Vicki Tanner?"

"Yes. Why?"

"She hasn't come home. Her husband's very upset."

"She isn't home?"

"No."

"That's ridiculous. What time is it?"

"It's after eleven."

"She should be home."

"She's not."

"It's not right," Cora Felton said. "And I'll tell you what you should do. You should call the police."

"The police know. They called me."

"They called you?"

"Yes. They're looking for her now. They didn't call there?"

"Sherry, did the police call?"

"Police? Aunt Cora, what's going on?"

"No, no one's called here. Why would they?"

"To find out where Vicki Tanner went when she left the Country Kitchen."

"I wouldn't know. I didn't leave then."

"Who did?"

"Iris and Lois. Stick-in-the-muds. Can't stay for one round."

Aaron Grant said, "Miss Felton, this may be nothing, but your friend Vicki Tanner is missing. The police obviously aren't taking it that seriously if they haven't even called you. But her husband's quite upset, and—"

"Of course he is. Let's go find her."

"What?"

"If the police aren't going to find her, we have to. Why don't you come pick me up."

"Now?"

"What, you're afraid of the dark? You'd like to wait till tomorrow, perhaps? Sherry and I will go with you. Come pick us up."

"Aunt Cora—" Sherry protested, but Aaron Grant had already hung up the phone.

23

"YOU'RE NOT GOING TO WEAR THAT DRESS."

Cora Felton lit a cigarette, took a drag, blew out the smoke. "I most certainly am. This is not a date. I'm working here."

"Drink your coffee."

"I don't need coffee."

"You need something. You can barely walk."

"Well, thank you very much."

"Aunt Cora. You've gotta understand. This is a newspaper reporter. *Newspaper reporter*. Those are the people we try very hard to make a good impression on."

"I think he likes you."

"Aunt Cora. You're not listening."

"Yes, I am. You're talking about that handsome young reporter." Cora Felton took a sip of coffee, cocked her head. "And you're afraid I'll mess up your chances with him."

"That is *not* what I'm afraid of. I'm afraid you'll blow your image. Then you won't have a puzzle column anymore, and then we won't be able to afford this house."

"You worry too much."

"Because you don't worry at all. I'm shouldering the whole load."

"And very nicely too, dear," Cora Felton said. She frowned at her cup. "Do you suppose you could spike this coffee just a touch?"

"Aunt Cora."

"Just a thought."

"What a nightmare. Won't you change that dress?"

"Why? He's not coming to see me. You can change if you want, but there's no need. You look good in a T-shirt and blue jeans. I bet he finds them sexy."

"Aunt Cora."

"I wonder what he's wearing this time of night. Surely not a suit and tie."

"Really," Sherry said. "The things you think of."

Headlights pulled into the driveway, cast shadows through the front window.

"Here he is," Cora Felton said. "No time to change now. It's a come-as-you-are-when-invited party."

She set the coffee cup down, shuffled through the living room, and went out the front door. Sherry trailed along behind.

Aaron Grant stood by the open door of his car. He was wearing a short-sleeved cotton pullover sports shirt with collar, and a pair of dark slacks. Sherry was irritated with herself for noticing, and blamed her aunt for bringing it up.

Aaron Grant waved. "Hi, are you ready? Let's go."

Cora Felton crossed the front lawn in long strides, talking as she went. "There you are, young man, nice to see you again. Please forgive my dress, Sherry said I should change, but then this isn't a social occasion, is it? I'll just sit in the back if you don't mind. Sherry, you sit up front. Hop in, hop in. You can tell us all about it as we go."

Cora Felton climbed into the backseat and slammed the door shut, leaving Sherry Carter alone with Aaron Grant.

Sherry didn't know what to say. She felt like apologizing for her aunt, but realized doing so would be wrong. She also felt like telling Aaron Grant this wasn't her idea, but then he knew that, and there was such a thing as protesting too much. So Sherry mutely marched to the passenger door, flung it open, and got in.

The engine was still running. Aaron Grant hopped in, threw the car into reverse, and backed out of the driveway.

"Where are we going?" Cora Felton asked.

"The Country Kitchen," Aaron Grant said. "I thought we'd start there, try to trace Mrs. Tanner's route home."

"Isn't that what the police are doing?"

"Probably."

"Then we should do something else."

"Like what?"

"Actually," Cora Felton said, "the Country Kitchen's not that bad an idea. I'll go in, interview the bartender, find out what time Vicki left."

"We know what time she left," Sherry Carter intervened. "You know when she left. *You* saw her leave."

"I didn't note the time. Wouldn't the time be an important factor in this case?" Cora inquired mildly.

"Perhaps," Aaron Grant said. "But you're right about not duplicating the police, Miss Felton. Questioning the bartender is the first thing they'll do, so we should do something else. I just thought the Country Kitchen was a good place to start driving from, but there's no reason to go inside."

"Is that so?" Cora Felton said. "But what if Vicki Tanner never left at all? What if she said good-bye and then went in the bathroom? Then she came out later after we'd gone, and she's sitting at the bar right now."

"Are you serious?" Aaron Grant said.

"No, she's not," Sherry said irritably. "She's just trying to get her own way."

"Well, I like that," Cora Felton said. "Here I am, only trying to help . . ."

"You can help with her car," Aaron said. "You happen to know what kind she drives?"

"Blue Nissan. I don't know the license number."

"Would you know it if you saw it?"

"The car or the license number?"

"Either."

"I'd probably know the car. The license number I never paid attention to."

"Then it's not a vanity plate. If she had a word on the license plate, you'd probably have noticed."

"I suppose."

"Anyway, let's keep a lookout for the car."

The Country Kitchen was on the other side of town. Aaron Grant cruised down the main street. The shops were all closed that time of night, and there were very few parked cars. Vicki Tanner's was not among them. Neither was Sam Brogan's. There was a light on in the police station, but no car out front.

"See," Aaron Grant said. "The police car's gone. Sam Brogan's out investigating this."

"Who?" Sherry said.

"Sam Brogan. That's the police officer who tipped me off. He's probably at the Country Kitchen now."

"Maybe we should go there," Cora Felton said.

Sherry took a breath, but held her tongue.

Just outside of town Aaron Grant spotted the police car coming from the opposite direction. He hit the horn, flashed his lights, and the police car braked to a stop. Aaron pulled up next to it, rolled down the window as Sam Brogan rolled down his.

"Any luck?" Aaron asked.

Sam Brogan shook his head. "No. Bartender says she left hours ago."

"Any chance he's wrong and she's still there?"

"Not at all. The place is empty. They're getting ready to close. I'm just trying to spot her car."

"Got a description?"

"Blue Nissan. Connecticut plate, M S seven nine six eight. If you spot it, call in. I don't feel like driving around all night." Sam Brogan jerked his thumb. "Who you got there?"

"One of the women she was playing cards with. And her niece. Where's the husband?"

"At home. He wanted to come along, but I told him what if she came back and no one's there?"

"You could have left a note."

"Hey, you think I want him driving me nuts? Anyway, you find her, you call the station so the chief can radio me to go home."

"Chief Harper's at the station?"

"No. He's home. Call forwarding's on. Just make sure you call. I don't need this."

Sam Brogan rolled up the window and drove off.

"Well," Aaron said, "that's that. We're duplicating his actions. But I don't know any other way to start. We're almost to the Country

Kitchen. Let's turn around there, start tracing her path like Sam is. And anything we can do different is all to the good."

In a couple of minutes they reached the Country Kitchen. The restaurant, styled to look like an oversized, sprawling log cabin, still had lights on, but the parking lot was nearly deserted. The few cars left probably belonged to the help. There was certainly no blue Nissan. Even so, Aaron pulled into the lot, circled it once before driving out.

"Okay," Aaron said. "Keep your eyes open. If you have any suggestions, please speak up."

They drove slowly back toward town. It was an open road, with only a scattering of houses. Nonetheless, in half a mile Cora Felton counted no less than four TAG SALE signs in the driveways, three proclaiming sales on Saturday and one on Sunday. Cora was sure some of the signs had been up ever since she'd moved in. A cynical New Yorker, Cora had an image of the Bakerhaven faithful assembling eagerly every weekend to buy each other's junk.

"Closed garage," Cora said.

"What?" Aaron said.

"That house has a closed garage. The car could be in there."

"There's a car in the driveway."

"Sure. That's the guy who owns the house. What if she drove up, put her car in the garage?"

"Why would she do that?"

"Are you kidding? So her husband wouldn't drive by and see her car."

"You think she's having an affair?"

"No, I don't. Frankly, it would be a huge relief. This isn't like her at all."

"Well, keep looking. We're not quite ready to start breaking into people's garages."

A mile down the road they caught up with Sam Brogan. He was driving slowly, and shining the searchlight into people's driveways.

"Not too subtle," Sherry commented.

"No, but effective," Aaron said. "If her car's there, he'll spot it."

A little farther down the road the Bakerhaven elementary school came up on the right. Sam Brogan drove on by.

"Turn in there," Cora Felton said.

"What?" Aaron Grant said.

"Let's check out the parking lot."

"There's nothing *in* the parking lot."

"I know."

"Then why do you want to check it out?"

"Because the cop didn't. Come on, let's check out the school."

Aaron Grant drove in and circled the parking lot. There were no cars.

"How about around back?" Cora suggested.

"There's no parking lot around back."

"So? Can you drive back there?"

"I don't know."

"Let's find out."

Aaron Grant drove to the edge of the school parking lot. The asphalt path continued on around the building. He drove onto it, circled around to the back.

His headlights lit up a car.

It was unanimous. All three of them said, "Look!"

All they could see was the bright lights reflecting off the back of the car parked behind the school. Aaron dimmed the headlights. Now through the back window they could see someone moving inside the other car. Quickly. Hurriedly. A minute later the engine roared and the car sprang to life and shot out of there.

"That's not her," Sherry said.

"No, it isn't," Aaron Grant said. "It's kids parking. We must have scared them to death."

"How do you know that?" Sherry asked.

"Don't be silly," Cora said. "He's obviously parked here himself."

Both Sherry and Aaron Grant chose to ignore this comment. Which only emphasized it. Into the awkward silence, Cora Felton said brightly, "What shall we do now?"

"Well," Sherry said, "we could drive out to Vicki's house and talk to her husband."

"I suppose we could," Aaron Grant said.

"What good would that do?" Cora said. "All he knows is she's not there."

"Well, what do *you* want to do?"

Cora Felton thought a moment. "Let's check out the high school."

"Huh?"

"Isn't the high school back the way we came?"

"Yeah. It's on the other side of the Country Kitchen."

"Fine. Let's check it out."

"The other side of the Country Kitchen?" Sherry said.

"Yeah," Aaron said. "About a half mile down the road."

"But—"

"But what?"

"That's the opposite direction she would have gone."

"If she went home," Cora said. "But she obviously didn't."

"Yes, but she was on her *way* home. Isn't that right? She said good-bye to you, and she was going home. There's no reason she would have gone the other way."

"Maybe not," Cora said, "but that's precisely the reason to check it out. We want to do what the police aren't doing. They are not looking in that direction. So let's go back to the Country Kitchen and ask ourselves, what if she came out the driveway and turned right?"

"Fine by me," Aaron Grant said.

He drove out of the elementary school parking lot and turned left, back the way they came. A few minutes later they passed the Country Kitchen. The lights were out and the last cars were leaving. They drove on down the road, checking the cars in the driveway of each house.

A couple of miles down the road they came to a soccer field in front of the high school, which was set back from the road. Aaron Grant turned in the drive, drove past the goal and up to the front doors.

The Bakerhaven high school had a circle out front for the buses to turn around in. The parking lot was in the back. Aaron Grant drove there, and once again they all said, "Look!"

Only this time it was a blue Nissan.

"Is that the plate?" Sherry asked.

"That's it."

Cora Felton was already out of the car. Aaron and Sherry were right behind.

"I wouldn't touch anything," Aaron warned.

Cora ignored him and tried the door handle. "Locked," she reported. "And it appears to be empty."

"Appears?" Sherry said.

"We haven't looked in the trunk."

"Cora!"

"It's not so far-fetched," Aaron Grant said. "Here's the car in a deserted parking lot. It doesn't look good."

"We better call it in," Cora said. "Where's the nearest phone?"

"Right here," Aaron Grant said. He went to his car, pulled his cellular phone out of the glove compartment, and called the police. With call forwarding on, he got Mrs. Harper, who wasn't eager to disturb her husband, but eventually Chief Harper came to the phone.

"Chief, it's Aaron Grant. You wanna tell Sam Brogan I just found Vicki Tanner's car."

"What?"

"We found her car. In the high school parking lot. It's locked, and there's no sign of her."

"Who's we?"

"I got Cora Felton and Sherry Carter with me."

"Oh? You mind telling me why?"

"Well, they were worried about her. Actually, it was Cora Felton who found the car."

"Uh huh. Any sign of foul play?"

"No, there's just the car. It's locked and there's nothing in it."

"Okay. I'll tell Sam."

Aaron Grant stuck the phone back in the glove compartment and turned around to find Cora Felton standing there. She had a strange expression on her face.

"What is it?" he said.

Cora Felton sighed.

"I know where Vicki is."

24

CHIEF HARPER PULLED HIS CAR TO A STOP IN FRONT OF THE CEMETERY gate and got out.

"Where is it?" he demanded.

Aaron Grant jerked his thumb. "Same place."

"Same grave?"

"That's right."

"Who's there now?"

"Sam Brogan and the women."

"And you found it?"

"We found it, we called you. Just like I said."

"When'd Sam get here?"

"Right before you."

"Uh huh. How do I get in?"

"Over the fence."

"Great."

It wasn't hard. The fence was only four feet high. Chief Harper hopped over, snapped on his flashlight, headed for the grave.

"Over here," a voice called.

He shone his light to see Cora Felton waving at him. He walked up, stopped, shone the light on the grave.

The body of Vicki Tanner lay facedown next to the gravestone, just the way the other body had lain. Her head was twisted to the side. Her eye was open. Her shoes and socks were missing.

Chief Harper felt light-headed, had to take a deep breath to steady himself. All right, he told himself. This doesn't seem real, but it is. So get a grip. Never mind how much it seems the same, how is it different?

The big difference was it wasn't raining. Chief Harper was grateful for that fact, although he actually felt a pang of guilt at how pleasant the thought was.

The other difference was her clothes. The girl had been wearing blue jeans and a shirt. Vicki Tanner wore a simple cotton dress.

"I haven't touched her," Sam Brogan told him. "This is just the way we found her."

"You call the doctor?"

"He's on his way. I called her husband too, to make the ID."

"Good," Harper said, but he wished Sam hadn't. The husband would just be in the way. Cora Felton could make the ID.

With that idea, he turned to her. "It is her, isn't it, Miss Felton?"

"It's her, all right."

"How'd you happen to find her?"

"We just looked and here she was."

"Uh huh. And how'd you happen to look here?"

"Just a hunch."

"A hunch?" Chief Harper repeated. Miss Felton seemed coherent, but he could smell liquor on her breath. "You want to elaborate on that?"

"When we found her car I was worried. I was afraid something had happened to her. Then it occurred to me, if something had, she'd be here."

"Her car's at the high school?"

"Yes."

"In the opposite direction? Out past the Country Kitchen?"

"Surely you know where the high school is."

"Yes. A good ways away in the opposite direction. You go out there, you find her car, and you conclude that she's *here?*"

Cora Felton smiled. "A faulty deduction, Chief?"

There came the sound of a siren in the distance. It grew louder, and headlights pulled up to the front gate.

"The ambulance can't get in," Chief Harper told them. "Sam, call the caretaker, get him over here to open up."

"Already done," Sam Brogan said. "Guy should be on his way." He pointed. "Maybe that's him now."

Another pair of headlights pulled up to the gate; a car door slammed. But it wasn't the caretaker, because moments later a figure climbed over the fence and began stumbling in their direction.

"Where is she? Where is she?" he cried.

Stuart Tanner hurried up. The young lawyer was distraught. His face was flushed, his eyes were wide. "Vicki!" he shouted. "Oh, my God, Vicki!"

He started for the body, but Chief Harper headed him off. "Easy there, Mr. Tanner. Take it easy. There's nothing you can do."

Stuart Tanner wouldn't listen. He lunged forward, stumbled, fell into Chief Harper's arms. Still he kept struggling, trying to get to his wife.

Chief Harper held him firm. "She's dead, Mr. Tanner. I'm sorry, but she's dead, and we can't touch her until the medical examiner gets here."

"Oh, my God!" Stuart Tanner moaned. "Oh, my God!" He was trembling. Sobs racked his lean body.

"Sam!" Chief Harper hissed. He rolled his eyes, said pointedly, "Sam, you want to take Mr. Tanner back to his car till the medical examiner gets here?"

Sam Brogan took Stuart Tanner by the shoulders, managed to pry him away, and led him off toward the gate. They passed the emergency medical team, who came up lugging the stretcher they'd lifted over the fence.

Chief Harper noted it was the same team who'd been on call the first time. "All right, you know the drill. Verify she's dead, but don't move her till Dr. Nathan gets here."

"He's not gonna wanna climb that fence," one of the medics said.

Chief Harper realized that was exactly right. He could imagine Barney Nathan standing in front of the gate, impatiently tapping his foot until the caretaker showed up to open it.

Harper looked over at the medics examining the body. Cora Felton was peering over their shoulders. It occurred to him he ought to get her out of there. Her and the other one.

Before he could, however, he was interrupted by a loud, peremptory voice, saying, "Dale!" He looked around to see the prosecutor come striding up.

"So," Henry Firth said, "you got another one."

"Yes, we do."

"The first one isn't even solved, and you've got another."

"It certainly seems inconsiderate," Chief Harper said.

Firth gave him a look. "What is that supposed to mean?"

Chief Harper shrugged. "Just pointing out the killer probably doesn't care how much he's inconveniencing us. That's probably the last thing in his mind."

"It isn't funny," Henry Firth said. "We have a situation here, where things are going from bad to worse with you in charge. It's time to concede you can't handle it, and step down."

Before Chief Harper could retort, there came the creak of the front gate swinging open, and a car drove into the cemetery. It stopped and Barney Nathan got out. The doctor had clearly been ready for bed when he'd gotten the call. He had put on his jacket, pants, and shirt, but not stopped to tie his bow tie. It was, Chief Harper noted, perhaps the only time he'd seen him in such disarray.

With barely a nod in his direction, Barney Nathan joined the medics examining the corpse.

Cora Felton peered over the doctor's shoulder.

Henry Firth grabbed Chief Harper by the arm. "Look at that," he said. "You let all these people run around your crime scene? I guess any tracks you find won't be much use."

"No," Chief Harper replied. "They'll probably be yours. Would it be asking too much for you to wait outside the gate?"

"Oh, now, look here—" Henry Firth began.

While they were arguing, Aaron Grant detoured around them and over to where Sherry Carter stood. "What's up?" he said.

She glared at him. "What's up? You're asking me what's up?"

"I don't mean for publication. I mean what's going on?"

"Can't you tell?"

"Yes, I can. Do I have to be direct? I went to call Chief Harper. I left you two alone with the body. Need I say more?"

"I don't know what you're talking about."

"Don't be dumb. I'm sure your aunt did everything but an autopsy. I wouldn't be surprised if she knew the body temperature."

Sherry pointed to the grave, where Cora Felton appeared to be conferring with the emergency team and the medical examiner. "No, I think she's getting that now."

"I'm sure she is," Aaron said. "Come on, did you find anything?"

Before Sherry could answer, Chief Harper joined them. "I'm going to have to clear you people out. I'm catching grief from the prosecutor. I just booted him and now I gotta boot you." He waved his hand. "Miss Felton, over here, please."

Cora Felton reluctantly left the body.

"You gotta do me a favor, wait outside the gate with everybody else. I'll talk to you when I get a chance. I don't know when that will be."

"That's fine, Chief," Cora Felton said. She came right up to him. "And you don't have to apologize. We understand exactly what you're doing." She took him by the hand, lowered her voice. "Of course, I couldn't say anything in front of the other cop. I know you want to keep this hush-hush. And I knew you didn't want that medical examiner to find it."

Chief Harper blinked. "Find what?"

Cora Felton smiled. "I knew you'd understand, Chief. Don't worry, we're cooperating, we'll be on our way. Come on, Sherry. You too, young man. Chief Harper has work to do."

With that she squeezed his hand shut, and shepherded them away.

As Chief Harper stood watching them go, he felt something in his hand.

He glanced over at the grave. Barney Nathan and the medics were busy with the body. There was no one else around.

He raised his hand, opened it.

In it was a folded slip of paper.

Chief Harper scowled. That damn woman. What had she done now?

He unfolded the piece of paper.

It read: 18) D — YES VOTE(3).

25

"WHAT WAS THAT ALL ABOUT?" AARON GRANT SAID.

"Now, now," Cora Felton said. "Let's be discreet until we get out of here."

They were coming out through the gate. The prosecutor stood off to one side, grumbling to himself. Stuart Tanner sat in the front seat of his car with his head in his hands. Sam Brogan stood next to the car, conferring with Dan Finley, who had just arrived. They were apparently discussing what they would do if the TV crews showed up.

Aaron Grant grimaced. The *Gazette* had already gone to press, and the morning edition wouldn't be reporting the murder. Aaron had called the managing editor right after he'd called the police. Bill Dodsworth couldn't have cared less. The bottom line was, no matter how good the story, the number of extra papers sold wouldn't cover the cost of another run. It was a bit of a disillusionment for Aaron to find he worked for a paper that wouldn't stop the presses even for a murder.

"So," Cora Felton said. "How about a ride?"

Aaron Grant was surprised. "You want to leave now?"

"Trust me."

Sam Brogan stopped them when they got in Aaron's car. "Where you going?"

"Taking the women home," Aaron said.

Sam nodded. "Good idea."

Aaron started the car and drove off. "Okay, we're alone. No one can hear us. Stop stalling. What did you find?"

"Hey, watch your tone," Sherry said.

"Now, now," Cora Felton said. "Can you blame him for being exasperated? You wouldn't shut up till I told you."

"I was right there, and there was no one around."

"You told me not to do it in the first place."

"Of course I did. You had no right touching the body."

"And I said, You wanna pretend I didn't touch her, you don't have to look at the clue."

"Clue?" Aaron Grant said.

"Yes. It was in the pocket of her dress. I just gave it to Chief Harper. I don't know what he'll make of it."

"What clue?"

"Eighteen D yes vote three."

"Yes vote three?" Aaron Grant repeated. "What does that mean?"

"You don't know?" Sherry said. "It's really too easy."

"It's easy for you. You've had it for half an hour and you got to discuss it with her. I just heard it. A yes vote. What's a yes vote?"

"Think motion."

"Huh?"

"Voting on a motion. If you don't vote nay, how do you vote?"

"Aye," Aaron Grant said. "You're right, it's too easy. So, does it fit?"

"I don't know. I haven't had a chance to play with it."

"How about it, Miss Felton, do you think it will fit?"

Cora shrugged. "It may."

"It may?"

"Yes. And then again, it may not. We'll have to see."

"Don't you have an opinion?"

"Yes, I do. My opinion, for what it's worth, is it doesn't really matter."

"Doesn't matter?"

"No. I think the killer's teasing us. And these clues don't mean as much as we think they do."

Aaron frowned. He wondered if Cora Felton really meant that, or if she was just trying to downplay her own role in the matter. "You're not going to try to put it in the grid?"

"Of course we are," Sherry retorted. "Cora just doesn't think it's going to help."

"And what would help?" Aaron Grant said.

"I think the physical clues are more important than the puzzle clues," Cora answered.

"Physical clues?"

"Yeah. The evidence. I don't think this clue is nearly as important as the physical evidence."

"How can you say that?"

"It's just my opinion. I'm sure Sherry wouldn't agree."

Aaron looked at Sherry Carter, but she just pointed and said, "That's our driveway coming up."

"I know."

"I wasn't sure you'd see it in the dark."

"It was dark when I picked you up."

Aaron Grant turned into their driveway, pulled up behind Cora Felton's car. He killed the engine, turned off the lights.

"Excuse me?" Sherry Carter said. "I don't recall inviting you in."

"I thought we were cooperating on this clue."

"Yeah. So?"

"Aren't you going to put it in the grid?"

"Eventually."

Aaron Grant grinned. "Eventually? Give me a break. You couldn't sit on this five minutes. You're turning the computer on right now. And we're cooperating and I want in."

"Of course you do, young man," Cora Felton told him. "Sherry, we have to honor our agreement. Let the man take a look at the grid."

Sherry grudgingly said, "All right."

"Fine." Cora nodded. "Just one thing. Could you back up a little bit so I could get out?"

"Excuse me?" Aaron said.

"You're blocking my car. If you could just back up a few feet."

"You're going out?"

"Yes, of course."

"What about the puzzle?"

"What about it?"

"You said I could watch you work on the grid."

"And you can. Only I'm not working on it right now. But that's all right. I'm sure you and Sherry will do just fine."

"But—"

Cora Felton leaned forward, patted him on the cheek. "There, there. Don't worry about a thing. This is not brain surgery. This is simply fitting three words into a grid. I'm sure you kids can get along without me."

"Where are you going?" Sherry demanded.

"It's probably better you don't know."

"What!"

"In case that nice policeman asks." Cora Felton smiled. "You wouldn't want to have to lie, would you?"

26

SHERRY CARTER PUNCHED UP THE ELEVEN-BY-ELEVEN GRID INTO WHICH
she'd inserted the words *queue* and *ewe*.

"You think we can do this without her?" Aaron Grant said.

Sherry impaled him with a look. "I can do it without *you* just fine.
Your car's out front, there's really nothing keeping you."

"You wouldn't want to disappoint your aunt."

"I beg your pardon?" Sherry said.

"Her matchmaking efforts. Haven't you noticed she's going out of
her way to put us together?"

"I'm sorry about that. When I get a chance, I'll tell her the facts of
life."

"Don't bother on my account. I'm not offended."

"No, just offensive. How about shutting up long enough for me to
work on the puzzle?"

"Suits me," Aaron said. "What do you make of it?"

"It doesn't fit."

"Oh?"

"Not an eleven-by-eleven grid. Not if the other answers are right
and this one's eighteen down."

"How do you know it doesn't fit? How can you tell that so soon?"

"Actually, I can't. What I mean is, it doesn't intersect. With the other two clues. At least, not in this grid. If *queue* is four down, and *ewe* is fourteen across. Look what we've got. There's a black square after *ewe,* so this has to be fifteen across. This has to be sixteen. This has to be seventeen down, under these three black squares. So eighteen down has to be here. You can put the word in, but it doesn't intersect with either of the others."

"Uh huh," Aaron said. "So are you saying the eleven-by-eleven grid won't work?"

"No. Only that the words don't intersect. But they're still close together. If we fill in eighteen down as *aye* in this grid we have here, it might be possible to find words that connect this all up."

"You think your aunt could do it?"

Sherry started to answer, stopped herself. "You don't know my aunt very well."

"No, I guess I don't. What's your point?"

"No point. I was just making a comment."

"I understand your aunt is reluctant to work on this. I'm not entirely sure why."

"Do you have to be?"

"No," he said. He exhaled heavily. It was the first trace of irritation he'd shown. "Still, I like to make *some* sense out of what I'm doing. It's quite clear your aunt pooh-poohs the idea that these murders have anything to do with a crossword puzzle."

"So?"

"So? Isn't that strange? Here it is, her field of expertise. I would think she'd want to jump in with both feet."

"You ever hear of a busman's holiday?"

"What?"

"When the bus driver goes on vacation, he does not take the bus. Doctors are *not* thrilled at cocktail parties when people tell them their medical problems. If all you do all day is crosswords, are you supposed to jump for joy when somebody brings you one?"

"No, but when it comes attached to a homicide—to two homicides—it's interesting as hell. It's not just an ordinary crossword puzzle. The killer is leaving a clue. You don't even write crosswords, and you can't wait to get it on the grid."

Sherry considered. "Maybe I'm not as smart as she is, and don't see immediately that it's meaningless."

"You think the clues are meaningless?"

"I don't know."

"But you're telling me your aunt does?"

"No. I think it's a simple case of priorities. You must understand, Aunt Cora's a bit of a romantic. She grew up on murder mysteries, reads them all the time. Now a real-life one suddenly drops in her lap. A puzzle's attached, but as far as she's concerned, that's merely incidental. Yes, it's the reason she's involved in the first place, but it's not that important to her. She's more concerned with physical clues. Time of death. Cause of death. And how that car got behind that high school. That's the type of puzzle *she* wants to figure out."

Aaron Grant was looking at her thoughtfully. "You make a good case. I'm not sure I buy it, but it's well thought out. Just like the work you do on these grids."

Sherry spun her chair around to face him. "I don't care if you buy it or not. You're here on sufferance, and largely on my aunt's account. You want to work on this, fine. You want to start impugning people's motives—"

"Impugning. Now there's a word you don't hear often."

"Or if you just want to criticize the way I speak—"

"I happen to *like* the way you speak. I don't always like what you *say,* but the way you speak is quite intriguing."

"Intriguing. Oh, there's a word. Straight out of your standard pickup line."

"I'm not trying to pick you up. That would make no sense. I'm at your house."

"Of course. I've misspoken again. Though I didn't expect to be taken literally."

"I'm not even going to touch the phrase *taken literally*."

Sherry looked at him. "As a double entendre? I would have thought that was beneath you."

"I'm not going to touch that either."

"Now how did we wind up talking about what you're not going to touch?"

Aaron smiled. "Well done. I hadn't even thought of that."

"I'll bet. Anyway, you want to talk about ulterior motives, let's talk about yours. I can't believe you're here because you're interested in me, despite how much banter you might indulge in." She put up her hand. "And please don't point out how quaint it is to use the word *despite*."

"Actually, I think it's more quaint to use the word *quaint*."

"I'm getting a headache." Sherry raised an eyebrow. "Now there's a phrase you must hear a lot from the women you date."

"How did we get on the women I date?"

"I'm not going to touch that."

"Or them," Aaron suggested.

"You're not going to touch them. I'm not going to touch *that*."

"I'm glad your sense of humor is returning," Aaron said. "Isn't this the point where you offer me coffee?"

"You want coffee?"

"Not really, but it helps with the social awkwardness."

"I wasn't aware of being socially awkward."

"You're not. But I get all flustered when women come on to me."

Sherry cocked her head. "And just when we were doing so well," she said ironically. "Yes, I guess we'd better have coffee. You can consider it one for the road."

"Is that a hint?"

"Of course not. I wouldn't expect you to *take* a hint. Don't worry. When I want you to leave, I'll throw you out."

"I appreciate that," Aaron said.

Sherry turned away to suppress a smile as she led him into the kitchen. She knew she was overdoing it, bantering incessantly with Aaron Grant, but she just couldn't help it. She told herself it was just because it wasn't often she had an intellectual equal who could give it back at her as good as he got. Irritating though Aaron Grant might be, she found sparring with him strangely exciting.

Sherry washed out the coffeepot in the sink, poured in water. Aaron Grant watched what line she filled it up to.

"Four?"

"They're small cups," Sherry said. "I always make two for one."

"Oh."

"I wasn't planning on us drinking coffee for hours, if that's what you thought."

"No, I would consider that slow, even for me."

"Can you utter a single phrase without sexual overtones?" Sherry demanded.

"I'd examine your *own* overtones. That phrase had none."

Sherry put in a new filter, measured four tablespoons of coffee, switched the coffeemaker on. It began to burble.

"There," she said. "That will take about three minutes. Do you suppose you can last that long?"

"No fair," Aaron said. "That one was deliberate."

"All right, that one was," Sherry said. "You wanna declare a truce?"

"Only if you do. I'm not sure we can communicate without word-play."

"Oh, that was wordplay? I thought you were just naturally antisocial."

"See what I mean?" Aaron said. "You can't control yourself."

"Oh, is that a fantasy of yours? And in your fantasy, what do I say?"

"How did you get in here?"

Sherry's eyes widened. "That's crude, even for you."

Aaron pointed. "And it's probably somewhat confusing to *him.*"

Sherry blinked. Turned.

Chief Harper stood in the doorway.

27

"SORRY," CHIEF HARPER SAID, "BUT YOU LEFT THE DOOR OPEN."

Sherry Carter found herself blushing bright red. "I what?"

"Left the door open," Chief Harper repeated patiently. "And your car's gone, and there's another car in the driveway. I was afraid you were being robbed."

"That's my car," Aaron Grant told him.

"Yes, I can see that now. You'll pardon me, Miss Carter, but where is your aunt?"

"She went out."

"Out? At this hour?"

"That's what *I* said. She insisted on going."

"Where?"

"To look for clues."

"But we *have* a clue," Chief Harper said. "That's why I'm here."

"And you want Aunt Cora to interpret the clue for you?"

"Of course."

Sherry frowned. "I think we have a problem here, Chief. There's a killer running around leaving crossword puzzle clues. It would be nice if these clues meant something. And maybe they do. But if you want Aunt Cora's opinion, she thinks they don't. She's out looking for more clues. But not this kind. The other kind. The muddy footprint. The distinctive tire track. The bloodstained knife."

"Vicki Tanner was struck with a blunt instrument."

"That was just an example. Though I'm sure Cora will be grateful for the information."

Chief Harper frowned, narrowed his eyes. "Are you telling me she's not going to help with the clue?"

"What help do you need, Chief? I mean, what do *you* think it means?"

Chief Harper shrugged. "A yes vote with three letters? Seems to me it has to be *aye.*"

Sherry turned to Aaron. "Now, don't you feel dumb?"

"He had time to think it over," Aaron said. "You spring it on me in conversation, then say, What's it mean? before I've even had time to consider."

"You think it *does* mean *aye?*" Chief Harper asked.

"Of course it means *aye,*" Sherry replied. "It's simple and obvious. At least to *some* people."

"And what does your aunt think?"

"Aunt Cora thinks it's a red herring. That the killer's just teasing us. That it doesn't mean anything."

"So you said. I mean about this particular clue. Does she think it means *aye?*"

"Let's put it this way: She doesn't think it means anything else."

"That's less than helpful." Chief Harper was scowling.

"Why don't you show him the grid?" Aaron suggested.

"Grid?" Chief Harper said.

"Crossword puzzle grid. Sherry's been laying out the letters."

"Really?" Chief Harper said. "I certainly *would* like to see that. Ah, is that coffee you're making?"

"Can't fool a policeman, can you?" Aaron said. "Good thing you made four cups."

Sherry poured coffee for the three of them, set milk and sugar on the table. Chief Harper and Aaron Grant added liberal helpings of both. Sherry took hers black.

They carried the coffee cups into the office, where the crossword puzzle grid was still up on the screen.

"Look at that," Chief Harper said. "They actually fit."

"They do so far," Sherry said. "Though you'll notice this last one doesn't intersect."

"Did your aunt work this out?"

"No. I did."

"Oh."

"Which doesn't necessarily mean it's wrong," Sherry said with a slight edge in her voice.

"Still, Miss Felton's the expert," Chief Harper pointed out. "Are you telling me she hasn't tried to solve the puzzle?"

"No, I'm not. Once again, I'm telling you her opinion is there is no puzzle to solve. Which is in itself a solution. But let's not get sidetracked here. The point is, if these *are* three genuine puzzle clues, and these words *are* the solution, they could fit together in a grid of this size."

"And no other size?" Chief Harper was staring at the screen.

Sherry grimaced. "That's not entirely accurate. This is the only size in which I've been able to intersect the words *queue* and *ewe*. There's no reason why I couldn't fit them into another puzzle where the words simply didn't connect. You notice, in this grid the word *aye* doesn't connect with either word. And there's no way that it could. It can't intersect with *queue* because both words go down. And it can't intersect with *ewe* because it has a higher number, so it must be lower in the grid. You see what I mean?"

"Not exactly, but I get the gist," Chief Harper said. "Listen, no offense meant, but I really need to talk to your aunt."

"Why?"

"Because she has to be the key. The killer's leaving crossword puzzle clues, and the Puzzle Lady lives right here in town. This can't be coincidence. There has to be a connection, and your aunt must be the key. Doesn't that make sense to you?"

"In a way."

"Oh? Well, in what way *doesn't* it? Because I have slightly more than a casual interest. I just left the crime scene. The prosecutor would like nothing better than to see me gone, and is just looking for an excuse to stab me in the back. And, guess what? Right now he's got all the ammunition he'd need."

Chief Harper paused, took a sip of coffee, and gestured with the cup. "I withheld the clue sent to the paper. No problem there. There was no reason to believe it was genuine. It was something that needed to be quietly checked out. No one could fault me on that. But now this." He spread his arms. "Here's a clue attached to a corpse. Pretty authentic, wouldn't you think? I mean, I'd be hard pressed to argue this could be the work of a copycat prank. This is not the type of thing I should be withholding from anyone. This is evidence removed from the crime scene. It's the type of thing that could cost me my job. Your aunt saw fit to steal it from the pocket of the corpse, and here I am."

"No, you're not," Sherry said.

That caught Chief Harper up short. "What?"

"That's a very pretty speech, but it's full of holes. *We* were there. Both of us. At the crime scene. When Aunt Cora gave you that paper. We left, you stayed. With the clue. You could have turned it in, you could have shown it to someone, you could have bagged it for evidence. You could have done any number of things you policemen do with clues. Instead you came rushing over here just as soon as you could to find out what it meant."

Chief Harper scowled. "Are you telling me I'm a bad cop? Are you telling me I should be off the investigation too?"

"Not at all. I'm just saying don't blame my aunt for everything. You're the one who bought into this withhold-the-puzzle-angle bit. It's up to you if you want to keep it up. If you don't, fine. You've got a newspaper reporter right here who'd be happy to print the whole thing as soon as you give him the go-ahead."

"Quite frankly, your aunt is driving me nuts. First she steals this off the body. Then she slips it to me as she's leaving. Then I come to see her and she's gone. And you tell me she's out looking for clues. I have to wonder what other evidence she might be messing up."

"Well, I like that."

Three heads turned at once.

Cora Felton stood in the doorway. Her face was dirty, and her hair was matted and greasy, but her eyes were bright. She was holding a paper bag.

She smiled. "If you keep talking about me like that, I won't show you what I found."

28

"THEY WERE IN A DUMPSTER," CORA FELTON TOLD THEM. "WHICH IS why I'm not at my sartorial best. You also might want to stand downwind."

"What have you got there?" Chief Harper said.

"See for yourself."

Cora Felton dumped the contents of the bag out on the table next to the computer.

They were a pair of brown leather shoes and a pair of white cotton socks.

"What's this?"

"Penny loafers," Sherry Carter told the chief. "Where did you find them?"

"Like I said. In a dumpster."

"Don't be a pain. Where is this dumpster?"

"Behind the high school."

Chief Harper gawked at her. "Are you telling me . . . ?"

"That these are Vicki Tanner's shoes?" Cora Felton said. "Absolutely not. I'm just bringing them to you. Identifying them is your job. But they certainly look like her shoes. She was in the habit of wearing penny loafers and white cotton socks. I couldn't swear Vicki was wearing these last night, but I bet someone else could."

"What were you doing in a dumpster at the high school? Don't tell me you were looking for these shoes."

"Actually, I was looking for the murder weapon," Cora Felton replied. "The shoes were just a bonus."

"You found the murder weapon?"

"I'm afraid not. I found the shoes. But I was looking for the murder weapon."

"Why?"

"Because that's the whole problem, isn't it? Where was she killed? If she wasn't killed in the graveyard, her body was brought there from somewhere else. Her car was found at the high school, so it might have been there. Not necessarily, of course, but it's something to be checked out. If she was killed there, the murder weapon might have been left at the scene. As far as I can determine, it wasn't. Unless it was left in her car."

"Her car?"

"Yes. Her car's locked. I couldn't search it. Of course, you can."

"Miss Felton, you can't go around searching crime scenes."

"So arrest me. You want these shoes or not?"

"That's not the point. The point is you can't continue to do what you're doing."

Cora Felton smiled. "Of course I can. The only question is, what are you going to do about it?"

"Cora, don't be rude," Sherry said.

"I'm not being rude. Just stating a fact. This started out as fun—with all due apologies to that poor young girl who was killed. But I didn't know her. Now it's personal. Vicki Tanner was my friend. And I intend to get to the bottom of this if it's the last thing that I do."

"Uh-oh," Chief Harper muttered.

"What?" Aaron Grant said.

"That never even occurred to me."

"What's that?"

The chief turned to Cora Felton. "That's right. Vicki Tanner was your friend. The killer taunts you with clues and then kills your friend. Is there a connection?"

Cora Felton sighed deeply. "I'd thought of that," she said softly. "I really hope there isn't."

Chief Harper said, "I *hadn't* thought of that. I'm thinking of it now.

And I don't like it at all. As if I didn't have enough to worry about. Now I gotta make sure your other bridge players are safe."

"Not to mention her," Aaron Grant said, pointing to Sherry. "If the killer really is targeting the Puzzle Lady, she'd be the main target."

Sherry gave him a look, but Aaron Grant seemed serious.

"See here now," Cora Felton said. "You're a nice young man, but I won't have you frightening my niece. In point of fact, she has nothing to worry about."

"Oh? And just why is that?" Aaron Grant said.

"Because Sherry's smart enough to stay away from the killer. Which Vicki wasn't. Which doesn't seem right somehow, though I guess I can understand it."

"What do you mean?" Chief Harper said.

"Well," Cora Felton said. "Obviously the killer is a handsome young man, attractive to women. Which is how he is able to get close enough to kill them. Picking up a runaway from the Midwest couldn't have been hard. Picking up Vicki Tanner would have been difficult. I still can't figure out how he could have done it. She leaves the Country Kitchen in her car intending to go home. Or so she says. Vicki would not be the first woman ever to tell a fib. Especially if she thought she was on her way to meet a young lover."

"Are you serious?" Chief Harper said.

"It's one possibility, and seems most likely. Vicki said she was going home. Instead she went to a rendezvous which got her killed. If that rendezvous was not planned in advance, if Vicki didn't know where she was going when she left the Country Kitchen, then how would the killer intercept her? Was he waiting in the restaurant parking lot? That would certainly be risky. If anyone saw him talking to her there, he'd be on the hook for murder. I can't imagine him taking such a risk."

"So if he didn't . . . ?" Chief Harper asked.

"Then we have an even bigger problem. Vicki Tanner leaves the Country Kitchen and heads home. Now the killer has to intercept her car. Get her to drive to the high school. And how is he going to do that?"

"I have no idea."

"Neither have I. And that's the thing we have to figure out if we have any hope of solving the case. But looking at it logically, everything points to the fact Vicki Tanner knew where she was going before she left."

Chief Harper snorted in disgust. "Fine. That's all well and good. You want to help me with my problem here? We have a puzzle clue—or rather, *I* have a puzzle clue, because as far as anybody else is concerned, I *don't* have a puzzle clue. Because they don't *know* I have a puzzle clue. Because you swiped it off the corpse. Now, if that comes out, it will cost me my job. And not just for not telling people about the clue, but for being so incompetent as to let you steal it in the first place."

"You weren't even there," Cora Felton said. "How can they hold you responsible for something that happened before you even got there?"

"Aunt Cora, I don't think he wants to debate this," Sherry said, glancing apprehensively at Chief Harper's face.

"I most certainly don't," he said. "What I *would* like is for you to tell me what it means. This clue you stole from the crime scene."

"No fair. I gave it to you," Cora Felton said.

"Right," Chief Harper said. "Making me an accessory to the crime. Tampering with evidence is usually not advisable for a police chief. It is not the best career move one can make."

"Your sarcasm is noted," Cora Felton said.

"Good. Now that we all understand the situation, do you think you could help me out with the clue?"

Cora pointed to the computer monitor. "It would appear you've already done that."

"Your niece has played around with the words. What do you think of her solution?"

Cora Felton smiled. "Sherry is extremely clever. I'm sure she's done well."

"That's not what I mean. Try not to be deliberately dense. If someone is sending you a message about these murders, I need to know if you're getting it. Have you decoded the clues?"

"No more than you see there. And as for fitting them into a grid, I don't see how that can possibly help." She gestured to Sherry. "Though you should certainly go ahead with your efforts because, on the other hand, it can't possibly hurt."

"Are you telling me you can't help me with this?" Chief Harper snapped.

"Well, I like that," Cora Felton said. "When I bring you the shoes. If you stopped to think, you'd realize they're ten times more valuable than some idle speculation about some possible clues."

"They're more than just possible now," Chief Harper insisted. "This last clue came from the killer. And while there's no proof as yet, it would appear identical to the one sent to the paper."

"You going to have them analyzed?" Aaron Grant asked.

"I certainly am. But there again, I'm in the position of having to do it so nobody knows about it."

"You want me to do it for you?" Aaron Grant said.

"Thank you, that's all I need," Chief Harper said ironically. "Just in case I was able to justify withholding these clues for a while, I'd also have to explain turning them over to a newspaper reporter. I will find an expert who can keep his mouth shut. I will also have this sheet of paper tested for fingerprints, though if they're able to find any, they will most likely be hers. And mine."

"I'm sorry about that," Cora Felton said, but she didn't look sorry. She fished a pack of cigarettes out of a pocket in her dress, pulled one out, and lit it.

"You smoke?" Chief Harper said it disapprovingly.

"Only in times of great stress," Cora Felton answered. She took a deep drag, smiled. "I smoked as a teenager. Managed to quit until my second marriage. Arthur got me started again."

"Your husband encouraged you to smoke?"

"No. Arthur hated cigarettes. My smoking annoyed him." When Chief Harper and Aaron blinked at that, Cora said, "Anyway, the clue's old hat. I would think you would want to get moving on the shoes."

"What about 'em?"

"Well, for one thing, fingerprints. If the killer took them off Vicki's feet, he might have left his prints. Granted, it's a long shot. The killer's probably too smart for that, the shoes are messed up from the garbage, any prints you find are probably mine." Cora took another drag, blew out more smoke, squinted thoughtfully. "Still, it probably ought to be done."

"It will be," Chief Harper said. "Anything else?"

"Yes. The other girl's shoes. You never found them, did you?"

"No, we didn't. What's your point?"

"It must be significant. The two women are killed in the same manner. In each case, the killer takes the shoes and socks, leaves his victim barefoot. There has to be a reason why."

"Can you think of one?"

"The obvious answer is he does it to leave her helpless, so she can't run away. But how effective is that? A woman facing death is going to be slowed down by her feet hurting on the pavement?" She gestured with the hand holding the cigarette. "That's assuming this happened in the high school parking lot."

"In Vicki Tanner's case?"

"Or the other. Everything else about the killing is the same. The other girl could have been brought there too. The only difference is, she's a runaway, so she doesn't have a car."

"Interesting," Chief Harper said.

Sherry Carter looked at him in amazement. He was actually buying this.

"You have any more theories for me?" Chief Harper asked Cora.

"Was the cause of death the same?"

"Uh huh. Blunt instrument to the back of the head. Does that fit in with your theory?"

"Yes, it does. The two crimes are identical. Beginning with placing the body at the grave. Because of that, I would expect to find as many similarities as possible."

"From which you conclude?"

Cora Felton shrugged. "The killer wants the crimes to be recognized as his. Which is the same reason for the puzzle clues. It's like an artist signing his work."

"That's an ugly thought."

"Yes, it is." Cora Felton took another drag. "That's all I have so far. Except for what I said before. The killer must be a handsome young man. Toward that end, you need to look to Vicki Tanner's husband. He's young, good-looking. And, if she was indeed having an affair—" Cora Felton put up both hands, "—though I don't have any reason to believe that was the case—but if she were, that would certainly make for some interesting possibilities. On the one hand, it would give her husband the motive. On the other hand, whoever she was having the affair with would probably be a much better bet. Because he would undoubtedly fit the description I'm talking about, a young man irresistible to women. In which case, I don't think you have to worry about my bridge group."

"Why is that?"

Cora Felton smiled. "Well, now, you don't know them, do you, Chief? Vicki Tanner was our youngest member. By a wide margin. I can't imagine Iris or Lois taking up with the young man I'm talking about. Assuming he is that young. Perhaps the killer's a dashing forty-five, but I don't think so. There's something youthful, almost childlike about this whole thing. Anyway, I don't think the other women are in danger. And as for Sherry here, needless to say she can take care of herself. I can't see her giving the killer the time of day."

Cora Felton blew a perfect smoke ring. She smiled, gestured to Aaron Grant. "Unless, of course, the killer was this young man here."

29

SHERRY DREAMED DENNIS WAS BREAKING DOWN HER DOOR. HE HAD found her somehow, and he had come to get her, and a locked door wasn't going to stop him. He was pounding and pounding in a drunken fury, screaming at her, trying to break the door in. Sherry was pushing against the door with all her might, but it was flimsy, would not hold, and any minute a fist would come crashing through and he'd be on her.

The door wasn't broken yet, it was still solid, but Sherry could see him through it, that's how she knew it was Dennis. She recognized him by his clothes, by his long stringy hair.

By his face.

But it wasn't his face.

It was Aaron Grant's face.

Aaron Grant was the one who was breaking down the door.

Sherry blinked. It couldn't be. She looked again. Who was it? Aaron? Dennis?

Neither.

It was the killer. A nameless, faceless killer, pounding relentlessly, trying to get in, pounding and ringing the doorbell.

The doorbell?

That seemed strange. Why would a killer trying to break in be ringing the doorbell?

Sherry woke with a start to find sunlight streaming in her bedroom window. She'd overslept, it was late, and someone was at the front door. Sherry pulled on a robe, staggered down the hall.

Cora Felton's door was open. There were dirty clothes on the floor and her bed was unmade. Her aunt was up and gone.

The doorbell rang again. Sherry yelled, "Coming!" hurried through the living room, and opened the door.

Standing on the front steps were a middle-aged couple. The man was solid, muscular, good-looking, with a broad face and graying hair. He wore a suit jacket but no tie.

The woman was a wreck. Her face was pale, her eyes were red. Her brown hair was tangled and uncombed. She clutched a handkerchief with which she dabbed her eyes. She was a frail woman, and clung to the large man, who had his arm around her protectively.

The man glared down at Sherry. "Cora Felton?" he demanded.

"I'm sorry. I think she's out."

"You *think?*"

"I just woke up. Her bed's empty. But she might be in the house. Let me see." Sherry leaned out, looked past the couple. A station wagon was the only car in the driveway. "No," she said. "Her car's gone."

"And who are you?"

Sherry frowned. While the man was clearly upset, she was not prepared for such rudeness. Especially before her morning coffee. "I'm Sherry Carter. Cora Felton is my aunt. Who are you?"

"I'm Raymond Burnside. This is my wife, Laura."

"What do you want?"

"You don't know?"

"No, I don't. I was asleep. You rang my bell."

"And your aunt didn't tell you?"

"Tell me what?"

Raymond Burnside had a folded newspaper under his arm. He thrust it at her.

Sherry took the paper, flipped it open. There on the front page was a huge headline, MURDER LINKED TO BURNSIDE TRAGEDY???

The story was by Aaron Grant. He led off with the subheadline, POLICE SHELVE PUZZLE THEORY.

In a surprising turnaround, the police today refuted the story reported Tuesday, June 1st, in the *Bakerhaven Gazette,* that the note found on the body of the decedent, eighteen-year-old Dana Phelps, of Muncie, Indiana, discovered Monday morning, May 31st, in the Bakerhaven cemetery by caretaker Fred Lloyd, might be a crossword puzzle clue. According to well-placed sources, even Miss Cora Felton, the nationally renowned Puzzle Lady herself, doubts that this is indeed a clue from a crossword. Miss Felton's speculation, reported Tuesday, that the notation, 4) D – LINE (5), might be a clue for the word *queue,* does not in fact reflect her opinion. Miss Felton concedes that *queue* might be a suitable solution if the note were actually a crossword puzzle clue. But it is her personal opinion that it is not.

The second paragraph was headed NEW THEORY EMERGES.

While rejecting the idea of a crossword puzzle clue, Miss Felton offered a new explanation for the note. In her opinion, the notation, 4) D – LINE (5), is much more likely to be a set of directions. She points out that Dana Phelps was found next to a gravestone, and that the graves in the cemetery are in rows. She thinks four down would be the fourth grave down from where the body was found, and line five would indicate the fifth line of graves over from the road.

The next subheading was BURNSIDE CONNECTION.

Four graves down in the fifth line over from the cemetery road is the grave of Barbara Burnside, tragically killed in an automobile accident fifteen years ago at the age of twenty-two.

The story was continued on page three. But Sherry didn't turn the page. She was looking at the two photos that accompanied the article.
Neither was of the dead girl, Dana Phelps.
One was a photo of Cora Felton.
The other was a photo of a young woman. It was a professional, retouched head shot, could have come from a yearbook or been a wedding announcement photograph. It showed a young woman with dark

hair, smooth skin, wide eyes, and a dazzling smile. It was a bright young face, full of promise.

The caption read: *Barbara Burnside.*

Sherry Carter looked up from the paper. Her eyes glistened and her lip quivered. "Oh, dear. Please come in. I'm so sorry."

"You're so sorry?" Raymond Burnside said.

"I don't know what to say. I had no idea. Please come in. I'll do anything I can for you." Sherry turned to the woman. "Mrs. Burnside. Please. I know how you must feel, but, please. Come in and let's talk about it."

The Burnsides allowed Sherry to usher them in the front door. Sherry shuddered at the thought of the living room, guided them instead into the kitchen.

The remains of a Bloody Mary were on the butcher block, the ice cubes melting, the tomato juice clinging to the sides of the glass. Sherry hoped the Burnsides wouldn't notice. "Please sit down. Can I get you coffee?"

"No, you can't," Raymond Burnside said. "This is not a social situation. You say you know how we feel. Well, I doubt it. You can't possibly know how we feel. Seven years in therapy. *Seven* years. And all we accomplished in that time was finally being able to stop therapy. Well, I guess we'll be starting again."

Laura Burnside had sunk into a chair. "Why would she do this to us? Why?"

Sherry took a breath. "Mrs. Burnside, this is all just a horrible misunderstanding. I know that doesn't help. But my aunt never had any intention of involving you or your daughter. The police came to her with a clue and insisted it was part of a crossword puzzle. She told them it wasn't. Said it could as likely mean four graves down in line five. But she didn't think it was, and she certainly didn't think someone would go to the cemetery and count the graves to see what that might be."

"Oh, no?" Raymond Burnside said. "Are you telling me she didn't go to the cemetery herself?"

"No, she did, but—"

"And did she find our daughter's grave?"

"She may have."

"She *may* have?"

"I don't know that she did, but I can't assure you that she didn't. I do know she didn't give it out for publication."

"Oh, of course not," Raymond Burnside snarled. "A woman like that, in the newspapers and on TV. Her smiling face everywhere. Like she'd pass up a chance to be on page one."

"You don't know my aunt."

"I know what she did to us."

"She didn't mean to."

"Of course not. You haven't *talked* to your aunt, but somehow you just *know*."

Sherry had turned away from the Burnsides. Now she turned back. Her eyes brimmed with tears. "It's my fault."

Raymond Burnside blinked. "I beg your pardon?"

"It's my fault," Sherry repeated. The tears overflowed, ran slowly down both cheeks. "That reporter came here after the first story, and I bawled him out for writing it. Told him how stupid he was. Made him promise to retract. Not write any more about crossword puzzles." She took a shaky breath. "I'm the one who gave him the other explanation. I didn't know he would write it, and I didn't know it would lead to you, but I did it. It's my fault."

Raymond Burnside snorted. "The hell it is."

Fresh tears welled in Laura Burnside's reddened eyes. It occurred to Laura for the first time how young Sherry was. Not much older than her daughter had been at the time . . . "Raymond," she said. "That's enough. Leave her alone."

"No, he's right," Sherry said. "And there's more you may not know. Have you spoken to Chief Harper this morning?"

"I called, he wasn't in," Raymond Burnside told her. "What do you mean, more?"

"There was another killing last night. Vicki Tanner. A young housewife from Bakerhaven." Sherry hated to say it. "She was found at the same grave."

Laura Burnside choked back a sob. "Oh, my God . . ."

Raymond Burnside's eyes were hard. "Then it just starts all over again. Tell me, was there another clue?"

Sherry couldn't bear to lie to him. But she couldn't tell him the truth either. "There was nothing about four d line five on the body. Nothing that would lead people to your daughter's grave."

"As if that mattered," Raymond Burnside said fiercely. "It's on the front page of the damn paper, and that ties it in. As far as anybody in town's concerned, my daughter's involved."

"Mr. Burnside, no one thinks that. I promise you it isn't true. These murders have nothing to do with your daughter's accident. There's no connection whatsoever. This is all my fault, and I will take care of it. I know that isn't good enough, but it's all that I can do."

Raymond Burnside didn't trust himself to speak. He put his arm around his wife again, helped her to her feet, led her out the door.

Sherry wiped her eyes, and stepped away from the counter, where she'd been standing in front of the vodka bottle Cora Felton had neglected to put away after mixing her breakfast drink. She followed the Burnsides out, watched while Raymond Burnside helped his wife into the passenger seat, then got in the driver's seat and started the car.

Sherry'd been so caught up in the Burnsides' problems that it was not until their station wagon backed out of the driveway that the implications of her aunt being on the front page of the morning paper caught up with her. It would not take much more publicity like this before her dream came true, before Dennis came knocking at her door.

Sherry looked at the empty driveway with mounting misgivings.

What mischief was that woman getting into now?

30

TONGUES WERE WAGGING IN THE BAKE SHOP.

"The Graveyard Killer," Sophie Singer said. A young music teacher at the high school, she had dropped in for coffee after her first class.

"That's right," Lydia Wakefield said. She had a baby in a stroller. "I heard it on the radio. The Graveyard Killer. That's what they're calling him. Because it was in the cemetery. Another murder in the cemetery just like before."

"Only this time it's local," Anna Furst said. An older woman with white hair in a fat bun, she had piercing eyes. "That's what I hear. This time it was one of us."

The women shuddered at the word *us*.

"Is that true?" Sophie Singer asked.

"Yes, it is," Mary Cushman said. The plump proprietor of Cushman's Bake Shop had the scoop. "She's local and she's important. In fact, I think she's a selectman."

"A selectman?" Sophie repeated. "Are you sure?"

"No, but I know she's important."

"She could be a film star," Lydia Wakefield pointed out. "Wouldn't that be something if she was an actress from the movies?"

"Well, why would you think that?" Sophie Singer demanded.

"Because she's someone important. So maybe she's someone famous. Like a film star."

"Wouldn't they have said?" Anna Furst said.

"Who?"

"The people on the radio."

"If they knew they would," Lydia Wakefield agreed. "But the police don't always release the information."

"That's true." Mrs. Cushman nodded. "They always leave so much out."

"From what I heard, he took her socks and shoes off," Sophie Singer said.

"Oh?"

"Killed her and took off her shoes. And left them in our parking lot."

"No!"

"Yes. Her car was in the high school parking lot, and her shoes were in it, and I think there was blood."

"Blood!"

"Well, I'm not sure about the blood. But the car was broken into."

"Is it still there?"

"No. The police towed it away." Sophie finished her coffee, threw out the paper cup. "Well, I gotta get back to class."

Sophie went out the door just as Julia Weinstein from the hairdresser's came in.

"Julia," Lydia Wakefield said, "did you hear what happened?"

"Who didn't," Julia said. "What's this I hear about he took her clothes off?"

"Took her clothes off?" Anna Furst said.

"That's what I hear. You didn't hear anything about that?"

"Sophie said her socks and shoes."

"There you are," Julia said. "I knew there was something to it. The way I hear, the killer stripped the body."

"Was she a movie star?" Lydia Wakefield said.

"Movie star?" Julia said. "I didn't know that. Is that right?"

"I don't know. I'm just asking."

"All we know is she was famous," Mary Cushman said. "Can I get you something?"

"I'll have a coffee and a blueberry muffin," Julia said. "Have they released her name?"

"Yes, and I didn't know it," Lydia Wakefield said.

"Then how could she be a movie star?"

"Oh, so you know the name of every movie star? What if it's one of those actors who's been in a million pictures and you know the face but you can't recall the name?"

The front door banged open as Betty Dunwood came in. A severe-looking middle-aged woman, Betty Dunwood was the town clerk.

"Ah, Betty," Mrs. Cushman exclaimed. "Just in time. You're the one who'd know. The woman found in the cemetery last night—you heard about it?"

"Who hasn't."

"So tell me, was she a selectman?"

Betty Dunwood was taken aback. "No, of course not. What makes you think that?"

"See," Lydia Wakefield said. "There you are. She must have been an actress."

"An actress?" Betty Dunwood was confused.

"Sure," Julia Weinstein said. "That would tie right in with the body being found naked."

"Naked?"

"Yes. We hear he took her clothes off."

In the corner of the bakery, Cora Felton sat, sipping her coffee and holding her tongue as misinformation swirled around her. Cora was grateful for the fact the proprietor still hadn't figured out who she was—somewhat remarkable, since her picture'd been on the front page of Tuesday's paper, not to mention today's, which gave an idea of how accurate Mrs. Cushman's assessments were.

Still, someone else might have recognized her, and every time one of the women glanced her way, Cora managed to have her head buried in this morning's *Bakerhaven Gazette*. As a result, she had read the Barbara Burnside story more than once. Which made rather interesting reading in counterpoint to the women in the bake shop discussing the crime.

Cora Felton sipped her coffee, tried to chase her hangover. She'd had a Bloody Mary when she'd first gotten up, and now she'd moved on to coffee. In her eyes, this was the difference between a drinker and a drunk. For a drunk, the Bloody Mary would be the first drink of the day. A drunk would stick with liquor, head for a bar. For Cora Felton the Bloody Mary was just to take the edge off. After that, she would straighten herself out with coffee and would not drink again until dinner.

Cora Felton was a social drinker, not a drunk.

It was something she told herself many times.

Cora Felton finished her coffee, tucked her paper under her arm, and headed for the door. She chose a moment to do so when the women's attention was diverted. She didn't want to be spotted, recognized, questioned about the crimes. At least not here. She made her way quietly to the front door, slipped outside.

Her car was parked across the street in front of the library. There was a crosswalk at the corner, but in a town this size, Cora couldn't really see the point. She stepped out between parked cars into the street.

A car turned the corner, came straight at her.

Cora had an instant of panic. The driver was trying to run her down. Then the car slowed to let her pass.

Cora Felton crossed the street, squeezed between two parked cars, stepped up on the sidewalk, and stopped dead.

Aaron Grant was sitting on the fender of her car. It occurred to her, for the amount of sleep he must have gotten, he didn't look bad. At least he'd managed to shave, shower, change his clothes.

"Hi," he said. "Thought this was your car. But you weren't in the library."

"No, I was in the bakery. But there wasn't a parking spot there when I drove up."

"Uh huh," he said, nodding. "You want to take a ride?"

"Where to?"

"It doesn't really matter. Just so long as no one bothers us."

"Oh? What's this?" Cora Felton said. "To pay me back for the you-might-be-the-killer remark? Or, wait, you *are* the killer, and I hit too close to home, and now you've got to eliminate me."

"Yeah, that's it," Aaron agreed. "You want to risk it?"

"I don't see why not," Cora said. "I'll drive. That way if you kill me, the car goes off the road."

"Sounds good," Aaron said. "Shall we?"

Cora Felton unlocked her car. Aaron Grant got in the passenger side. Cora got in, started it up. She pulled out of the parking space, headed out of town in the direction of the Country Kitchen.

"Okay," she said. "I'm driving as far as the high school and turning around. If you've got something to say, young man, say it by then."

"You see this morning's paper?"

"How could I miss it? I have it right here."

"I see that you do. I'm wondering if you read it."

"I read it. You took the Barbara Burnside story and ran with it. I'm not entirely sure why."

"It's part of the deal," Aaron said. "I did it to pooh-pooh the puzzle angle."

"Well, I bet you get little thanks for it," Cora said. "You are rather young, you know."

"What's that supposed to mean?"

"You're impetuous. You do things without considering the consequences."

"That's a youthful trait?"

" 'Older and wiser' isn't just an expression. You learn not to do things after a while."

"Uh huh. That's not what I want to talk about."

"I'm sure it isn't. So what's your pleasure?"

"I was hoping you could help me with a puzzle."

Cora Felton grimaced. "We've been over all that. Or has there been another clue?"

"No, there hasn't. And that wasn't what I meant."

"Oh? What did you mean, then?"

"In the paper. In today's paper. That's why I asked if you read it. I was hoping for some help with that."

"With the *Barbara Burnside* story?"

"No," Aaron Grant said. "I told you. With the puzzle. With today's puzzle." He took the paper, folded it open to the page. "Here we are. Today's Puzzle Lady column. Today's puzzle is entitled SHORTCAKE SHORTS. It tells the story of a woman who served shortcake to her luncheon guests, and had one more guest than pieces of cake. A rather amusing story, I must say."

"What in the world are you talking about?"

"I'm talking about your column. Your Puzzle Lady column. I need help with today's puzzle."

"You have to be kidding."

"Oh, but I'm not. I started solving today's puzzle, and I'm stuck on fifty-two across. Civil War boat. Seven letters. First letter *m*. Can you help me with that?"

"Now, see here," Cora Felton said. "You did not hunt me up in the middle of a murder investigation to help you with crossword puzzles."

"Oh, but I did," Aaron Grant said. "It's suddenly become one of the more intriguing aspects of the case. It's a fact I need to know, and I'm going to have to insist on an answer. In today's puzzle, what is fifty-two across, a seven-letter word for Civil War boat, beginning with *m?*"

"I have no idea. You think I remember all these puzzles?"

"No, I don't. But I think you could help me with a perfectly straightforward clue."

"If I happened to remember it. Which I have no particular reason to do."

"Uh huh," Aaron Grant said. "Well, it seems to me a seven-letter word for Civil War boat beginning with *m* would have to be the *Monitor*. Wouldn't that be right?"

"If you know, why are you asking me?"

"To see what you'd say. Look here, Miss Felton. I'm a newspaper reporter. When I get a hold of a story, I don't let go. You're not going to get around me, and you're not going to put me off. So why don't you just come clean?"

"I beg your pardon? Come clean about what?"

"You can't *do* crossword puzzles, can you?"

31

"ORANGE JUICE?" AARON GRANT ASKED.

Cora Felton grimaced. "Yes, I know. It's too early for a *real* drink, and if I have any more coffee I think my head will come off. Besides, I need to keep my wits about me."

"Surely it's not as bad as all that."

"Oh, no? I'm sitting here with a reporter. The one thing Sherry warned me about. And here I am, talking to the media."

"This is off the record."

"That's what they all say. And the next day you're in the *National Enquirer.*"

"You talk as if this has happened before."

"Only once. And it went away."

"How was that?"

"I sat tight and the guy gave up. After all, it's a very small story."

"Not really. You're a celebrity."

"In a TV commercial. Big deal. That's not the same as a movie star. It's the difference between an amusing tidbit and a shocking revelation."

"Uh huh. Wanna tell me about it?"

"Do I have a choice?"

"Absolutely. You can clam up and tell me to go to hell."

"What would you do then?"

"Go see Sherry."

"That would not be good."

"So here we are."

Cora Felton took a sip of her orange juice, made a face. "God, that's bad. Jerry, my first husband, got me on the wagon, made me drink this stuff. I've hated it ever since."

"Bad associations?"

"No. I loved Jerry. It's orange juice I can't stand." Cora took another sip, grimaced, and considered. "I don't know what I can tell you. You seem to know everything already. It's as if you're here just for confirmation. Which is what reporters do before they print the story."

"I'm not printing this."

"So you say. Okay, let's not go around again. So I can't do crossword puzzles. Big deal. You gonna blow the whistle?"

"No, I'm gonna hear your story. As you say, I'm gonna hear it from you, or I'm gonna hear it from Sherry."

"Sherry will not be inclined to talk to you. She'll be inclined to talk to me. I don't want that."

"So you talk to me."

"Yeah." Cora Felton took another sip of orange juice, frowned. "Sherry always was a bright girl. Did well in high school, went to a good college. Dartmouth. Did well there too."

"And?"

"Her junior year she met Mr. Wrong. Young, self-absorbed, played the guitar, wanted to be a rock star."

"Oh."

"Yeah. Oh. A walking disaster. The type of guy everyone can see is bad news, except the girl involved."

"What happened?"

"They got married, Sherry dropped out of school, took a job, supported him while he launched his career."

"Did he launch it?"

"In a manner of speaking. He managed to put a band together that performed just enough small gigs to attract a few groupies. He also used the money Sherry earned to buy enough drugs to keep up the pretense that he was in a successful band."

"How long did that last?"

"Till she got pregnant."

Aaron Grant blinked. "Sherry has a kid?"

"No."

"Oh."

"No, not like that."

"What happened?"

"What happened was Golden Boy came back from a night of carousing stoned out of his mind and took exception to Sherry asking him where he'd been."

"No."

"Yes. He beat her up pretty bad. You'd think a musician would be more careful with his hands. But this guy wasn't much of a musician."

"She had a miscarriage?"

"If you can call it that. She got beat up and lost her baby, as a result of trauma. Basically, the creep killed their kid."

"She left him?"

"And never looked back. Good thing too. I don't think she could trust herself around him."

"How'd he take it?"

"About how you'd expect. Swore he'd be good on the one hand, blamed her for everything on the other, and refused to let go. He still hassles her from time to time."

"When did this happen?"

"The split-up?"

"Yeah."

"It's been a couple of years."

"And he's still around?"

"In a manner of speaking. He's the kind of guy gets loaded, feels persecuted, wants to avenge all wrongs."

"I know the type," Aaron said thoughtfully. "So what did Sherry do, after she lost the baby?"

"Moped around for a while. She took it hard. She really wanted that kid. She finally pulled herself together and went back to school."

"She went back to Dartmouth?"

"Yeah."

"What did she study?"

"Linguistics."

"Uh huh. How did she do?"

"Graduated with honors. Came to New York, found an apartment, got a job."

"As what?"

"Copy editor. Right up her alley. It was freelance work, wasn't steady, but it left her time to do other things."

"Like what?"

Cora Felton glared at him. "You know like what. Crossword puzzles. She had a real knack for 'em. Solving 'em, and making 'em up."

"So?"

"So, she tried to sell 'em."

"How'd that go?"

"About as well as her marriage. Another huge disillusionment."

"Why?"

"Maybe she set her sights too high. I don't know. I'm sure if she tried hard enough she could have sold a few puzzles. Maybe even got one in the *Sunday Times*. But that wasn't what she was after. She wanted a full-time job."

"How was that?"

"A syndicated column. In the national papers."

"Like you have now?"

"Right. Only she couldn't get it."

"Why not?"

"I don't know. Why does one movie get made and a hundred others don't? It certainly isn't the quality. There was nothing wrong with Sherry's stuff. It was terrific."

"But?"

"You gotta understand Sherry's head. She's coming off a bad marriage, she's bitter, she's disillusioned. She's had it up to here with men."

"I kind of got that."

"Did you?" Cora regarded him thoughtfully. "Well, that's what was in her mind. And that's how she took her rejections. She regarded it as a sexist thing."

"Was it?"

"Maybe. I mean, there is that mind-set. An editor looks at her and she's so young and attractive how could she possibly be any good?"

"That's a little simplistic."

"Yes, it is. I'm sure there's a zillion factors involved, but the bottom line is Sherry couldn't sell her puzzles."

"So what happened?"

"She gave up her apartment, moved in with me."

"Where?"

"I had an apartment in Manhattan. Still do, actually. It's just sublet. It's a great apartment, I'll never give it up."

"Uh huh. And the column?"

"It just happened. Sherry came up with the concept. As a result of having struck out. Came to the conclusion it was all hype and all image. She needed a new image." Cora shrugged. "I happen to photograph well. Look like somebody's sweet old grandmother." She made a face. "Truly revolting concept, but there you have it. Sherry went to work, put together the Puzzle Lady column. Wrote it around my picture, had me submit it under my name."

"It was an instant hit?"

"I wish. It took months of hard work. And it didn't get syndicated overnight. First one small paper picked it up. Then another. Then another. Then the whole thing really took off."

"Uh huh. Why'd you move?"

"I lived in New York all my life. I have a lot of friends. Not that many do crossword puzzles. But they all have TV. When the ad came out, my phone was ringing off the hook. That's when that reporter found me, by the way, the one I told you about. Anyway, I made a lot of money off of that ad. And it occurred to me I could sublet my apartment for twice what I pay. It seemed like a good time to get out of town."

"How'd Sherry feel about it?"

"Well, you have to understand. This happened to coincide with one of Dennis's little visits."

"Dennis?"

"Her husband."

"Husband or ex-husband?"

Cora waggled her hand. "Sherry spoke to a lawyer, went back to using her own name. Whether it's finalized or not, I couldn't say. Sherry doesn't talk about it."

"Uh huh," Aaron Grant said. He frowned. Considered. "So this whole business—the crossword puzzle clues—they don't really mean anything?"

"Well, not to me," Cora Felton said. "They never did. But they do to Sherry, and that's all that matters. She is the Puzzle Lady. As for me . . ." She smiled, shrugged. "I'm just a pretty face."

"Must be tough."

"Hey, I don't mind. Just a little inconvenient now and then. Particularly with the police expecting me to solve two murders for them."

"You came up with the shoes."

Cora grinned. "Yes, I did. That I can do just fine. Murder mysteries are my element. Just keep the wordplay out of it, I'll be happy as a clam."

"And that's the only reason you came up with the four-graves-down theory—because you didn't want to talk about a crossword clue?"

"Don't you know it," Cora Felton said. "Imagine having the chief of police sitting there saying, Tell me what this means. The I'll-work-on-it-and-get-back-to-you bit isn't going to work forever."

"Tell me something," Aaron Grant said.

"What?"

"Why'd you do it?"

"What?"

"Agree to be the Puzzle Lady?"

Cora shrugged. "I couldn't talk her out of it."

"Why didn't you just say no?"

"And break her heart? Sherry's like a daughter to me. I'd do anything for her. Anything I could." Her eyes narrowed. "I wouldn't let anyone hurt her, either."

"I wouldn't hurt her."

"You will if you keep putting my picture on your front page. Sherry likes hiding behind the facade. Plus Dennis doesn't know where she is, and she doesn't want to tell him. She's phobic about the media, and terrified of publicity."

"So you think she won't care for my Barbara Burnside piece?" Aaron said.

Cora smiled and cocked her head.

"I would say that was a pretty safe bet."

32

SHERRY CARTER SAT AT THE KITCHEN TABLE, DRINKING HER COFFEE and cursing Aaron Grant. Wasn't that just like a man? After everything they'd been through the night before—driving around in the car, finding the body, calling the police, and deciphering the clue—never once did Aaron think to mention the one tiny detail, that he'd put her aunt on the front page again.

The *Bakerhaven Gazette* lay on the table in front of her. The headline, MURDER LINKED TO BURNSIDE TRAGEDY???, in bold, black type.

Gee, Aaron, you think you might have mentioned that?

And how could he have done this to the Burnsides? Yes, of course, it was long ago. He'd been a child at the time of the accident. Too young to know Barbara Burnside, way too young to know her parents. But still, he should have known better. What an insensitive lout. She'd read him the riot act the next time he came around. If he had the nerve to show his face around here again.

Sherry heard a car turn into the driveway. Could it be him? No, most likely Cora. Which would be good. They could talk this over, figure out what they were going to do.

Sherry went to the window, looked out. But it wasn't her aunt. The car in the driveway was a news van from Channel 8. As Sherry watched, three men piled out, and the big, beefy one in the jeans and T-shirt began to unload a camera.

Sherry's heart skipped a beat. This couldn't be happening. Without stopping to think, she stormed out the front door onto the lawn.

"All right," she said, "hold it right there."

The youngest of the three men wore a tie and a Channel 8 blazer. He saw her and smiled a dazzlingly white smile that must have cost a fortune in dental caps. "Hi," he said. "Is Cora Felton at home?"

"No. And even if she were, she's not interested in doing an interview, so I'm afraid you're out of luck."

"And who might you be?"

"It doesn't matter. I'm not doing an interview either."

The young man's smile never lessened in intensity. "Most people like being on television."

"I am not one of them." Sherry pointed at the cameraman, who was focusing on her. "You can tell *him* to put *that* down. I don't wish to be filmed, I'm not a celebrity or a criminal, I didn't consent to an interview. This is private property, you're trespassing, and if you violate my right to privacy, I will prosecute you to the fullest extent of the law. Need I be more clear?"

"No, I think you made your point. Ernie, ditch the camera. You and Phil take a break." The reporter in his Channel 8 blazer turned back to Sherry, smiled again. "Before we were interrupted, I was asking you your name."

"Yes," Sherry said. "You were. And I was telling you why it couldn't possibly matter."

"Because you don't want to be interviewed. No problem." He spread his hands. "Look, ma. No camera. No mike. No reason why we shouldn't be friends."

"I don't recall inviting you here."

"You didn't. I came to see Miss Felton. Our meeting—yours and mine—is accidental. Anyway, let me introduce myself. I'm Rick Reed. I work for Channel 8 News. I'm young, I'm ambitious, and I happen to be single."

"Am I supposed to swoon?"

"No, but you could tell me your name."

"And have it wind up on television?"

"Not unless you've done something newsworthy. Am I to gather you haven't?"

Sherry straightened to her full height and glared at him. "I'm Sherry Carter. Cora Felton happens to be my aunt. She does not wish to appear on television, and she has nothing to tell you."

Rick Reed nodded. "I appreciate that. You understand I will have to verify that with Miss Felton herself."

"She's not here."

"So you said. So, Cora Felton's niece, eh? I don't believe you mentioned being single."

"It's not one of the first things I tell people."

"Too bad. Then I'll have to ask directly. Are you single?"

"Why do you want to know?"

"I don't like to ask married women out to dinner."

"Had a problem with it, have you?"

Rick Reed frowned momentarily, immediately smiled again. "Wrong response. You're supposed to say, Are you asking me out to dinner?"

"Sorry. I'm obviously not up on your standard pickup lines."

"Well, let me clue you in. You would probably have a fairly good shot at dinner, if you played your cards right."

"With a real TV star? Be still, my heart."

"Okay, so it's only local," Rick Reed said. "I see it as a stepping-stone."

"I'm sure you do. I believe you also mentioned you were ambitious?"

"That's right."

"Then what are you doing hitting on me when you've got a double homicide to deal with? Or were you aware there was another killing?"

"Oh, we're aware of it. The cops aren't granting any interviews, and neither is the husband. The crime scene's exactly the same, and nothing's happening there, which means we've got until tonight to get out there and shoot a thirty-second lead-in. In the meanwhile, I got a much more promising angle."

"What's that?"

"You didn't see? It's on the front page of the *Bakerhaven Gazette.* Burnside connection, courtesy of your aunt. Which I can't wait to ask her about."

"There *is* no Burnside connection. It's got nothing to do with anything. It's a nonstory."

"It's a nonstory on page one, and I'm going after it. Your aunt gave a statement to the press, that makes her fair game."

"Oh, for goodness sakes."

"Plus, your aunt *is* a celebrity, which makes her fair game to begin with. But that's just how I see it. I'd be delighted with any career guidance you'd care to give me."

"I suggest you lay off my aunt."

"That's interesting advice. Perhaps we could discuss it over dinner."

"Are you offering to drop the interview if I go out with you?"

Rick Reed smiled. "Young lady, are you trying to bribe me?"

Sherry caught herself, choked back the scathing retort she'd been building up to. Told herself this was not the man she wanted to antagonize, this was not the man she wanted to tell off. She had to be calm, cool, and collected. She had to reason with him. Be polite to him.

Go out with him?

Sherry caught her breath. How far would she go to stay out of the news? To keep Dennis from finding her again?

To keep her promise to the Burnsides?

It crossed her mind that this was entirely Aaron Grant's fault.

That thought somehow made it easier to say yes.

She didn't, it just would have been easier.

That realization infuriated her, made it easier saying no.

Which she did. Politely, yet firmly, in no uncertain terms.

She would have felt a certain satisfaction in doing so, were it not for the Burnsides. As she watched the news crew back their van out of the driveway, Sherry wondered just how much her refusal had cost the Burnsides. Not much, she figured. It was, like she had told the reporter, a nonstory. It was much better to ignore the Burnside story than to try to cover it up. Nobody really cared about it, not with another murder to contend with. The reporter had even said he was only after it because he couldn't get anything else.

Sherry calmed herself with the thought the Barbara Burnside story meant nothing to anyone.

Just leave it alone, and it would go away.

33

AARON GRANT HUNG UP THE PHONE WITH HIS EARS RINGING. HE pushed back in his chair, shook his head to clear it. He certainly had a new appreciation for Barbara Burnside and what her family had gone through. And he had given Chief Harper a clear promise he would not touch that story again. Not that he wanted to. Especially now that he knew the Burnside connection had been manufactured by Cora Felton simply for the purpose of trying to keep Sherry Carter's secret. Well, he had learned his lesson. That was the last he would have to do with the Burnside affair, with the possible exception of issuing a private apology to her parents.

Which left him with a great big problem—what was he going to write today?

"Aaron Grant?"

Aaron looked up. The man standing by his desk was not happy, but that was par for the course. No one seemed happy today. The man was in his mid-thirties, early forties, it was hard to tell—his bald head might make him look older than he was. He had a plumpish face and wore wire-rimmed glasses. Aaron Grant recognized him vaguely. He had seen him around town, but couldn't place him.

"Can I help you?" Aaron said.

"Can you help me? That's a good one. Can *you* help *me?*"

Aaron stood up, faced the man. "All right. I'll try again. Who are you and what do you want?"

"I'm Kevin Roth," the man said, and waited for a response.

"Oh?" Aaron said. After a moment, he said, "Oh."

"That's right," Roth said. "You mentioned me in your story. In passing. Like a footnote. Well, I was more than a footnote. I was her boyfriend. And she meant something to me."

"You were with her that night."

"Earlier that night," he said. "Yeah, I was at the party. We had a fight, Barbara and I, and she took off in the car. She'd had a little too much to drink."

"You're the one who found her."

"I was worried about her. I borrowed a car, went after her. She didn't get far."

"You're the one who called the police."

Kevin Roth ran his hand over his bald head. "This is all a matter of record. And it's also ancient history. Why do you have to dig it up?"

"I'm not digging it up."

"You wrote that story."

"That's all it is—a story. Just reporting the facts."

"Yeah, sure. But you tie it in with these other murders, get the police to reopen the investigation."

"I'm not doing that. I just got off the phone with Chief Harper. He assures me there's nothing to it and they're not reopening the investigation."

"He might be saying that just to throw you off the track."

"Well, he isn't. I have it on good authority the police attach no credence to that theory of the case."

"You mean the Graveyard Killings?"

"Yes, of course."

"But your theory is there is a connection."

"It's not my theory."

"You wrote it."

"I reported it. I'm sorry I did. I could print a retraction, but that would only bring it up again. It's probably better to drop the whole thing, just let it alone."

"So you won't retract?"

Aaron Grant controlled himself with an effort. "I'm sorry you're upset, but I don't wish to be willfully misunderstood. The only reason I would not print a retraction would be to spare her parents' feelings. That and the fact any retraction is going to be inconclusive."

"Inconclusive?"

"Yes. I can say there was no foundation to the story, but people will still wonder if it's true."

"So tell them it isn't."

"I can't do that. I have no basis to make such a statement. For all I know this guy killed two girls to cover up the fact he was involved in Barbara Burnside's death years ago."

"What are you talking about, involved in her death? She had a car accident, for God's sake."

"Exactly my point. There is absolutely nothing to connect the one thing to the other. By the same token, there is nothing to prove these events are unrelated. The best course of action is no action at all. Just let it go. The police are not investigating, I'm not reporting, it's not happening. Even the woman who came up with the theory in the first place admits there's nothing to it. I can give you my personal assurance, all parties have agreed to let the matter drop."

Kevin Roth rubbed his head again. What Aaron Grant had told him clearly wasn't good enough. He frowned, seemed to be searching for something to say. He looked around the newsroom, at the door, at the wall, at Aaron Grant's desk, at the bulletin board. At the managing editor back in his office, visible through the glass partition.

Aaron Grant followed his glance. "Go ask my editor if you don't believe me. He'll tell you the same thing. We're not following up. If you let it drop, we'll let it drop. The only thing that's gonna keep it alive is if someone makes a fuss."

"Damn it to hell."

"Your coming here is off the record. I assure you I'm not writing it up."

Kevin Roth seemed hopelessly torn, as if he didn't know what to do. He glanced around again, looked at Aaron Grant. Aaron got the impression the man wanted to brush by him, shove him out of the way. He didn't, however. After another moment, he turned and stalked off.

Aaron watched until Kevin Roth went out the door. He heaved a sigh of relief and slumped into his desk chair. What a day. No, what a week. He'd certainly learned his lesson. He'd never write an irresponsible column like that again. No more idle speculation. Stick to hard news, get something on the murders. He'd head over to the police station, see what he could turn up.

First to business. There were letters in his in-basket, compliments of the ever-efficient Mary Mason. Aaron pulled them out, riffled through them. While his expectations were not high, it occurred to him the killer might send another clue.

A glance showed that he hadn't. At least none of the envelopes matched the typewritten one he'd gotten the day before.

Aaron got to the last one, stopped, and stared.

It was typewritten, but not like the one with the clue. There was no stamp and no address. Just his name.

While he was looking at it, Mary Mason walked by.

"Mary," Aaron said. "Did you put this in my basket?"

She looked down at the letter. "Yes. Why?"

"Where did you get it?"

"It was under the door."

"The door?"

"When I came in this morning it was lying there. Someone slipped it under the door."

"That's odd."

"Why? They saved a stamp and made sure you got it the same day. What is it?"

"I don't know. I haven't opened it yet."

Mary's eyes twinkled. "Oh, well, why do that? You'll spoil our fun guessing where it came from."

"Yeah," Aaron said absentmindedly. He ripped the envelope open. Inside was a single sheet of paper. He pulled it out, half expecting it to be another crossword puzzle clue.

It wasn't.

It said: DROP THE BARBARA BURNSIDE STORY.

34

"YOU'RE THE PUZZLE LADY?"

Cora Felton frowned. She'd been on her way to the police station to talk to Chief Harper when the young girl had stopped her with the question. And it was one that she hated to answer. At least, directly. "I'm the woman on TV," she replied. It was one of her favorite deflections.

"Uh huh," the girl said. "And the one in the paper, talking about the murders."

"That's a misunderstanding," Cora told her. "I really have nothing to do with it."

The girl pouted. "Don't be like that. That's how my father acts."

"Your father?"

"Yes. Chief Harper. He's my dad."

"Oh. Yes." Cora remembered seeing the girl at the town meeting with her mother, standing by the chief. "Then you know more about it than I do."

"Maybe I do."

"I beg your pardon?"

Clara Harper leaned in conspiratorially, told Cora Felton about her suspicions of Jimmy Potter the librarian's son and her father's refusal to listen to them. "So, what do you think?" she demanded.

Cora Felton thought Clara Harper was pretty young, but she wasn't about to say so. "I'll tell you what I think. It's probably nothing, but I've read enough murder mysteries where someone has an important clue, and no one will listen to them."

"So?"

Cora Felton smiled. "So, I think I'll go and check out a book."

Cora Felton crossed the street and went up the front steps into the library. She smiled a greeting at Edith Potter at the front desk, but swept on by to look for her son. She found him straightening up the magazines in the reading room.

"Excuse me, young man. Can you tell me where the Agatha Christie mysteries are kept?"

Jimmy Potter looked up from his work. His eyes widened and his mouth fell open. "You're the woman on TV!"

"I'm Cora Felton. You must be Jimmy Potter."

He seemed amazed she knew his name. "Yeah. That's me." His eyes grew wider still. "It was in the paper. You're working on the killings." He lowered his voice. "There's been some killings and it's very sad, but we still have to do our work." He nodded in agreement with himself, looked at her solemnly.

"That's very true," Cora Felton said placidly. "Tell me, do you know anything that would help?"

Jimmy frowned. "Help?"

"Yes. Do you know anything about the murders?"

Jimmy's face twisted in alarm. "Me? Why me?"

Cora Felton put her hand on his arm reassuringly. "I just thought you might have seen something because you're in the library all day long, and you see everyone who comes in and goes out. So you'd be in a good position to see things."

Jimmy considered. "That's true," he said. The fact that his being in a good position to see everyone who went in and out of the library was not even remotely connected to the murders did not seem to occur to him.

"So, if you see anything, please let me know," Cora Felton said. She turned to go.

"Don't you want a book?"

"I'll get it later," Cora called over her shoulder. "I just remembered something I have to do."

Cora Felton could understand why Clara Harper suspected Jimmy

Potter, though she did not suspect him at all. She wondered how to tell young Clara without disillusioning her too badly.

Cora Felton stepped out onto the library front porch and looked across the street. Clara Harper wasn't there, but her father was. Aaron Grant's car was parked in front of the police station, and he and Chief Harper were standing in the street next to it. Chief Harper was holding a sheet of paper. He didn't look happy.

Cora Felton came down the steps and crossed the street.

"Hi," she said. "What have you got there?"

Chief Harper groaned.

Aaron Grant grimaced and shook his head. "You wouldn't believe."

35

SHERRY WAS DEVASTATED BY THE NEWS. SHE'D BEEN WATCHING OUT the window for her aunt, come out to meet her when she'd driven up the driveway. She leaned against the fender of the car, ran her hand through her glossy hair. "This is awful."

"Isn't it?" Cora Felton agreed happily. "I come up with a wacky theory, and now it appears it means something."

"That's not the point."

"What's the point?"

"They were here."

"Who?"

"The Burnsides. They were here this morning, looking for you."

"Oh."

"Yeah. And, Cora. They're nice people. I promised them this was nothing and it would go away."

"Maybe it will."

"Are you kidding? Those TV sharks are on to it. I had a news crew in the driveway this morning looking to interview you."

"What'd you tell 'em?"

"I told 'em to take a hike. The reporter wouldn't take no for an answer, and tried to hit on me."

"Really? What's he like?"

"Aunt Cora! I'm not in the mood. The Burnsides lost a daughter. It's years ago, and the scars are healed, but this reopens them all again. If you'd been here this morning, if you'd met them, if you'd met the mother . . ." Sherry blinked back tears. "I felt so bad."

"I know."

"I assured them you never meant to involve their daughter. I promised them there was nothing to it."

"I'm sure there isn't."

"Maybe not. But if someone's sending anonymous letters, Chief Harper's not going to let it go."

"Maybe not, but he's killing the story. He ordered Aaron Grant to lay off. Me too. He made me swear up and down I wouldn't look into it."

"What about him?"

"What *about* him?"

"He's looking into it, isn't he?"

"He's tracing the letter. That's all."

"How's he doing that?"

"He's getting typing samples from everyone involved."

"Like who?"

"The boyfriend, for starters. Kevin Roth. He's the most likely suspect. Particularly after going to the newspaper to confront Aaron Grant."

"Who else?"

Cora grimaced. "Well, of course, the parents."

"He should leave them alone."

"How can he? They're involved. They could have written that letter."

"I don't think so."

"Maybe not, but he has to know."

"It's not fair. Cora, if you met these people, you'd feel like I do. They've suffered enough, and they deserve to be left alone."

"Which is exactly Chief Harper's point. That's why he's killing the investigation. Except for finding out who wrote the letter."

Sherry frowned. "That's not right either."

"What do you mean?"

"If there's any connection between these murders and the Barbara Burnside accident, it should be looked into."

Cora Felton looked at her in exasperation. "Sherry. How could there be? *I made it up.* Or do *you* think the four-graves-down theory means something?"

"I know it doesn't. But if someone wants the story killed, there must be something there."

"What are you saying?"

"Aunt Cora. I gave the Burnsides my word that this meant nothing. If I'm wrong, I have to know it. If I told them wrong, I have to fix it. These people deserve the truth, whatever it is."

Cora Felton put up her hands. "Sherry, Sherry, Sherry. This is the most convoluted reasoning I ever heard. You promised the Burnsides no one would investigate their daughter's death, so you *want* it investigated?"

"I promised them the article in the paper was wrong. I have to make sure that's true."

"Well, there's no way to do that," Cora said. "Because the story is killed. No one's going after it. Chief Harper made that perfectly clear. I gave him my word I wouldn't touch it."

Sherry's skin tingled. It all came to the surface—her fear of publicity, her fear of Dennis. The things she'd been conditioned to avoid. And it was very hard, very unnatural for her to do what she was about to do.

Sherry shivered. She looked at Cora Felton, sighed.

"But I didn't."

36

SHERRY CARTER FOUND ED HODGES WORKING IN HIS GARDEN. THE former chief of police lived in a modest ranch house on a wooded lot on the north side of town. The house had fallen into poor repair. Sherry noted cracked shingles, peeling paint, and a drainpipe dangling from the roof.

The garden, on the other hand, was beautiful. Ed Hodges might have let the house go, but he certainly cared for his plants. The vegetable garden had neat green rows of carrots, radishes, and lettuce, according to the upside down seed packets on stakes at the end of the rows. There were also tomato plants carefully attached to sticks, a patch of summer squash, and a raspberry bush.

The flower garden was even nicer. There were marigolds, geraniums, several varieties of coleus plants, daisies, and petunias. As it was way too early in the season for any of them to have grown from seed, Sherry knew the flower garden represented frequent trips to the local greenhouse and many hours of careful planting.

Ed Hodges was digging when Sherry came up. He'd dug up one corner of the flower garden, and was planting ground cover from a cardboard box.

"Ed Hodges?" Sherry Carter asked.

The man did not even glance up from his work. "Go away."

"I'm Sherry Carter. I'd like to talk to you."

He glanced up then. Ed Hodges was about seventy, had no doubt at one time been a bull of a man. Now the skin of his broad face sagged a little, but the eyes were still hard. "I'll bet you would. You from the newspaper?"

"No."

"TV?"

"No."

"Then you're not here about Barbara Burnside?"

"Actually, I am."

"Then you can leave."

Sherry Carter smiled. "Mr. Hodges, don't be like that."

"Well, how do you expect me to be? Bunch of rubbish in the morning paper. I've been expecting someone to come around."

"When they do, just say, No comment."

Ed Hodges scowled. "And who are you?"

Sherry hesitated. She knew her aunt would be quick on her feet, would hand the man a line, get him to open up. Sherry had none of those skills. She was no detective, didn't know how to play the game. She wasn't versed in subterfuge and deception. Her only weapon was the truth.

"I'm Sherry Carter. The woman quoted in that story is my aunt."

"Yeah, well, your aunt is a fool. I'm sorry, lady, but that's a fact."

Sherry nodded. "Then you see my problem. My aunt shoots her mouth off, and there's hell to pay. Now, I can tell you what's already been done. Chief Harper's talked to the reporter who wrote the story, told him not to write another. He's also told my aunt if she issues anything more than a retraction the next headline she reads will be BUSYBODY SNOOP ARRESTED FOR MEDDLING IN CASE."

Ed Hodges smiled in spite of himself.

Sherry pressed her advantage. "Now, can you help me out here? The Burnsides came to me this morning, all upset because of my aunt. I assured them there was nothing to the story."

"So?"

"So, I'd like to hear it from you."

Ed Hodges jabbed his trowel into the ground, let it stick there. He brushed his hands off, got to his feet. Standing slightly bent, he still towered over Sherry Carter. "Close," he said. "Very close."

"What do you mean?"

"Young lady, you almost had me sold. You're young, pretty, come across as sincere. And I can tell. After a lifetime of hearing stories, I know which to buy. And yours holds up until right at the end. If the story is killed, then why are you here?"

Sherry hesitated. Then she said, "Because someone wants it killed."

Ed Hodges frowned. "How's that?"

"The reporter who wrote the story. He got an anonymous letter telling him not to write another."

Ed Hodges made a face. "And that's all?"

"That's not enough?"

"An anonymous letter's not worth the paper to print it on. It could be a nut, it could be a crank, it could be some kid."

"That's true," Sherry said. "And it could be—and, granted, this is a real long shot—it could be someone who wanted the Burnside story killed."

"Why?"

"I don't know. But I promised the Burnsides it meant nothing, and I need to make sure I'm right. They're good folks, and they don't deserve this. So, can you help me out?"

Sherry Carter had beginner's luck. Ed Hodges wouldn't have fallen for deception. But sincerity got him. "Let's go up on the porch."

He led Sherry Carter up onto a screened-in back porch with faded wicker chairs and a rickety card table. "Here, sit down. Just let me wash my hands, I'll be right with you."

Ed Hodges pushed through the screen door into the kitchen. Sherry could hear him in there, banging around. He was gone several minutes, returned carrying two tall glasses.

"Ice tea," he said. "Took a chance you could stand it, nice sunny day like today. The way I like it, lemon, no sugar, but I can get you some if you like."

"Not for me," Sherry said. "This is fine."

Ed Hodges sat down at the table, took a sip from his glass. "Okay," he said, "what can I tell you?"

Sherry considered. Smiled. "What were you thinking in there while you were making the tea?"

Ed Hodges laughed. "I'm thinkin' you're pretty sharp. I was goin' over it in my head, thinkin' what I wanna say."

"Why do you have to do that?"

"Because it's been a long time, and I don't wanna tell you wrong. Like you said, these are good folks. Not that I think it matters, but for what it's worth, ask your questions."

"Okay," Sherry said. "Let's get right to it. Was there anything suspicious at all about the Barbara Burnside fatality?"

Ed Hodges shook his head. "Absolutely nothing. Typical drunk driving accident. Blood alcohol on the girl was well over the legal limit. I don't remember the exact figures, but it's a matter of record, you could look it up. Anyway, it was way over point one percent. She wasn't slightly drunk, she was very drunk. It's a wonder she was able to drive at all. As it was, she didn't get more than half a mile."

"From where?"

"The Timlin place. That's where the party was. Young kids. Drinking age, but still kids. Early twenties maybe. And maybe some of them not even that. *She* was over twenty. That I know for sure. It was important to know. The state of Connecticut raised the drinking age to twenty in the fall of '83. If she was under twenty, the Timlins were on the hook, serving liquor to a minor."

"I thought the drinking age was twenty-one."

"It is now. Ever since '85. But at the time of the wreck it was twenty."

Sherry nodded. "And there was nothing suspicious about where Barbara's car went off the road?"

"Not at all. The Timlin house is up on a hill. You know the place? Out on Locust, two miles out of town, just past the vet's. You know the house I mean?"

"I'm new in town."

"Well, the first big curve down the hill she didn't make. Right through the guardrail, hit a tree, threw her from the car. Messy." Chief Hodges looked away and grimaced.

"And the boyfriend reported the accident?"

"That's right. Kevin Roth. He called it in."

"You questioned him?"

"Yes, I did."

"What was his story?"

Hodges shrugged. "What you know. He went to the party with her. They had a fight. She got angry, took off in her car. He was worried she was too drunk to drive. He borrowed a car and went after her. Found the accident, phoned it in."

Sherry hesitated. Frowned.

"What's the matter?"

"I'm new at this. I don't know what to ask."

Ed Hodges smiled. "Sure. 'Cause you don't know what's important. When you investigate, you don't worry what's important, you ask everything. Until you find something. In this case, it's hard, 'cause there's nothin' much to find."

"Maybe not," Sherry said. "But I gotta try." She took a sip of ice tea. "Okay. I'm gonna take you at your word and ask everything. When the boyfriend found the wreck—he was alone at the time?"

"Yes, he was."

"And when he saw the car off the road, did he get out of his car? Did he go and look?"

"Yes, he did."

"She was thrown from the car. Did he find her body? Try to revive her? Realize she was dead?"

"That's what he said."

"Her injuries were extensive?"

"Very. She went through the windshield, hit her head on a rock. It wasn't pretty."

"So there was no question about it. He'd have known right away that she was dead."

"Oh, yes. It was perfectly obvious."

"Was there blood on his clothes?"

"Blood?"

"Yes. If he touched Barbara, tried to help her, wouldn't he have messed himself up?"

"He would, and he did. The car jumped a guardrail, went down an embankment, hit a tree. He went in after it. Snagged his pants, ripped his shirt, got blood all over himself. I had a feeling he got to her, grabbed her, before he knew what was what. You know, like she was facing away, and he couldn't see how much damage had been done."

"Uh huh. And was he drunk at the time?"

"He'd been drinking. I could smell it on him. He was a little out of it, but part of that would be shock. I didn't do a blood level on him because he wasn't driving. Well, he was, actually, when he found her.

But he didn't have an accident. He probably shouldn't have been driving a car, but no one made an issue out of it in light of the other thing."

"His story checked out, that he was worried about Barbara, borrowed a car, and went to look?"

"Yes, it did."

"Who'd he borrow the car from?"

"Kid at the party. Billy Spires."

"And Spires confirmed the story?"

"Yes, he did. Somewhat reluctantly, as I recall, but he confirmed it." Sherry pounced on that. "Reluctantly?"

Ed Hodges shrugged, sorry to let her down. "Sure. He was a kid. Kids hate to admit to anything. If you were a cop, you'd know. Billy Spires didn't want to admit to loaning his car to someone who might be drunk. I had to convince him that wasn't what I was after. Once I did, he backed the story up. That's one witness. For the rest, practically everybody at the party saw Kevin Roth come running in after he found her. He called us, and the kids all went to look."

"The kids at the party were all there at the scene when you got there?"

"Yes. Just like I said."

"So they could have tampered with the evidence?"

"*What* evidence? I know you're trying to make a mystery out of this, but you're barkin' up the wrong tree. There was no evidence to hide. Nobody strangled this girl and then made it look like an accident. These are not criminal masterminds here, these are a bunch of drunk kids. The car ran off the road. No one staged that. If you'd seen it, you would know. No one ran it off the road to make it look like that's how she died. You'd have to be crazy to try that. 'Cause more than likely you'd get killed doin' it."

"Uh huh," Sherry Carter said. She frowned. "I'm not getting anywhere."

"Because there's nowhere to get."

"Maybe," Sherry said. She took another sip of ice tea, looked through the dirty porch screen into the backyard. A bluejay on a trellis seemed to be eyeing the garden. Sherry watched the bird while she tried to focus her thoughts. She replayed the conversation in her mind, searching for a thread. She asked: "Anyone confirm the fight?"

Ed Hodges had been looking at the backyard too. "What?"

"The fight they had that made Barbara run off—was there a witness to that?"

"No, there wasn't."

"How come?"

"The way I understand it, there wouldn't have been."

"Why is that?"

"Well, the way the boyfriend tells it, the impression I got—because this is not exactly how he tells it—but the way it seems to me is, the fight was the type that was apt to occur when they were alone." The old chief was trying to choose his words carefully.

Sherry Carter's bright eyes narrowed. "You care to elaborate on that?"

"That's my impression," Hodges said. "From the way Roth acted. And the fact that she was so drunk—considerably drunker than he was—I had the impression maybe he tried something with her and she didn't like it. You know, that it was *that* kind of fight. Which he would naturally not want to admit."

"You have any evidence of that?"

"No, I don't. But when you asked me about this—was there anything about it that didn't seem right—my first reaction is no, absolutely not. And my personal opinion is still, no, absolutely not. But if you want any part of it that don't add up total, one hundred percent, well, it's the bit about that fight. Because there's no confirmation because it happened when they were alone. And the boyfriend isn't supplying the details that would explain *why* they were alone. So I'm supplying them from what *I* think happened. Not that it makes any difference one way or another. It was still an accident. You're not gonna get away from that."

"Uh huh," Sherry Carter said. "Can you think of anything else that might help?"

"I don't see how any of this helps."

"I'm not sure it does. But thanks anyway." Sherry got up. "And thanks for the tea."

"Don't mention it. Wish I could have been more help."

Sherry drove off, feeling somewhat ambivalent about her performance. She hadn't gotten much, but as Ed Hodges had said, there probably wasn't much to get.

Still, she couldn't help wondering if Cora Felton could have done better.

37

CORA FELTON PACED THE KITCHEN LIKE A CAGED TIGER, AND WONdered how Sherry was doing. She wished she were with her. It was so frustrating, being stuck without a car. Cora felt like she was back in college, grounded, campused, confined to her room. And just when things were getting good.

The Barbara Burnside business was certainly interesting. Cora knew the old accident had nothing to do with the murders, that simply made no sense. Still, it was certainly significant that someone didn't want it investigated. That had to indicate something was wrong.

Unless.

Unless, it was *the murderer* who was warning people off the Barbara Burnside investigation in order to draw attention *away* from himself.

Cora Felton mulled that explanation over, liked it a lot. Wished there was someone to share it with.

The sound of tires in the driveway brought her to life. Sherry back so soon. Thank goodness.

Cora was halfway to the front door before it occurred to her it might be the TV people again. She peered out the window to see a police car coming up the drive.

Great. Chief Harper. She'd tell him her theory and give him a piece of her mind.

Cora went outside to meet the chief, but it was a young officer who climbed out of the car. He was wide-eyed, and seemed somewhat awkward and self-conscious.

"Miss Felton?"

Cora's thoughts leaped to Sherry. Sherry alone investigating. Sherry out in her car. "What's wrong?" she said.

The officer put up his hands. "I'm sorry. I didn't mean to alarm you. There's nothing wrong." He grimaced, took his hat off, held it in front of him. "Oh. Gee. That's pretty stupid. I guess I can't say that today. I mean nothing *else* wrong." The young policeman was particularly gawky, seemed to be falling all over himself. "I'm sorry, Miss Felton. I've seen you around, of course, but I don't think we've officially met. I'm Dan Finley. I was at the cemetery last night."

"Yes, of course," Cora said.

"Terrible thing," Dan said. "I understand you knew Vicki Tanner?"

"She was my bridge partner," Cora said. She looked the young officer over, trying to account for his nervousness. "How about you? Did you know her?"

"Sure," Dan said. "Since high school. Nice girl. As a matter of fact, she was in my class."

"Oh?"

That was all the prompting Dan needed. "That's right," he said. "She was Vicki Johnson then. Poor thing. Lived here all her life. Well, except for college. She went away for that. Smith, as I recall. She came back, lived with her parents right up till she got married. They're both dead now. Her parents, I mean." Dan shook his head. "I was at her father's funeral just last year. Good man, Mike Johnson. Ran the Old Mill Inn on Clemson Drive. Best food in town. Been closed up ever since he died."

"I see," Cora said.

Dan Finley blushed. "I'm sorry. Here I am, rambling on, and I didn't tell you why I'm here. I'm collecting typing samples, and I need to get one of yours."

"Typing samples?"

"Yes. Chief Harper says you know, and I can just ask you direct. Which is a pleasure, believe me. Everyone else I've had to trick."

Cora Felton smiled. "Let's be sure we're communicating here, young man. What is it I know that you don't have to trick me about?"

"The letter. Aaron Grant got a letter, telling him to lay off Barbara Burnside. Chief Harper wants to know where it came from, he's got me collecting samples from every typewriter in town."

"In town?"

"Maybe that's an exaggeration. But from interested parties. Plus any typewriter in any public place anyone could go in and use."

"I see," Cora Felton said. She smiled to herself. Chief Harper had told Dan Finley he was collecting samples to compare with the Barbara Burnside letter. Of course, the chief also wanted samples to compare with the two typed puzzle clues. In that way the Barbara Burnside letter had been a godsend, giving him a legitimate excuse for collecting the samples.

And for keeping quiet about collecting them.

"Anyway, no one's supposed to know about it," Dan Finley said. He hesitated, then ducked his head, shuffled his feet, and acted embarrassed again. This time Cora recognized the behavior, and figured she knew why.

She was right.

"I have to tell you, Miss Felton," Dan Finley said. "I'm a big fan of yours."

"Oh, really?" Cora said. Fans made her nervous, because there was always the danger they might want to discuss some recent crossword puzzle which she of course knew nothing about.

"Yes," Dan gushed. "I guess that's why I was rambling on before. Celebrities make me nervous. And, like I say, I'm a fan."

When meeting a fan, Cora always found a way to change the subject. This time it was easy. Eyes twinkling, she said, "But you still want my typing sample?"

Dan Finley put up his hands. "I know it's stupid. You're the nationally famous Puzzle Lady. No one suspects you of anything. But the chief said get it, and what can I do?"

Cora patted him on the shoulder. "Don't be silly. Of course you can have a sample. Come in."

She led Dan Finley through the living room and into the office, wondering what it would do to the young officer's assessment of her as the nationally famous Puzzle Lady when he found out she wasn't even sure how to turn on the computer.

Fortunately, it was on. Sherry had left the computer running, although the screen was blank. Cora knew how to deal with that—*It's a screen saver, hit any key.* Cora touched the space bar, the computer hummed, and moments later a bunch of icons faded onto the screen.

Cora moved the mouse, clicked on the icon *WordPerfect.* Cora had actually written letters on the computer before, but always when Sherry was there. This was her first solo flight.

She was gratified when a new document came up. "What would you like me to type?" she asked.

"The quick brown fox jumps over the lazy dog."

"I beg your pardon?"

Dan Finley grinned. "That's what the examiner of questioned documents said to ask for. *The quick brown fox jumps over the lazy dog.* It has every letter in the alphabet."

"Really? Did you have everybody type that?"

"No, of course not. Because I couldn't tell 'em. You, I could tell. And any machines I type on myself, that's what I type. So, if you wouldn't mind."

Cora Felton typed *The quick brown fox jumps over the lazy dog.* She took care to do it, hoped he wouldn't notice how slow she was.

"Now I have to print it out," she said.

Cora had printed things before, again with Sherry's help. She clicked on the printer icon, checked the screen that came up, verified that it was set for *Print* and not *Fax,* and the number of copies was listed as *1.* Cora moved the mouse and clicked *Print.*

The printer whirred, spat out the page. Cora pulled it out, tried not to look as amazed as she always felt when the machine actually worked. She gave the page to Dan Finley, who sealed it in a plastic bag.

"Okay, thanks a lot, Miss Felton," he said. "I wish they were all this easy."

As Cora watched him back out of the driveway, it occurred to her how lucky she was the reporters hadn't shown up while he was there. It would have been a little awkward denying her involvement in the case with a policeman right in the house, not to mention explaining her interest in quick brown foxes and lazy dogs.

Cora remembered she'd left the printer on. Plus she hadn't exited from the document, or from *WordPerfect,* or done any of the things Sherry was always asking her to do.

Cora went back into the study, switched the printer off. She clicked the mouse on *Exit,* and the computer asked her if she wished to save her document. Cora couldn't think of a reason to do so, clicked *No.* The document imploded, and *WordPerfect* shrank back to a tiny icon, nestled among the others on the computer screen.

One icon caught Cora's eye. A tiny black and white checkerboard, labeled: *11×11.* Cora clicked on it. The icon vanished, and moments later a crossword puzzle grid appeared on the screen.

Cora looked at it, realized it was the grid Sherry had been working on. Aside from that, it meant nothing to her.

Underneath the grid, Sherry had typed:

4) D — LINE (5)

14) A — SHEEP (3)

18) D — YES VOTE (3)

The puzzle clues.

It occurred to Cora if she were really the nationally famous Puzzle Lady they might mean something to her.

But they didn't.

Cora sat down, rubbed her head.

It was torture, in the middle of an actual murder investigation to be stuck at home with nothing to work on but a crossword puzzle. And an electronic one at that. The ultimate insult to one who regarded the computer with distaste, considered it a natural enemy, would have preferred an old-fashioned Smith-Corona.

But there was nothing else to work on.

Cora Felton leaned back in her chair, cocked her head, studied the screen.

38

SHERRY DID MUCH BETTER THIS TIME. MAYBE SHE'D LEARNED SOME-thing from Ed Hodges, or maybe she was just more confident the second time around, or maybe it was because the man she was question-ing gave the impression there might be something to get. But, whatever the reason, Sherry gained confidence, zeroed in, and actually began to enjoy herself. After all, she realized, it was basically a logic problem. You asked questions, and you looked for discrepancies, contradictions, and omissions, then you boiled them down and asked more questions. If the witness was hiding something, you ferreted it out. Easy as pie.

Of course, it helped that Billy Spires wasn't all that bright.

Billy Spires worked in a used-car lot in Danbury. A little man in a shiny blue suit and polka dot tie, Billy Spires thought Sherry Carter could use a new car.

"Nothing against the Japanese," Billy Spires said, "but you really ought to go American."

"I'm not here for a car."

Billy Spires nodded enthusiastically. "I know the feeling. Half the people walk on this lot, they're not looking to buy. They think they're set, they think they're doing fine, but then, why are they here?"

"I'm here to see you," Sherry said.

"And I appreciate it," Billy Spires said. "And I'm grateful to who-ever gave you the recommendation."

"That would be Ed Hodges."

"Who?"

"Ed Hodges. From Bakerhaven. Former chief of police."

"Oh, yes. And he recommended me?"

"Let's say he remembered you. With regard to an accident."

"An accident." Billy Spires put up his hands. "Hey, look, we're not responsible once they leave the lot."

"I'm sure you're not," Sherry Carter said. "Let's try this again. My name is Sherry Carter. I'm from Bakerhaven. I'm looking into the Barbara Burnside accident."

Billy Spires' mouth fell open. "Barbara Burnside."

"Yes."

"But that was years ago."

"Yes, it was."

"I don't understand."

"You heard about the murders in Bakerhaven?"

"Yes, of course."

"You happen to see this morning's *Gazette*?"

"No, I didn't. This is Danbury. Why would I get the *Gazette*?"

"Well, there was a column this morning about Barbara Burnside. I'd like to follow up."

"Follow up on what?"

"The story. There's always a story. And I figure you'd be the one to know."

"Know what? What the devil are you talking about?"

Sherry Carter smiled. "Come on, Billy. I talked to Ed Hodges. And now I'm talking to you. Piecing together what happened that night."

"What happened that night. Everyone *knows* what happened that night. Barbara Burnside got sloshed, ran her car off the road."

"And why did she do that?"

"What?"

"Why did she get in her car, drive away, and run off the road?"

"She had a beef with her boyfriend. Kevin Roth."

"How do you know that?"

"Everybody knows that. That's what happened."

"Did you see the fight?"

"It wasn't a fight. Just an argument."

"Did you see the argument?"

"Nah."

"Then how do you know?"

"Kevin told me."

"And who found the wreck?"

"Kevin did."

"Uh huh. How did that happen?"

"What do you mean? He was real worried, and he went to look for her."

"On foot?"

"What?"

"When he went to look for Barbara—was he on foot?"

"No. He took my car."

"You let him take your car?"

"Yeah. Why shouldn't I?"

"I'm not saying you shouldn't. I'm just asking if you did."

"Yeah, I let him take my car."

"He wasn't drunk?"

"No, he wasn't drunk."

"But he'd been drinking, hadn't he?"

"It was a party. We'd all been drinking."

"And he wasn't too drunk to drive?"

"No, he did fine."

"So," Sherry Carter said. "Kevin Roth and Barbara Burnside had an argument. She took off in her car. Kevin came to you, told you about it, said he was worried about her, and asked to borrow your car. You said, sure, and gave him your car keys."

"That's about right."

"About right? What's wrong with it?"

"Well, you're making up a conversation."

"You didn't have that conversation?"

"Not like that."

"What conversation did you have?" Sherry asked patiently.

"Well, almost like that. We talked about the car. About him taking it. About how it was all right."

"That he took it?"

"Yeah."

Billy Spires seemed interested in a button on his jacket. Sherry Carter watched him fiddling with it, and pondered.

"But not the bit about the car keys?"

"What?"

"Well, that's the only thing you left out. You talked about him taking the car and how it was all right. The only thing you didn't talk about was giving him the keys."

"Oh."

"Is that right? You didn't talk about the keys?"

"No."

"Why not?"

Billy Spires continued to play with the button. "The keys were in the car."

"Oh, is that what you told him?"

"No. He told me."

"He told you your keys were in your car?"

"Yes."

"How did he know that?"

"I don't know. Maybe he didn't tell me that. It's been a long time. How can I remember?"

"You seem to remember pretty well, Mr. Spires. I told you a conversation, you said it wasn't quite right."

"Well, it wasn't."

"So you remember that. If you know what's wrong, you must know what's right. So what was the bit about the keys?"

Billy Spires looked up from his button then. "Hey, wait a minute. You'll pardon me, but why are you asking? You're interested in Barbara Burnside, well how come? Here's something happened a long time ago, over, done with, finished, and you're bringing it all up again. And you said something about the murders, but you didn't say what. I *asked* you, and you didn't say. And you expect me to talk to you?"

"Well, actually," Sherry said, "I asked you if you happened to read the *Gazette*. And you pointed out this is Danbury. But there's an article in the morning paper how the two killings in Bakerhaven might be connected to the Barbara Burnside accident."

"That's ridiculous."

"That's what *I* said. Only problem is, every time I try to dismiss the theory someone keeps it alive. By stonewalling and covering things up.

So, when I see you doing the same thing, it makes me say, hey, maybe there's something to this stupid idea after all."

"I'm not covering anything up."

"So what's the bit about the car?"

"There's no bit about the car. It happened just the way I said."

"And the way you said is Kevin Roth told you about the keys. Which doesn't make much sense. At least, not the way you tell it. Because how would he know the keys were in your car?"

Billy Spires said nothing, set his jaw.

"No," Sherry said, "the only thing that makes sense to me is if Kevin Roth took your car without telling you. He had an argument with his girlfriend, she took off in her car. Your car was sitting there with the keys in it. Kevin hopped in and went after her. He was right behind her. He didn't come along later and find the wreck. He *saw* her go off the road."

"You're making that up. You don't know that happened."

"You're telling me it didn't?"

"I'm not talking to you anymore. You twist a person's words. You make things up. You're not quoting me in the paper, because I'm not saying squat."

"You already told me about the keys."

"I didn't tell you nothing. You made a lot of guesses, and they're probably all wrong."

"Oh, I doubt that," Sherry said. "If they were, you wouldn't have stopped talking. So, that's very interesting. From your refusal to discuss this matter, I can assume there's something to the supposition. Kevin Roth was there when Barbara's accident happened. Is it possible he ran her off the road?"

"No, it's *not* possible," Billy Spires said. His hands tightened into fists. "If you're asking me if he banged up my car, the answer is no. That's the stupidest idea I ever heard."

Sherry Carter suppressed a smile. Speaking of stupid, Billy Spires was not the swiftest person in the world, either. Anything he knew wasn't true he was happy to deny. Which made his refusal to talk on certain points all the more illuminating.

"So, he didn't bang up your car," Sherry agreed, "but he still could have spooked her off the road."

"You think he killed her? Is that really what you think?"

"You tell me."

"Don't be dumb. He loved her. He wouldn't have hurt her for the world."

"But he did."

"He didn't. It was an accident."

"Yeah, but if it weren't for the argument, she wouldn't have run away."

"You blame him for that?"

"No. But maybe he blames himself."

"Maybe he does. But so what? Arguing with someone ain't a crime."

"No, it isn't. But murder is."

"Who said anything about murder?"

"Well, that's the thing," Sherry said.

She smiled. Shrugged.

"Too bad you don't read the *Bakerhaven Gazette,*" she told Billy Spires.

39

CORA FELTON SMILED. "THAT'S RIGHT. THERE IS ABSOLUTELY NO FOUN-dation to the story in the *Bakerhaven Gazette* today. I never meant to suggest that the tragic death of Barbara Burnside was in any way con-nected to the murders. I merely used it as an example of how meaning-less the note found in the dead girl's pocket was. People were suggesting it was a crossword puzzle clue. I said it would be just as logical to assume it meant the fourth grave down in line five. But please understand I am not advancing either of these theories. I think they're utterly ridiculous."

The TV picture cut to Rick Reed of Channel 8 News standing in front of the town hall. "And there you have it. The Puzzle Lady, herself, insisting that there is no puzzle. Yet the police are baffled, and have no clue as to the identity of the perpetrator or perpetrators of these two dastardly crimes that have traumatized this peaceful little commu-nity, leaving the townspeople afraid even to walk the streets at night. To the residents of Bakerhaven, it is an intolerable situation. County prosecutor Henry Firth feels something should be done."

The prosecutor appeared on the town hall steps. Belligerent, righ-teous, aggrieved. "This can't go on," he declared. "I won't stand for it. The good citizens of Bakerhaven deserve better. We must act, and act now, before more lives are lost. If our police cannot handle this on a local level, then we must appeal for help from outside. We are a small town, with limited resources. If our police chief is not up to the task, he should step down, before it is too late, before this maniac strikes again."

Cora Felton switched the TV off. "Can you believe that," she said. "The man actually said *strikes again.*"

Sherry Carter wasn't amused. "Why did you do that—give a TV interview?"

Cora Felton smiled. "Sherry, darling, I didn't go looking for them. I was out on the front lawn, they came up the driveway, stuck a microphone in my face."

"You could have said no comment."

"That would have been worse. They would have run the Barbara Burnside story and my refusal to comment on it. Insinuated there must be something there. I'm ten times better off saying, No, there's nothing to it, if I want it to go away."

"Yeah, I know. I'm just touchy. I mean, I could have prevented that interview." Sherry said it glumly.

"That guy really asked you out?"

"Asked me out? You call that asking me out? The guy tried to pressure me."

"Men are like that. I remember my fifth husband—"

"Aunt *Cora!* Please!"

Sherry got up from the couch, went into the kitchen, took out a mixing bowl, and lit the oven.

Cora Felton trailed in behind her. "Oh, oh," she said. "Cake or brownies?"

"Brownies."

"Brownies? You must be *really* upset."

"Please, don't start that again."

"Start what? You bake when you're stressed. It's no big deal." Cora Felton took a gin bottle out of the cupboard. "I drink when I'm stressed. It's the same thing."

"You're not stressed."

"And you *are?*"

"Aunt Cora, give me a break."

Sherry Carter took out flour, sugar, milk, eggs, started mixing them in the bowl.

Cora Felton poured gin in a glass, added tonic and ice. Took a sip. "Not bad. Could use a little lime."

Sherry said nothing, stirred the batter.

"You know, I think that newspaper reporter likes you."

"Aunt Cora, *puh-lease.*"

"*Puh-lease?* You sound like a teenager. You want me to slip him a note in English class, see if he thinks you're cute?"

"You're not funny."

"You're stirring that batter awfully vigorously."

"Good thing you said *vigorously* now, before you start slurring your words."

Cora Felton raised an eyebrow at her. "Oh. Cheap shot. Did I hit a nerve?"

Sherry added chocolate syrup, stirred it around. Said nothing.

"I thought Chief Harper did pretty well," Cora Felton said. The chief, in a brief TV interview, had denied the Barbara Burnside story, reported on the lab analysis of the Vicki Tanner shoes, and declined further comment, even when Rick Reed snidely and none too subtly hinted Harper was not up to his job. "Didn't you think he did well?"

"Just great," Sherry said.

"What are you so upset about?"

Sherry poured the batter into a baking pan, put it in the oven. She straightened up and turned around. "What am I so upset about? What *aren't* I so upset about? On the one side, the Barbara Burnside case won't go away. I made a promise to the parents that I can't fulfill. I keep getting information that is inconclusive and leads nowhere. Not that there's anywhere to lead. But what I want is for people to tell me, no, there's nothing to it, Sherry, forget about it, get on with your life. Instead, I come up with some insignificant witness, who didn't even see the accident, who only loaned the guy the car, but who couldn't act more guilty if he'd killed the girl himself."

"Maybe I should go talk to him."

"No, you *shouldn't.* You shouldn't, and I shouldn't either. We're way too visible in this case. You were just on TV. And I'm upset about it, but here I am poking around in the case too. And imagine what would happen if that bloody TV reporter were to find out about that."

"You mean you might have to have dinner with him?"

"That's not funny." Sherry walked out of the kitchen back into the living room. Sat on the couch, snapped on the TV.

Wheel of Fortune was on. There was a new puzzle on the board, with no letters filled in. The category was *Quote.* The puzzle was:

"I came, I saw, I conquered," Sherry said.

From the kitchen doorway, Cora Felton said, "You can't solve the puzzle with no letters showing."

"Of course I can," Sherry said. "It has to be a famous quote, one everyone would know. That's the only one that fits."

"Uh huh," Cora Felton said. She watched as a young housewife, an airline pilot, and a plump woman with an enormous smile tried to solve the puzzle.

The young housewife said, *"T."*

There was no *t.*

The airline pilot said, *"L."*

There was no *l.*

"She'll guess *r,* which is third from the last," Sherry said.

The plump woman with the enormous smile did indeed guess *r,* which was exactly where Sherry said it would be.

"Now she'll get the *s* in *saw,"* Sherry said.

The woman spun the wheel, got five hundred dollars for one *s,* the first letter in the three-letter word in the second line.

"Now," Sherry said, "she'll buy a vowel, because she hasn't got a clue. The *i* would give it to her, but she'll buy the *e*'s in *conquered* and *came* which won't help her at all."

The woman did just as predicted. She spun again, got two hundred for an *n,* spun again, and lost her turn for guessing *g.*

It was nearly five minutes later when the airline pilot finally solved it to thunderous applause. He'd have made a thousand dollars more if he'd been able to supply Julius Caesar as the source of the quote.

"Unlucky," Sherry Carter said sourly.

"Gee, even I knew that one," Cora Felton said.

"So, why don't you go on the show?" Sherry said. "Let the whole world see how quick you are at puzzle solving."

"It wouldn't be the end of the world."

"No. Just the end of the series."

"I don't think it would be that bad."

"Oh, no? People don't like being duped, Aunt Cora. It gets them rather upset."

"I can see that."

"What's that supposed to mean?"

"It doesn't mean anything, but are you capable of being nice?"

"What?"

"Can you control your temper, act civil, not treat me with contempt?"

"What are you talking about?"

"That young reporter—the one I mentioned—the one I think likes you."

"You're going to start that again?"

"Absolutely not. I just thought you'd like to know."

"Know what?"

Cora Felton pointed. "He's here."

Sherry shot to her feet, looked out the window. Aaron Grant was climbing out of his car.

"For goodness sakes," Sherry said. "What does he want now?"

"That's a complicated question."

"Don't start with me," Sherry snapped.

On the TV, *Wheel of Fortune* had come back out of commercial. The new puzzle was:

— — —   — — — —

— —   — — — —

— — — — — — —

The category was *Book*.

"*The Firm* by John Grisham," Sherry said. She picked up the remote control, snapped off the TV.

The front doorbell rang. Cora Felton went to the door, ushered in Aaron Grant.

"Hi, there," Aaron said. "You seen the evening news?"

"Yes, we have," Cora said.

"I've also seen the morning paper," Sherry said dryly.

"Oh. Sorry about that."

"Well, you're not sorry enough. I had the Burnsides here this morning. You happen to know them? Nice people. A little upset, but nice, decent people."

"I know," Aaron said. "I was wrong, and I feel bad. But I assume your aunt told you about the letter?"

Sherry shot a look at Cora Felton. "She told me. I suppose you think the letter makes it all right?"

"No, but it certainly makes it interesting. Particularly the way Chief Harper's playing it."

"He's withholding it."

Aaron Grant grinned. "He's *officially* withholding it. That is the part he's withholding that the police *know* he's withholding. Then there's the part he's withholding from everybody *including* the police. I'm telling you, I don't envy that man his job."

"I don't envy you *yours,*" Sherry said. "What are you writing about for tomorrow?"

"Oh, it's all written," Aaron said. "This time of night I'm usually done. The paper's mostly set in type, they just wait on the ball scores to go to press."

"What'd you write about?"

"Nothing. I took a dive. For the benefit of all concerned. A general rehash, with a spotlight on the Tanner shoes. Nothing more than Harper gave out in his interview."

"And you're here looking for something better?" Sherry said. Her tone was not pleasant.

"I'm here to fill you in," Aaron said. He looked at Cora Felton. "And I happen to need some puzzle-making expertise. Not for publication, but just for my own sanity. Nothing in this case is right-side up. The puzzle clues, which should mean something, don't. The clue to Barbara Burnside's grave, which should be meaningless, is pay dirt. But if that's pay dirt, what are the other clues all about? You see what I mean?"

"Yes, I do," Cora said. "What about it, Sherry? You think you could fit that information into a grid?"

"No, I don't," Sherry said. "But it's your theory. What do you think it means?"

Cora Felton considered. Aaron Grant watched her with some

amusement, knowing she was making it up. And knowing she knew he knew. He smiled slightly.

"Frankly," Cora said, "I don't think it means anything."

"Really?" Aaron said. He turned to Sherry. "Do you think she's right?"

Sherry looked at him, tried to read the expression on his face. His nostrils quivered. The thought occurred to her, just like a horse.

"Something in the oven?" Aaron said.

"Oh," Sherry said.

She went in the kitchen, checked the oven. The brownies were not quite done. Another ten minutes, she figured. She straightened up to find Aaron Grant standing in the doorway.

"Cake?" he said.

"Brownies."

"Oh. I like brownies. Duncan Hines? Betty Crocker?"

"No."

"What, then?"

"Just brownies."

"You made them from scratch?"

"You make it sound like a crime."

"No. I just didn't realize you were a cook."

"Please."

"Nothing wrong with that," Aaron Grant said. "I'll bet they're good too. Are they almost done?"

"No. They just started."

"They smell like they're baking. What do you think, another fifteen minutes?"

"Were you planning to, stay that long?"

"Are you kicking me out?"

"Don't you have a job to do?"

"I told you. My column's already in."

"Too bad. You could have done a human interest story on my baking."

"I may anyway."

"You do, and I'll kill you."

"There's a thought," Aaron said. "You know, everyone is assuming it's a man, because it's young women being killed. That's rather sexist. What if the killer was actually a woman?"

"I'm so flattered that you consider me in that category."

"As a woman?"

"No, as a killer."

Cora Felton stuck her head in the door before Aaron could reply. "Sorry to interrupt, but did you mail a letter?"

"What?" Sherry said.

"Did you mail a letter this afternoon?"

"No. Why?"

"The flag is up."

"What?"

"On the mailbox. I looked out the window just now, and the flag is up on the mailbox. I don't recall seeing it up when I got home."

"It was up when I got here," Aaron said. "I remember seeing it. I figured Sherry was posting another Puzzle Lady column."

Cora Felton gave him a look, said, "Well, if no one mailed anything, then why is it up?"

"Well, that's one puzzle we can solve," Aaron Grant said. "You want me to go and take a look?"

"I think I can handle it," Cora said. "You kids bake your brownies."

Aaron Grant watched her go, turned back to Sherry. "She's getting a real kick out of this."

"I suppose so."

"Well, it's right up her alley, isn't it? Just a big puzzle."

"A murder is not a puzzle," Sherry said sharply. "A puzzle has one correct solution."

"And a murder doesn't?"

"Not in the same way. You can have a murder that's solved, you can have a murder that's not solved. You can have a killer who goes to jail, you can have a killer who gets off. You can have a killer who's convicted, but it's the wrong killer."

"Interesting," Aaron said. "You have a very analytical mind."

"Is that meant as a compliment? Are you trying to charm a brownie out of me?"

"Did it work?"

"Oh, that *was* insincere flattery?"

"A compliment doesn't have to be insincere to work."

"Just discussing whether it worked or not makes it insincere."

"You're the one who brought up that concept."

Before Sherry Carter could retort, Cora Felton burst into the kitchen. Her eyes were bright. There was a letter in her hand.

"Take a look at this," Cora said.

Sherry and Aaron crowded around, peered over her shoulder.

It was a typewritten letter. The envelope was addressed to the Puzzle Lady.

The letter read:

Don't give up yet. Your theories aren't wrong, you just haven't gone far enough. Suppose four down line five was the grave of Barbara Burnside. Then what comes next? Have you followed the clues? I don't think so. That's the only grave I've heard mentioned. What comes next?

The signature was also typed.

The Graveyard Killer

40

AARON GRANT PULLED THE CAR TO A STOP IN FRONT OF THE CEMETERY gate.

"I don't like this," Sherry said.

"Relax," Cora told her. "We're just checking it out."

"We shouldn't check it out. We should give it to Chief Harper."

"If it checks out, we will. Okay, let's go over the fence."

"Just as if we had every right to," Sherry said. She walked up to the fence, put her hands on the top, hoisted herself up, and hopped over.

Aaron Grant boosted Cora Felton up.

"Thank you, young man." She smiled at him. "I certainly hope you don't turn out to be the murderer."

Before Aaron could retort she'd hopped down the other side. He climbed over the fence and followed. The women had already gone on ahead.

"Hey, wait for me, I got the light," Aaron said, but the moon was nearly full, and the women were having no problem making their way through the tombstones. By the time Aaron had caught up they'd reached the grave with the new crime scene ribbon.

"Okay," Cora said. "Let's start again. Count four down, then count five over from the road."

Aaron Grant shone the light on the gravestones as they counted.

"And that should bring us to Barbara Burnside," Cora said.

It did. Aaron Grant's flashlight lit up the gravestone of the young woman who had died in 1984.

"Okay," Cora said. "If this letter is for real, telling me I haven't gone far enough, then let's go a little farther. The next clue was fourteen across. *Sheep three.*" Cora held up her hand. "Now, admittedly, *sheep three* is not like *line five*. We can't go three sheep over."

"I'm glad to hear it," Sherry said.

"Yes," Cora said. "But the three-letter word for sheep is *ewe*. So instead of *sheep three*, we have *ewe three*. Which is a homonym for *you three*. So *we three* should go fourteen across."

"*We three?*" Sherry said. The contempt was evident in her voice.

"Okay, forget the *we three*," Cora said. "But let's count fourteen across."

With Aaron shining the light, they counted over fourteen graves.

"Okay," Cora said. "Who have we here?"

"Ann Pascal, eighteen eighty-eight," Aaron said.

"*Eighteen* eighty-eight?" Cora repeated. "That probably shouldn't concern us. Let's push on. Next was eighteen down. *Yes vote three.*"

"Don't tell me," Sherry said. "A *yes vote* was *aye*, so *I* go eighteen down."

Cora smiled. "Couldn't have said it better myself. Come on, let's count eighteen down."

"Won't that take us back to the road?" Aaron objected.

"Practically," Cora said. "If there are eighteen graves down. Otherwise this won't work."

It did. Eighteen graves down left them about a half a dozen short of the road. They could see the car over by the gate.

"Great," Cora said. "No one's spotted us yet. What have we got here?"

Aaron Grant shone the flashlight on the weathered gravestone. "Roger Dunnley, nineteen forty-two."

"What's that?" Sherry said.

"What's what?"

"That," Sherry said. She pointed to the side of the gravestone.

Aaron shone the light.

Next to the tombstone was a cardboard box.

It was a small box, about a foot square. It was sealed with masking tape.

There was something written on the top of the box in Magic Marker.

Aaron Grant shone the light, lit it up.

It was one large symbol.

A question mark.

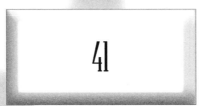

41

CHIEF HARPER SHONE HIS FLASHLIGHT ON THE CARDBOARD BOX.

"You didn't touch it?"

"Absolutely not," Aaron assured him. "We left it for you."

"How come?"

"We recognized your authority as the chief of police," Sherry said.

"Come again?"

"We thought it might be a bomb," Cora Felton said.

Chief Harper looked at Cora, tried to see if she was kidding. Wasn't sure. "Great," he said.

Chief Harper turned, shone the light around the cemetery, and found a crooked stick. He picked it up, and joined the others at the grave.

"Okay," he said. "The proper procedure would be to call the bomb squad. Only we don't *have* a bomb squad. Even if we did, I wouldn't want to call them. This is the next best thing. Anyone who doesn't like loud noises better move back."

Chief Harper approached the small box. He edged up on it from the side, as if that would make any difference if it actually were a bomb. Standing as far away as he could, he reached out with the stick.

Touched the box.

Nudged it.

And immediately flinched, dropped the stick, and covered his head.

Nothing happened.

He looked up.

The box had moved about an inch.

He heaved a sigh, picked up the stick, reached it out again.

This time he gave it a bigger push.

And a smaller flinch.

The box moved a half a foot.

"Okay," he said. "At least it's not rigged to explode on contact. Next order of business is to pick it up."

"You really want to do that, Chief?" Aaron Grant asked.

"I don't want to do that at all, but I can't leave it here." Chief Harper looked around. "I wonder if there's anything I can pick it up with."

"Oh, for goodness sakes," Cora Felton said. "It's not a damn bomb." She walked over, picked up the box. "See?"

The others flinched back in alarm, but nothing happened.

"How could you do that?" Sherry demanded. "What if it blew up?"

"I'd be dead, and I wouldn't know," Cora replied. "But I don't think it's a bomb. It's not heavy enough." She frowned. "It could be a stick of dynamite, however."

"Would you please put that down," Chief Harper said.

"I could, but I thought we wanted to take it with us." Cora held the box out toward Chief Harper. "Or would you care to carry it?"

"Fine, bring it along," he said, surrendering.

"Where are we going?"

"I think we better open it where no one can see it."

"Oh? Where is that?"

"I was thinking of your house."

"Nice guy," Sherry said. "You think it might be a bomb, so you wanna open it at our house."

"It's not a bomb," Cora said. She shook the box. "See. It rattles."

"Please don't do that," Chief Harper said. "Okay, come on, let's go."

They made their way back to the front gate, negotiated Cora and the box over the fence, and piled into the cars. Cora got in with Chief Harper, who clearly would have preferred to have her ride with Aaron

Grant, but didn't want to have to say so. "Just hold that steady," he cautioned.

"Steady as a rock," Cora said. She sat in the passenger seat, held the box on her lap.

Chief Harper slammed the door. He got in the car, started the motor, and took off.

Very slowly.

Chief Harper followed Aaron Grant's car straight back to the house. He stopped the car, shut off the engine, tried not to appear in too big a hurry to get out the door. He went around the car, helped Cora Felton out of her seat.

Sherry Carter had the front door open. "Right this way," she said. "Bring the bomb right in here."

"It's not a bomb," Cora said.

She brought the box into the house, took it into the kitchen, set it on the butcher block table. The others gathered around.

At a safe distance.

"Okay," Chief Harper said. "You got any tongs, or long-handled pliers, or anything we can open this with?"

"Aw, phooey," Cora Felton said. She ripped the strip of masking tape off the top.

The others flinched, but, once again, nothing happened.

"Okay," Cora said. "You want to stand back, you can. I'm lifting the lid."

The top of the box consisted of two cardboard flaps that had been held down by the masking tape. Cora put her finger under one, lifted it up. Then lifted the other. She peered inside, then reached in and lifted the two end flaps that had been folded underneath. She craned her neck, peered into the box.

"There's something in the bottom, all right. Let's see what it is."

With that she tipped the box over.

A object clattered out onto the butcher block.

It was a hammer.

On the head of the hammer was something dried and red.

"Oh, my God," Sherry murmured. "Is it . . . ?"

"The murder weapon?" Cora Felton said. "I would imagine it is."

Chief Harper, who realized he'd been holding his breath, exhaled loudly. "All right," he said. "We don't know this is the murder weapon, but it certainly could be. The important thing is no one touches it. I've got an evidence bag in the car."

"Uh oh," Cora Felton said.

Chief Harper frowned. "What?" He looked, saw that she was bent over, peering into the box, which was now lying on its side. "What are you doing there?"

"There's something else in the box."

"What?"

"A piece of paper. Looks like another note."

"Don't touch it," Chief Harper said. "I'll get something, pull it out."

"Here's a paper towel," Sherry said. "Will that do?"

"Fine." Chief Harper took the paper towel, reached into the box, pulled out the piece of paper.

It was typewritten, just like the second and third clues.

It read:

48) D — EARL GREY (3).

"Earl Grey three," Chief Harper said. "Isn't that tea?"

"Yes, of course," Sherry said. "It's entirely too simple."

"Simple," Chief Harper said. "It makes no sense at all. The guy has us running around the cemetery counting gravestones following clues, now he gives us forty-eight down. There *is* no forty-eight down. Forty-eight down would be way across the road."

"Never mind that," Aaron Grant said. "If forty-eight down is tea, Sherry, can you fit it in the grid?"

"I have no idea," Sherry said. "And even if I could, it couldn't possibly intersect with any of the other words."

Chief Harper, who still deferred to Cora Felton as the Puzzle Lady, turned to her now. "Is that right?" he said. "Is tea the right word, and can you fit it in a grid?"

"Oh, it's the right word, all right," Cora Felton said. "And, no, I can't fit it in a grid. But there's really no need. It's a much simpler puzzle than that, and the message is quite clear."

Sherry looked at her aunt as if she'd taken leave of her senses. Sherry seemed about to speak up, but Chief Harper said, "What do you mean?"

Cora Felton shrugged. "I guess the killer doesn't think much of our abilities. Sends us the murder weapon, tells us even so we can't catch him."

"Tells us? Tells us how?" Chief Harper said.

"With the puzzle," Cora said. "He just completed the puzzle. Four down is *queue*. Fourteen across is *ewe*. Eighteen down is *aye*. Forty-eight down is *tea*. That's your message.

"*Queue, ewe, aye, tea.*"

Cora Felton shrugged.

"*Quit.*"

42

CHIEF HARPER PUT THE HAMMER IN ONE EVIDENCE BAG, AND THE TWO letters in two others. He sealed the bags, heaved a sigh. "Okay," he said. "What do I do now?"

"What do you mean?" Sherry Carter said.

Chief Harper pointed to the last clue. "Do you have any idea what sort of position this puts me in? I got the prosecutor pressuring me to get off the case. Everyone in town's convinced I'm not capable of doing my job. And, lo and behold, I'm not. Here I am, through no real fault of my own, withholding a whole bunch of puzzle clues. Which just happen to be evidence in a double murder case. I had a good reason to withhold them when I started withholdin' 'em. That reason got shakier and shakier as time went on. I stood my ground, because it seemed like anything else would be a disaster." Chief Harper laughed bitterly. "Well, I can't imagine any bigger disaster than this. By an unhappy coincidence, the clues I'm withholding are all telling me to quit."

"You know, those might be aimed at me," Cora Felton said. "Telling me to quit trying to solve the puzzle."

"You *solved* the puzzle," Chief Harper pointed out. "There *was* no puzzle. Just a painfully obvious message, mocking me and suggesting I give up."

"So, what are you going to do?" Aaron Grant said.

"Do?" Chief Harper echoed. "The first thing I'm going to do is I'm gonna have these two notes analyzed, see if I can match 'em up."

"Why wouldn't they match? They're obviously from the killer."

"Yes, and no," Cora Felton said.

Chief Harper looked at her. "What do you mean by that?"

"Well," she said, "I have no doubt about the fourth puzzle clue. It looks just like the other two typed ones." She pointed. "But this letter to me is something else. It was obviously typed on a different typewriter."

"You're kidding," Chief Harper said.

"Not at all. Take a look. Some of the characters are different. The letter *s,* for instance. It's a whole different style of type."

"You're right," Chief Harper said. "This *was* typed on a different machine."

"You noticed this just now?" Sherry asked her aunt.

"Actually," Cora replied, "I noticed it when we got the letter."

"And you didn't feel it was worth mentioning?"

"I didn't want to distract us from our task."

Aaron Grant grinned. "Nice euphemism. You figured if we thought it wasn't from the killer, we wouldn't go."

"Oh, I'm sure you would have eventually," Cora said, "but time was of the essence. Suppose some teenagers got into the cemetery, found that box?"

Chief Harper put up his hands. "All right," he said. "If we could please not squabble. The fact is, you did go, and you found it. Which makes no sense if the note isn't genuine."

"It's clearly genuine," Cora Felton told him. "For some reason, the killer used another typewriter. And that's rather revealing."

"How so?"

"The puzzle clues were obviously prepared in advance. With the exception of the first one. But the other three would all appear to be typed on the same typewriter. The killer had them typed out, ready to deliver his special message. This letter, telling us where to find the box, was done on the spur of the moment. At a time when the killer did not have access to the original typewriter. So he had to use a different one. One he had access to today. And it's gotta be nearby, because he typed that letter, put it in my mailbox, and put the box in the cemetery all in a very short space of time. If we can just find the typewriter he used, we should be able to nail him."

"I have Dan Finley collecting samples of type now."

"Dan Finley?"

"One of my officers."

"Would that be the rather young officer who came by to get a typing sample?"

"That's Dan. Why?"

Cora Felton shrugged. "Just making an observation. After all, our premise is the killer is a young man."

Chief Harper looked pained. "You suspect Dan Finley?"

"I don't know Dan Finley. I just remarked that he's young. Like our reporter friend here. And Dan knew who I was. Said he was a big fan. Does he have any interest in crosswords?"

"Yes, he does, but it's not what you think. He's the one who sent me to you in the first place."

"Oh?"

"When we got the first clue. He was the one who thought it was a crossword puzzle clue, and suggested I consult the Puzzle Lady. He knew you from the TV ad, heard you were in town."

"From the TV ad?" Cora Felton said. "Not from the puzzle column?"

"He knew that too. Showed me your picture in the paper."

"Interesting," Cora Felton said. "So he was the one who pointed out the crossword clue. Did you know he knew Vicki Tanner?"

"Oh, come on," Chief Harper said. "It's a small town. *You* knew Vicki Tanner."

"Yes, but he knew her well. They were the same age, were in the same class at school. He went to her father's funeral."

"So what?"

"And it occurs to me, he was off that night."

Chief Harper frowned. "What do you mean?"

"When we found Vicki Tanner. It was the older officer who was out looking for her. What's-his-name."

"Sam Brogan."

"Right. So if Sam was on duty, I would assume Dan Finley was off. In other words, Dan was free at the time Vicki Tanner was killed. Dan showed up later at the cemetery, but that was after we found the body. But we don't know where he was before."

"Now, look here," Chief Harper said. "I assure you, Dan Finley has nothing to do with this."

"I'm glad you're so sure," Cora Felton said. "That will make your investigation easier."

Chief Harper gave her a look, but her expression remained serene. "All right," he said, "here's the bottom line. We have discovered the murder weapon—if it is indeed the murder weapon, and I think we can assume it is. It was discovered tonight in the cemetery in a cardboard box. I discovered it. I went to the cemetery, found the cardboard box next to one of the graves, found the hammer in it. That is essentially true. It leaves out a few small details, but it is essentially true. And that is the official version I'm giving out to the media. As for the rest of it, I am assembling typewriting samples and having them analyzed as quickly as I possibly can. I figure I have a day or two at best before this all blows up in my face. If I can solve the murders by then, I'm off the hook. If not, I might as well just take the killer's advice and quit. If this blows up, I'll be lucky to keep my job."

Chief Harper looked at Aaron Grant. "You're sitting on this?"

"I'm sitting on this, Chief. I expect an exclusive the minute you crack the case. And if you fail, I'll have to report that fact. But I won't be the one to bring you down."

"Practically a vote of confidence," Chief Harper said. He gathered up his evidence bags, nodded grimly, and went out the door.

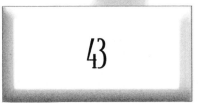

43

FRIDAY BEGAN WELL.

Too well.

For once Cora Felton woke up without a hangover, due to the fact she'd been so busy finding the murder weapon the night before she hadn't had time to drink. Sherry Carter didn't care what the reason was. She was delighted to see her aunt in such good shape, and she decided to celebrate by making Cora her favorite breakfast, blueberry pancakes.

Sherry mixed the batter in the bowl, dumped in fresh blueberries, stirred it around, and spooned it out on the stove. Sherry's stove had a built-in grill, large enough that she was able to lay out strips of bacon too. She also started coffee perking, and soon the most wonderful medley of odors was wafting through the house.

Cora Felton stuck her head in the door. "Pancakes and bacon?"

"*Blue*berry pancakes and bacon," Sherry said.

"I'm in heaven," Cora said. She went to the refrigerator, took out the tomato juice, set it on the counter. She filled a glass with ice, opened the cabinet, took out the vodka.

Sherry frowned. "Going to spoil your breakfast?"

"Not at all," Cora replied. "I'm going to enjoy my brunch."

Cora Felton mixed the Bloody Mary and sat down at the kitchen table just as Sherry slid a plate of pancakes in front of her.

"And we've got real maple syrup," Sherry said. "Which wasn't that easy to find. Can you imagine that? I would have thought here in the country it would be all they have. But the supermarket just had the processed kind."

"Which I positively detest," Cora said. "But I'll eat it if I have to." She poured syrup on her pancakes, cut off a bite, popped it in her mouth. "I think that's the difference between us. You *wouldn't* eat it if you had to."

"Oh? Is that a criticism or a compliment?"

"It's an observation." Cora bit a strip of bacon in half. "You're the one who makes value judgments."

"Value judgments?" Sherry said.

"I don't mean value judgments. I'm not sure what I mean. Aren't you going to sit down and eat?"

"I'm still cooking," Sherry answered. She adjusted the flame on the grill, flipped the pancakes. When they were done she put them on a plate and brought them to the table where her own plate of pancakes was waiting.

"Eat the hot ones," Cora said. "Yours are cold."

"That's okay."

"No, it's not. You cooked the stuff, you should enjoy it. You eat the fresh batch. When I'm ready for seconds, I'll stick 'em in the microwave."

"Okay," Sherry said. "Thanks."

She poured herself a cup of coffee and sat down.

Cora Felton fed another bite of pancakes into her mouth, chewed it. "So, are you asking yourself the question?"

"What question?"

"Is it cause and effect?"

"What do you mean?"

"You start investigating Barbara Burnside. You question Ed Hodges and Billy Spires. Next thing you know the killer's sending you letters and drops the murder weapon in your lap."

"Wait a minute," Sherry said. "The killer sent *you* the murder weapon. You're the Puzzle Lady as far as he's concerned."

"Yes," Cora said. "I don't know how smart this guy is, but I'll grant you that. On the other hand, it ties right in. The killer even says so in his letter. Suppose it *was* Barbara Burnside. You have to ask yourself, was that letter a reaction to what you did?"

"Are you saying I did something wrong?"

"Not at all. I'm saying maybe you did something right."

"So, what do I do now? Go back to Ed Hodges, get a list of the kids involved that night, poke around some more? If I do, it won't be long before Chief Harper finds out."

"You want me to tell you to stop?"

"No, I want you to tell me what to do next."

Cora smiled. "I wish it were that easy."

The phone rang.

Sherry frowned, got up, and picked the receiver off the wall. "Hello."

"Cora Felton, please."

"Who's calling, please?"

"NBC News."

Sherry felt a sudden rush of fear. She must have shown it, because Cora Felton asked, "What's the matter?"

Sherry covered the mouthpiece, said, "It's NBC News."

"I'll handle it."

"Cora."

"I'll handle it."

Cora walked over, took the phone from Sherry, said, "Yes, this is Cora Felton."

"Miss Felton. This is Simon Blackwood. I'm with NBC News. Are you the woman who writes the Puzzle Lady column?"

"That's my picture on it," Cora said.

"Yes, I know. I've also seen your TV ad. You photograph well."

"Whereas in person I look just dreadful," Cora said, dryly.

Simon Blackwood laughed. "I guess I deserve that. You're right, Miss Felton, I've never seen you in person, so how would I know? Anyway, I understand you're involved in a couple murders."

Cora Felton laughed. "Well, Mr. Blackwood, you make it sound like the police just read me my rights."

"I'm sorry. That was not my intention, Miss Felton. Let me re-phrase that. I understand the police investigating two murders have asked your help with a puzzle clue."

Cora Felton laughed again. "Well, you're a day late and a penny short. Or whatever that expression is. The police asked my help at one time. They've since come to the conclusion they don't need it."

"Even so. The idea that a murder involved a crossword clue—it's just too good to pass up. It would be perfect for the closing feature of the nightly news. You know, those fascinating, unusual little tidbits we like to end the program with."

"You mean the *national* news?" Cora said.

Sherry, who had been listening intently, came up out of her chair.

Cora raised her hand as Mr. Blackwood said, "That's right, Miss Felton. We'd love to have you do it."

"Well, I'm afraid I can't."

"Why not?"

"For just the reason you said. What was it, the fascinating tidbit? There's nothing fascinating about it. Two women are dead. One of them I knew. I don't want to profit from their death in any way. In particular by gaining national TV exposure."

"I'm sorry you feel that way."

"Me too," Cora said. "But it's the only way to feel. Thanks for asking."

She hung up the phone, went back to the table. "Well," she said, "I just kissed off NBC."

"I knew it," Sherry said. "I knew they'd get on to us."

"They're not on to us. They're on to a story. The story isn't there, they're gonna go away."

Cora Felton tossed off the rest of her Bloody Mary. She got up, took the glass to the counter, opened the refrigerator, poured some tomato juice.

Then she took the vodka bottle out of the cabinet.

"Aunt Cora."

"What?"

"You don't need another drink."

"How do you know what I need?"

"Aunt Cora. Don't be like that."

Cora Felton unscrewed the top from the vodka bottle. "What's the first rule?"

"Aunt Cora."

"What's the first rule? When we started living together. What was rule number one?"

"I don't tell you what to drink."

"Fine," Cora said. "Just so you remember."

"But if the TV people are after you—"

"No one's after me. Sherry, I turned it down. I could see you getting upset if I'd *done* the interview, but I turned it down. You've got nothing to worry about."

As Cora Felton poured the vodka into the Bloody Mary, Sherry knew she had a lot to worry about. When Cora chose to violate her one-drink-before-dinner rule, there was usually no stopping her. And it couldn't have happened at a worse time, what with the TV people sniffing around. NBC had been forestalled, but the other networks might be more persistent. If they called, Sherry wouldn't know what to tell them. Stall them, of course, but for how long?

Sherry watched Cora Felton sip her Bloody Mary and prayed for a miracle.

That Chief Harper would solve the murders.

44

DAN FINLEY SHOOK HIS HEAD. "I COULDN'T GET IT."

"Get what?"

"The typing sample. From Kevin Roth. I feel bad, because I know that's the one you really wanted."

"One of them," Chief Harper said. "What's the problem?"

"I guess I blew it. I went out to Roth's house, told him the police would like to issue a formal apology to him for bringing up the Barbara Burnside accident." Finley made a face. "Well, that was the wrong thing to do. He pounced on that, said he thought the police were denying they ever had anything to do with bringing up the Barbara Burnside accident. Which, I guess, is true, it was that reporter who brought it up, but, picky, picky, picky. 'Cause we got the credit for doin' it anyway."

"Yes, yes," Chief Harper said, impatiently. "But what happened?"

"Well, I tap-danced around all that, said we weren't investigating the Burnside accident, never had been, but since it had come up we wanted to issue an apology anyway, and we'd be glad to issue a formal, written apology if he would care to request one. If so, all he had to do was make a simple, written request. If he would type one out and sign it, I would be happy to see it processed."

"Not bad," Chief Harper said.

"Yeah, if he was biting. Only he wasn't. The suggestion just made him uncomfortable and suspicious. The end result was he threw me out. No chance of getting a peek at his typewriter. No chance of typing out your quick brown fox. I couldn't even tell you if he *has* a typewriter, 'cause I never got past his front door."

"Uh huh," Chief Harper said. "What about the others?"

"Much better. That same line worked on Barbara Burnside's father. He wants a letter of apology, and issued a written request. It's a full page long, tells us pretty much what he thinks of the whole police department. It should be all you need."

"Who else?"

"Stuart Tanner. Both machines. The one in his home, and his New York office."

"How'd you get the office one so fast?"

"Fax machine. I had his secretary fax me a letter. That's good enough for comparison, isn't it? I mean, isn't a fax just the same as the original?"

"It's not the same ink, but it would be the same typeface. I imagine it'll do. Who else you got?"

"Iris Cooper and Lois Greely. That's the women Vicki Tanner was playing bridge with before she left the Country Kitchen. Then you got the rest of the Burnside people. Ed Hodges, police chief at the time. And the witness in the case, Billy Spires—the guy who loaned the boyfriend the car when he went and found her. The guy lives in Danbury. I didn't catch up with him till late last night."

"And you got him?"

"Yes, I did. At least I got his typewriter at home. Spires works at a used-car dealer—if there's a typewriter there he could use, I don't have that."

"Let's hope we don't need it," Chief Harper said. "I'll let you know."

"Then there's typewriters in public places—that is what you asked, isn't it? Well, I tried the library. There is one at the front desk, of course, but I don't see how anyone could use it, the librarian's almost always there."

"Did you get it anyway?"

"Sure I did. And there's another one in a little office just off the downstairs reading room. Her son was using it. You know, Jimmy. He's helping out, typing up file cards."

"You got a sample from that?"

"Sure thing. Jimmy typed it up himself."

"He didn't mind doing it?"

"No, he seemed proud to show off his typing."

"Is that it?"

"Oh, no. I got a whole bunch more." Dan Finley pointed to the file folder on his desk. "They're all sealed in plastic, they're all labeled where they're from."

"Then we don't need to go over them," Chief Harper said breezily. He was afraid it would occur to Dan that there was no reason to be interested in any typing that obviously didn't match the Barbara Burnside letter. "Okay, hold down the fort, I'm going to New Haven to drop the hammer off at the lab. If anyone should ask, that's where I went. I'll also be taking these typing samples to the examiner of questioned documents, but you don't have to mention that."

"Gotcha," Dan Finley said. "Anything else?"

"Yes. I need that typing sample from Kevin Roth. If we can't get it the easy way, we'll get it the hard way. Draw up a search warrant, empowering you to search his premises and seize any and all typewriters. Get a judge to sign it, and go and serve it."

"Are you serious?"

"Absolutely."

"What grounds do we have for a warrant?"

"Plenty. We suspect Kevin Roth of obstructing justice, compounding a felony, and conspiring to conceal a crime."

"We do?"

"We most certainly do. And I'm counting on you to impress that fact on the judge, Finley. The reason for the warrant is to determine whether the suspect wrote a letter in an attempt to impede a police investigation."

"Kevin Roth's going to be furious."

"I'm sure he is. At this point, I don't care."

"Okay, I'll give it a try."

"Give it a good one. Also, call Officer Crocket in Muncie, Indiana, see if he's got anything more on the runaway girl. If he hasn't, see if you can get him to make another pass at the boyfriend."

"Okay. Anything in particular you want to know?"

"Actually, yes. If possible, ask him about Dana's shoes."

"Her shoes?"

"Yes. The killer took her shoes off. At least that's what we assume. At any rate, we never found them. It would help to know what kind they are. See if the boyfriend remembers what kind she was wearing."

"How will that help?"

"It might help to find them. If we could find them, maybe we could figure out why. In both cases, the killer took the victim's shoes off. There's gotta be a reason. I have a feeling if we can just figure out why he did that, it would go a long way toward solving the crime."

"Yeah, maybe," Dan Finley said. "Is that it?"

"No. Type me a note on your typewriter."

"What?"

"Type me a note. Type anything. Type the quick brown fox jumps over the lazy dog. Mine too. And the one at the other desk. Did you give me samples from them?"

"No, of course not."

"Then do it now. We're not always here. I don't want to overlook the obvious."

"When no one's here, the place is locked."

"I know. I want them just the same."

Dan Finley typed two samples and Chief Harper typed the other one. They labeled them, added them to the folder.

Chief Harper gathered up the folder of typing samples, nodded to Dan Finley, and went out. He drove to New Haven, confident that, aside from Kevin Roth, he had typing samples of everyone else in the case.

45

SHERRY CARTER SWITCHED ON THE COMPUTER, LOGGED ONTO THE Internet, and tried to forget about life.

Her aunt, after finishing off the last of the vodka and searching in vain for another bottle, which Sherry had had the presence of mind to hide, had marched out the front door and taken off in the car, leaving Sherry to her own devices. The device that suited her best was the computer, and Sherry sought solace in that.

Sherry scrolled through the CRUCIVERB-L digest, a daily compilation of posts discussing crossword puzzles. Some of the subscribers were merely puzzle enthusiasts, but many were constructors looking for help, and these were the posts Sherry liked best.

Sherry checked the thread that had been started the day before by Word Man, the on-line name (or nom) of a constructor who had used the five-letter sequence *youto* in a puzzle, and wanted suggestions for a good clue. In particular, Word Man wanted to know if the words *you to* were in any song, poem, or quote memorable enough to be fair.

Today there were several responses. The most inventive was *Irish rock group, sort of,* though Sherry knew it wouldn't fly. The rock group was U2. *Sort of* was the fact the answer was only a homonym for their name. Most puzzle editors would throw it right out.

Ordinarily, Sherry would have found this amusing. Today, she couldn't even concentrate on the screen. Sherry told herself it was because she was worried about her aunt, but she knew that wasn't the case. And it wasn't even the Barbara Burnside business, either. No, Sherry was bothered by the nagging thought that wouldn't go away.

Dennis.

And it wasn't just the idea that he might find her.

No, it was the idea that had been germinating in her mind ever since her friend Brenda had put it there, offhandedly, inadvertently, with a casual, facetious comment.

What was it Brenda had said?

You're glad he's on tour and not strangling young girls.

That had been days ago. But all that time it had been ticking around in her subconscious. Bouncing around the corners of her brain, trying to come to the forefront.

Not strangling young girls.

Dennis.

Strangling young girls.

Sherry pushed herself back from the computer.

There. She had finally voiced the thought. At least to herself.

Could her ex-husband be a killer?

Could her ex-husband be *the* killer?

Could her ex-husband be behind all this?

The minute she had that thought, a million other thoughts assailed her. Ugly thoughts, buffeting her from all directions.

Yes, Dennis was violent; Dennis had a history of violence.

Yes, Dennis hated her, hated her almost as much as he loved her.

Yes, Dennis was handsome, personable, would be attractive to young girls.

But was he sick enough to kill?

Drunk, he was. Sherry knew that for a fact. Drunk, Dennis was capable of anything.

But sober, she couldn't see it. Somehow, she just couldn't see it. And yet, she realized, the reason she couldn't see it was because Dennis, sober, was so suave, sophisticated, charming, and pleasant. And if that was an act—and didn't she know well enough that most of his posturing was an act—well, then, would Dennis be capable of murder? Could he lure and kill a young girl?

The answer tortured Sherry.

It was not that the answer was yes.

It was that the answer wasn't no.

It was possible.

In her heart, she knew it was possible.

She had to get it out of her head.

Sherry told herself if it were *really* possible, she would have thought of it before, it wouldn't have taken this long. Why wouldn't she have realized the moment she heard?

Unfortunately, she had the answer. Brenda'd said *strangling* young girls. Sherry had corrected her—the girl had been hit with a blunt object—leading the discussion away from Dennis and back to the crime. But more than that, the original remark, in being wrong, hadn't registered. Brenda had referred to strangling young girls. No one was strangling young girls. Therefore, her remark had not connected Dennis to the murders.

Yes, it was pure semantics. But Sherry dealt in semantics. Her brain processed words in a very precise, selective manner. If a premise was misstated, it would take a long time for the truth to penetrate.

The truth?

Dennis?

Did she really believe it was Dennis?

Sherry told herself she had to think this out rationally. Because, rationally and logically, she knew it *couldn't* be Dennis. It simply didn't make sense. So, if it wasn't Dennis, she merely had to convince herself of that fact by simple, irrefutable logic. Calmly, coolly, work it out.

Could Dennis kill the girls?

Yes, he could.

But why would he kill the girls?

Unfortunately, Sherry knew why. He would do it to get at her. To scare her. To demonstrate his superiority, strength, intelligence, cunning, ruthlessness, ingeniousness, and persistence.

All right, grant him that. Was there anything in these two murders that pointed to him?

Unfortunately, there was.

The puzzle clues.

Sherry's ex-husband was one of the few people in the world who knew that Sherry, not Cora Felton, was the Puzzle Lady. So far, it had not occurred to him to threaten to reveal that fact. Sherry prayed it never would. But he knew it, and he could certainly use it. And if he was killing these girls, as Sherry feared he was, to get at her, then didn't it follow that he would taunt her with the puzzle clues?

No, it did not, Sherry told herself. And for the first time since she had had the paranoid thought that Dennis might be behind this, she was comparatively calm. Because the logic here was forceful. Although Dennis might be capable of committing the murders, he was not capable of leaving the puzzle clues. For the same reason his band would never get anywhere. Dennis was not that creative. His songs were mediocre at best. As a performer, he had gotten by on charisma, not talent. But to create a puzzle based on several words that were homonyms for letters spelling another word—Dennis simply couldn't do it.

So, unless Dennis had an accomplice—which made no sense—he could not be the killer. Dennis might have killed in a drunken rage. He might even have lured young girls like the spider and the fly. But not like this.

So, the very thing that implicated Dennis also exonerated him. The puzzle clues, which he would have known to send to her, he could not have made up.

In Sherry's mind it was very clear.

Because of the puzzle clues, Dennis could not be the killer.

46

OFFICER CROCKET, WHO WAS SOMEWHAT OVERWEIGHT, RESENTED THE stairs up to Timothy Rice's room. Timothy lived above his parents' garage in a housing development on the outskirts of Muncie, Indiana, and while that might have been cool for a teenage boy, the steep, narrow stairs were ill suited for a portly policeman. So Officer Crocket began the questioning slightly out of breath.

Fortunately, he had a good chance to recover while Timothy protested that he'd already told the police everything he knew. Crocket let the boy ramble, glanced around the room.

It was your typical teenage room, clothes on the floor, rock stars and baseball and basketball players on the wall. No pinups, Crocket noted. Timothy's mother probably collected the laundry once a week, prohibiting calendar art. Timothy had a TV with some video game or other—Crocket was not clear on the various distinctions—a hi-fi system for cassettes and CDs, and a computer and modem. The computer, centrally placed, seemed to dominate the room. Crocket got the impression that for all the sports posters, not to mention his Indianapolis Colts T-shirt, Timothy Rice was more nerd than jock.

"All right," Crocket said, when the boy finally ran down and stopped complaining. "I know this is difficult for you, but I just have a few more questions. I'm sure you want Dana's killer caught."

"Of course I do. I just don't see how I can help."

"Well, why don't you let us be the judge of that. Just help us any way you can."

Timothy Rice had sandy hair and tortoiseshell glasses. He pushed the glasses back up on his nose and said, "What do you want to know?"

"Do you remember her shoes?"

"What?"

"When Dana came to see you, just before she left—what kind of shoes was she wearing?"

"Why?"

"Because there weren't any on the body, and they've never been found."

Timothy shuddered. "Body."

"I know. It's upsetting. But if you could help us out. You happen to remember her shoes?"

"Sure. She was wearing sneakers."

"Are you sure?"

"Yeah. Dana always wore sneakers."

"Do you happen to know what kind?"

"Nike."

"Are you sure?"

"Sure I'm sure. She wore Nike. I wear Reebok. See?" Timothy hiked the leg of his blue jeans, lifted his foot. "See. Reebok. We used to kid about it. You know, like a commercial parody. Anyway, that's what she wore."

"What about her socks?"

"What about 'em?"

"What kind were they?"

"White, of course. What else do you wear with sneakers?"

"Uh huh," Crocket said. "And when she came over here—the last time you saw her—did she give you any idea she was going to leave?"

"No, she didn't," Timothy said. "I've been over this a hundred times. She was upset, she was real unhappy, and she was complaining. But she never said anything about running away."

"Why was she upset?"

"About her grades, of course."

"Her grades?"

"Yeah. She had terrible grades."

"Lots of kids get bad grades. They don't run away."

"I know."

"Well, can you think of any reason why Dana did?"

Timothy Rice sat in his desk chair, swiveled it around, typed idly on the keyboard of the computer. The computer was off. "I guess it was Mr. Foster."

"Who?"

"The math teacher."

Officer Crocket felt a sudden rush of adrenaline. Good God. Something concrete. At last. The girl was involved with her teacher.

He tried not to sound too eager. "What do you mean, Timothy?"

"Oh. The math teacher scared her off. She flunked his course. Flat out flunked. Her other grades were bad, but this was the worst. He gave her a straight F."

That was not what Crocket wanted. Now he tried to hide his disappointment. "Too bad," he said. "But no reason to run away."

"Yeah, I know," Timothy said. "It was the way he humiliated her."

"I beg your pardon?"

"Foster offered her a chance to pass. Just barely, with a D minus, but still, better than flunking the course."

"Wait a minute. Her teacher offered to change her grade?"

"That's right. If . . ."

"If what?"

"She did what he wanted."

"And what was that?"

"Corrected her final."

Crocket blinked, stunned by the anticlimax. "What?"

"He gave her back her final, asked her to correct it."

"Her final?"

"Yeah. Her math final. The one she flunked. Foster asked her to correct everything she had wrong and hand it in again."

"Why didn't she do it?"

"She was going to. She just couldn't bear it."

"How do you know?"

"That's why she came over. To ask me to help her. You gotta understand, Dana wasn't very good at math."

"She came here to ask you to help her with her final?"

"That's right."

"And you wouldn't do it?"

"What do you mean, I wouldn't do it? Why wouldn't I do it?

Actually, there was nothing to do. I got an A on that final. All she had to do was copy my answers."

"She didn't have to write out the problems?"

"No, just the answers. Pretty stupid, huh? Did he really think she wasn't gonna get 'em from somebody else?"

"And she came over here to do that?"

"Right."

"Then why did she run away?"

"I don't know."

"Yes," Crocket said, trying hard to be patient. "But when I asked you why she ran away, you said this teacher might have been a reason. But, if all she had to do was write the answers, and she came here to get 'em, and you were willing to give 'em, well, what went wrong?"

Timothy thought a minute, then swiveled his chair around. "I think it got to her. The sheer stupidity of it. See, it was multiple choice, *a, b, c,* or *d.* So if the guy only wanted the answer, that's all you gotta write. But, no, just to be mean, the guy says you gotta write out the whole answer. As if the answer meant anything without the question. See, I think Dana would have been willing to write the letters. Or even write out the problems, though it would have been more work. Because there would have been a point. But writing the answers, just for the sake of writing them—well, that's like writing 'I was a bad girl' on the blackboard a hundred times."

"So Dana never corrected her test?"

"She started, got fed up, and quit. That's why I say, maybe that was the last straw, made her run away. I don't really think that, I think it's pretty stupid, I only say it 'cause you're pressing me for a reason."

"Uh huh. But you say Dana started to correct her test?"

"That's right."

"And that's when she got upset and left?"

"Yeah. 'Cause it was stupid."

"I see," Officer Crocket said. He furrowed his brow. "Was there anything in the test itself that might have upset her?"

"No. How could there be?"

"I don't know, I'm just wondering. Do you happen to have the test?"

"Of course."

"Could I see it?"

"Sure."

Timothy Rice jerked open the drawer of a file cabinet by the desk. Crocket noted that despite the clutter in the room, his papers were neatly filed.

Timothy pulled out the math exam. "Here we go."

Officer Crocket came, looked over his shoulder.

It appeared to be a typical final exam. Half a dozen pages, typed, mimeoed, and stapled together. On the top it said: *Algebra II Final Exam, Mr. Foster.* Next to that, circled in red pencil, was the inscription: 96 — A.

Timothy noticed Crocket looking at the grade. "Got one wrong," he said. "Careless. Misread a sign."

"Ninety-six isn't bad," Crocket said. "So, Dana started copying off this?"

"Right," Timothy said. "Writing down the answers. As I recall, she got the first three right. Actually, not that bad. Three out of four. Seventy-five percent. If she kept up like that, she'd have had a C. Unfortunately, she had the next four wrong. Her grade on the test was forty-six. That's pretty bad when you consider it's multiple choice. Even if you didn't know anything and just guessed, by the law of averages you'd get a twenty-five."

"Uh huh," Crocket said. "Show me what Dana did."

"She just did problem four. She started five, never wrote the answer. This is the one she did."

He pointed to it.

Crocket looked over his shoulder, read:

4) The graph of $2x = 3y + 5$ is a:
    a) circle
    b) parabola
    c) hyperbola
    d) line

"That's the one she did," Timothy said. "Then she started number five and quit." He grimaced. "It was a little my fault. She started writing number five on the same line, instead of underneath. Foster's a real stickler, would have made her do it again. When I pointed that out, Dana got mad. Said, 'I circled it, for goodness sakes, that's not good enough?' She folded her paper up, crammed it in her pocket. Wouldn't look at it again. She left right after that. That's why I say, it's stupid, but maybe that had something to do with it. Running away, I mean."

"Uh huh," Crocket said. "So, what did she write, exactly?"

"The answer. And the start of the next question. Here, I'll show you."

Timothy Rice took a piece of paper and a ballpoint pen. He wrote on the paper, held it up for Crocket.

Officer Crocket took the paper, read what Timothy Rice had written:

4) D — LINE (5).

47

HE SAT ON THE STOOL, SIPPING HIS DRINK, AND PRETENDED NOT TO notice the young girl at the end of the bar.

She wore shorts and a tank top a size too small, and wasn't that revealing in more ways than one? Her blonde hair was curly, her eyes were blue. An all-American girl. Young. Very young. Old enough to be in the bar, but just barely. She'd be carded if she wasn't known, maybe even had a fake ID.

Very young.

Good.

He liked them young.

He smiled, sipped his drink.

She was watching him. Even without looking he could tell. She was interested. And he didn't even have to make a move. He could just sit here, wait till she came up to him.

He raised his glass, sipped his beer. Casually, arrogantly. Gave her a little profile. He swallowed, exhaled, leaned back. Crooned a few notes. Soft, low, but audible enough to carry across the bar.

I'm the pied piper, follow me.

He knew she would.

It was just a matter of time.

He picked up his glass, tossed down the rest of his beer, signaled to the bartender to draw another. He never once considered sending one to the girl. That was for losers. Not for him. Women bought *him* drinks. She'd buy him one before long. Maybe even pick up his tab.

He smiled at the thought.

A businessman came in and sat at the bar.

Between him and the girl.

Bang, right in his line of sight.

What arrogance! What colossal gall! Couldn't the guy see what was going on here? Comes in, plunks his briefcase down, opens it up—why didn't he just build a *wall* between them?—takes out a newspaper, unfolds it, and holds it up.

Unbelievable.

Who was this, the girl's *father* come to protect her? The guy couldn't do a better job of screening him off if he tried.

He was saved from having to say something by the bartender, who arrived to take the businessman's order—martini, very dry—and the fact after placing the order the guy found the page he wanted and folded the paper up.

And took out a pen.

It drew his eyes like a magnet to the newspaper on the bar.

To the black-and-white grid.

The familiar face of Cora Felton.

He frowned. His smile became a sneer. He inhaled, exhaled, clenched his fists.

The Puzzle Lady.

Thought she was such hot stuff, didn't she?

The Puzzle Lady.

Thought she was too smart for him.

Well, he'd show her a thing or two.

He snatched up his beer, took a sip, wiped his mouth. He wasn't concerned if the girl was watching him. She was no longer an object. He'd completely forgotten about her, didn't even notice. There was only one woman on his mind now.

Sherry.

She should never have done this to him. She should have known better. She should have learned.

She *would* learn.

He'd see to it.

She'd be sorry.

Dennis drained his glass, and called for another beer.

48

MORTIMER PINKHAM, THE EXAMINER OF QUESTIONED DOCUMENTS, raised his eyebrows. "All this? You have to be kidding."

"I'm not," Chief Harper said. "How long is it going to take?"

"A detailed analysis would take some time. I assume you're only interested in a match."

"That's right," Chief Harper said. He opened his briefcase, took out two letters encased in plastic. "Here's two more samples to match up."

"Oh?"

"One's another puzzle clue. I assume it will match the two you have. The other's something else."

"And what is that?"

Chief Harper passed it over. The examiner took it, turned it around, read the letter. His eyes widened. When he looked up, it was without his usual supercilious air. "This is a letter from the killer?"

"It would appear to be."

"How do you know it's not a prank?"

"I don't think you want to know that."

"I beg your pardon?"

"There are things I'm not releasing to the media, and things I am. I'm releasing something today. When you hear it, if you put two and two together, I can't stop you, but it's probably better you don't know for sure."

Pinkham's eyes were still wide. "I see."

"I gotta run over to the crime lab. I'll be grateful for anything you can tell me when I get back."

Chief Harper drove to the crime lab, created a small sensation by dropping off the hammer. He fended off all questions, and left instructions that it be processed for fingerprints, and that blood and hair samples should be recovered and tested against those of the decedents.

"This is the murder weapon?" the lab technician said incredulously.

"You tell me," Chief Harper said.

Not really expecting much, Chief Harper drove back to the examiner's office to find Mortimer Pinkham was actually through.

"Well, you're lucky," Pinkham said.

"How so?"

"Your three samples—the puzzle clues, the Barbara Burnside letter, and this new one, the one sending you back to the cemetery—were all typed on typewriters."

Chief Harper was confused. "That's lucky?"

"It is in this day and age. Everyone's got computer printers. Three out of three typewriters is a real stroke of luck."

"You can't match computer printouts?"

Pinkham looked offended. "I didn't say that. With a laser printer the paper is marked by the belts, pinchers, and rollers. And toner can have unique chemical composition. It can be done. It's just much easier with a typewriter."

"And in this case?" Chief Harper prompted.

"We've got three separate typewriters. I got an electric courier, a non-electric courier, and this new one, a non-electric elite. Knowing that, I could throw out half these samples right away."

"Fine, but did you get a match?" Chief Harper said.

"I sure did. Unfortunately, I only got one, but I guess that's better than nothing."

"What is it?"

"It's the elite non-electric. I couldn't match up the puzzle clues, and I couldn't match up the Burnside letter. But this new one, the one about the cemetery, I matched up just fine."

Chief Harper could feel his pulse racing. "Who is it?" he asked. "Which typewriter did you match it up with?"

"This one here," Pinkham said.

He passed over a paper encased in plastic. Chief Harper took it, turned it around.

It read: *The quick brown Fox jumps over the lasy Dog.*

The word *lazy* was misspelled *l-a-s-y*. And the *F* in *Fox* and the *D* in *Dog* were capitalized.

Chief Harper looked at the tag on the top of the plastic envelope. On it, Dan Finley had neatly written: *Library reading room annex.*

49

JIMMY POTTER WALKED ALONG THE ROAD, HUMMING TO HIMSELF. HE felt slightly guilty about leaving work, but there were priorities. Jimmy didn't actually think the word *priorities,* but that was what he meant.

The two killings bothered him. That was an understatement. The killings *should* have bothered him. But it was more than that. They fascinated him too. The idea of the two girls lying there, stretched out in front of the gravestone. It just didn't seem real, somehow. It just didn't seem like it could really be.

Or that it could be connected to him. That he could have anything to do with it. That made no sense. He would never, never do anything like that. So why should anyone think so?

Why should anyone suspect?

How did they get after him?

Snooping around. Asking him questions. Making him type stupid things on his typewriter. What was that all about?

Jimmy had to figure it out. And soon. So he could stop the feelings he'd been having. Bad feelings. Feelings that shouldn't be.

He'd liked helping that reporter. That had been fun. Finding him microfilm. Looking up facts.

Pointing him at someone else.

But it wasn't his fault. That's what people had to understand. It wasn't his fault. There were things he could not help, things over which he had no control.

Things for which he should not be blamed.

That man. What's his name? Kevin Roth. That was the one they should be looking at. That was the one they should suspect. He was the one Aaron Grant suspected, wasn't he?

He was the one who got mad.

But why did he have to get mad at him? Make him so uncomfortable he had to get out of there. Had to go somewhere. Had to find some answers. See how it felt.

Jimmy Potter walked along the street, lost in thought.

If he was aware of the young girl following him, he gave no sign.

50

"I COULDN'T GET HIM," DAN FINLEY SAID.

"Oh?" Chief Harper said. His head was spinning. He'd just given the news crews a brief statement about finding the murder weapon, then ducked into the police station as the reporters shouted questions. His abrupt departure had not pleased them. Rick Reed of Channel 8 News had nearly attempted to physically restrain him.

"Yes," Dan said. "I'm sorry. I know how bad you wanted him."

"What are you talking about?"

"Kevin Roth. I couldn't serve Kevin Roth."

"The judge wouldn't give you a warrant?"

"No, he did. I just couldn't serve it."

"Why not?"

"He didn't answer the door. I went out to his house, rang the bell, no answer." Dan Finley shrugged. "What was I supposed to do? This wasn't a no-knock warrant. It allows me to search, not to break and enter. So if the guy doesn't answer the bell . . ."

"Was Roth there?"

"I think so. His car was there. I tried to look in the windows, but I couldn't see anything. I rang the bell, I called out his name, I got no response. I gave it my best shot, and came up short."

"You call him on the phone?"

"When?"

"When you couldn't get in. When no one answered the bell."

"No, I didn't."

"Try him now."

Dan Finley looked up Kevin Roth's number, punched it in. He listened a minute, covered the mouthpiece, said, "Answering machine."

"Hang up."

Dan Finley obeyed. "You don't want to leave a message, Chief?"

"Like what? *This is the police, would you please answer your door so we can serve a warrant?* Somehow I think not."

"So what do you want to do?"

"I don't know. I could put a man on his house, wait for him to come out. I could go back to the judge, try to get a no-knock. At the moment, I'm just not sure."

"So you couldn't match the typewriter?"

"Huh?"

"To the Barbara Burnside letter. If you matched the typewriter, you wouldn't want Kevin Roth. So I guess you didn't get a match."

"No, I couldn't match the Barbara Burnside letter," Chief Harper replied. "Tell me something, Dan."

"What's that?"

"When you got the other samples, did you say Jimmy Potter typed the one in the library for you?"

"Yes, he did. Why?"

"Did you notice he misspelled *lazy* and capitalized *fox* and *dog*?"

"I didn't pay much attention. Why?"

"I just stopped by the library. Jimmy's not there, and his mother doesn't know where he went."

Dan Finley frowned. "What's Jimmy got to do with anything?"

Chief Harper waved it away. "No reason. This case is just driving me nuts. Everything bothers me."

"Oh, yeah. Well, I got some good news for you too."

"What's that?"

"That officer called from Muncie. Crocket. 'Cause I called him, told him to find out about the shoes."

"He did?"

"Yeah. He spoke to the witness, who says she was wearing Nikes. He says the guy's pretty sure about it, so at least we know what we're looking for."

Chief Harper frowned. "Sneakers."

"Yeah. I suppose you were hoping for penny loafers, like the other one. But, no, the shoes are different. Same socks, though. White cotton. Oh, and the puzzle was a wash."

"What?"

"Yeah, the famous puzzle clue. *Four d line five.* Turns out it's not a puzzle clue after all. It's an algebra problem. Or at least the answer. It's part of the girl's final exam. She was copying corrections from her boyfriend's paper, gave up and stuck it in her pocket."

Chief Harper's eyes were wide. He felt very light-headed. He put up his hands. "Hold on. Hold on. What are you saying?"

"I'm just telling you what Crocket said. And he's just reporting what the boyfriend said. But Crocket said it's pretty definite. The boyfriend showed him his paper. You know, his final exam. In algebra. And it's all right there. What the girl wrote is straight off the test paper. So it never was a puzzle clue at all."

"You're kidding," Chief Harper said. He went to his desk, got out his notebook, looked up the phone number, and called Officer Crocket.

The Muncie police officer seemed rather pleased with himself. "That's right," he said. "It's right off the final exam. The kid showed me the problem, showed me what she wrote. Of course, the puzzle angle didn't make the papers out here, so it didn't mean anything to him. He didn't know we found it in her pocket. But he described it to a T."

"So there never was a puzzle?"

"No. The word *line* was the answer to a problem. The graph of some equation was a line."

"I see."

Chief Harper hung up the phone with nerveless fingers. Officer Crocket had confirmed Dan Finley's story. Not that he suspected Dan Finley of lying, but still.

Dan Finley had been the one to get the typing sample from the library. He claimed Jimmy Potter typed it. But what if Dan typed it himself when Jimmy Potter wasn't there? And at the same time, he'd typed the note about the murder weapon. Wouldn't that be a colossal double bluff, typing out the note, and, at the same time, typing a sample so that Chief Harper could identify it. And then, just to play with his head, telling him the puzzle clues weren't puzzle clues. After all, it was Dan Finley who had said it was a clue in the first place. If Finley were the killer, as Cora Felton had suggested, might he get some perverse pleasure out of suddenly denying his own handiwork?

But, no, Officer Crocket had confirmed Dan's story. The first puzzle clue was *not* a puzzle clue. And all investigations leading from it were meaningless.

Except they weren't. The puzzle clues had arrived with the murder weapon, with the second dead girl. The killer was for real, even if the clues weren't.

Nothing made any sense.

Chief Harper flipped back a page in his notebook, picked up the phone again, punched in a number.

Sherry Carter answered the phone.

"Hi, it's Chief Harper. Is your aunt there?"

"No, she's not. What's up, Chief?"

"I really need to talk to your aunt. Do you know where she is?"

"No."

Her voice was cold. Chief Harper suspected her in some way of covering up for her aunt. "All right, look," he said. "I want you to find her. There's been a development that she needs to know."

"What is that?"

Chief Harper chose his words carefully, well aware that Dan Finley was listening to his end of the conversation. "The puzzle clue," he said. It took a conscious effort to avoid saying *first* puzzle clue. *"Four d line five* has been identified. We now know exactly what it is. It's the answer to an algebra question."

There was a silence.

"The girl wrote it herself," Chief Harper continued. "It's the answer to a problem on an algebra test. This has been confirmed by the Muncie police. When it gets out, the media may have some questions for your aunt. I would like to talk to her first."

"Good lord, Chief. Do you know what this means?"

"I don't have time to go into all the implications now, Miss Carter. If you can get a message to your aunt, I need to talk to her as soon as possible."

Chief Harper hung up the phone, rubbed his head.

"I guess I got you into that one," Dan Finley said. "But, hey, it's no big deal. It's not like she ever insisted it was a puzzle. In fact, the interview last night, she said she thought it wasn't. So she won't be that upset."

"Right," Chief Harper said.

Dan Finley didn't know the half of it. Unless, of course, Dan Finley set this whole thing up. Unless Dan Finley was the killer.

Chief Harper's mind was going in circles. He was having trouble collecting his thoughts.

The phone rang.

Chief Harper wasn't ready to deal with anyone. He let Finley answer it.

"It's your wife," Dan said.

Chief Harper picked up the phone, pushed the button. "Hi," he said.

Her words went through him like a knife.

"Clara didn't come home from school."

51

CLARA HARPER WAS THRILLED. THIS WAS EXCITING. DOING DETECTIVE work. Following somebody. Just like on TV.

She'd staked out the library after school, checked casually to make sure Jimmy was still working there and hadn't knocked off early and gone home, or simply not come in. But, no, from the front porch she'd seen him inside carting books back and forth. She'd retreated down the street to a safe vantage point in front of the pharmacy, purchased a newspaper to hide behind when he went by, like in the movies. She'd thrown it in the trash when he'd finally come out and gone the other way.

Now she was following him at a discreet distance, keeping him in sight, but never getting close enough to be seen. If she had been spotted, it would not have been good, because she was not walking along like a girl on her way home from school, but was darting furtively from doorway to doorway and tree to tree. Fortunately, no one seemed to notice.

The first place Jimmy went was home. Clara's hopes sank when she saw this. If he just went home and stayed there what was she going to do? Sit on the sidewalk and watch? Boring. But, no, Jimmy was out six minutes later, slamming the screen door and skipping down from the front porch so quickly Clara was sure she'd been spotted. She ducked behind a maple tree, peered at him from across the street.

To her surprise, Jimmy went neither right nor left, but turned the corner and went around the back of his house.

Clara crept from behind the tree and darted across the street. Jimmy was out of sight, so Clara had to either wait for him to come back, or creep around the side of the house.

Creeping was scary, but waiting was dull.

Clara crept.

She reached the far corner of the house, peered around, just in time to see Jimmy go into his clubhouse, a little wooden shack next to the tidy flower garden in his mom's backyard. The shack could have been a toolshed, but Clara recognized it as a clubhouse from the sign on the door. The sign said NO GIRLS ALLOWED!!!!! Really, Clara thought. Jimmy was what, nineteen, maybe twenty years old? And he still had a clubhouse with no girls allowed? Her father should hear about *this*.

Clara was once again faced with the prospect of waiting, but once again Jimmy rescued her, emerging from the clubhouse four minutes later. He headed right at her, and Clara fell all over herself ducking behind the building and rushing back to the street. She got there just in time to hide behind a neighbor's bush as Jimmy came out the driveway, turned right, and headed out of town.

As he walked, he fished something out of his pants pocket. Clara, tagging along behind, craned her neck to see what it was. She wasn't sure until he flipped the blade open.

A knife!

Jimmy Potter had a knife!

Clara could hardly contain herself. As she watched, Jimmy Potter flipped the knife carelessly from hand to hand, then lazily snapped it closed, slipped it into his pocket, and continued down the road.

Clara, ever vigilant, was right on his tail.

Clara was doing this for her father. At least, that's what she told herself. She was doing this for him, because her father, like most fathers, was pigheaded and wouldn't listen to reason.

It stood to reason that Jimmy Potter had committed these crimes. If her father refused to accept that, he was never going to solve them.

And he needed to solve them. The family honor was at stake. If her father knew what the kids were saying at school, maybe he wouldn't be so obstinate. Maybe it would provide a little motivation, make him solve these murders.

But her father wouldn't do anything without proof, so it was up to her to get it. She was convinced Jimmy Potter was guilty. And Jimmy wasn't the brightest boy in the world, so he was sure to give himself away. All she had to do was follow him long enough. He was bound to do something stupid. Clara was sure of it. And when he did, she would be there, on the spot, to bail out her father and save the family name.

Not to mention stopping any more young girls from being killed.

Clara's mission was commendable, earnest, righteous, full of high moral purpose.

It was also fun.

52

SHERRY CARTER'S HEAD WAS REELING. THE PUZZLE MADE NO SENSE. This to Sherry made no sense. How could it be? Two young women were dead, the murder weapon had been dropped in her lap, the police chief had been told to quit, and yet all of that meant nothing.

Sherry Carter was not used to puzzles that made no sense. Having a logical mind, Sherry was used to puzzles that could be figured out, puzzles that had one and only one solution. Not only that, the puzzles that Sherry dealt with followed a strict set of rules. Any puzzle that violated those rules was considered unfair.

Here was a puzzle that followed no rules, wasn't fair, was too hard on the one hand, too easy on the other, and then turned out to be based on a premise that wasn't even a clue. To a logical person like Sherry, this simply didn't compute.

It occurred to her that it would take an illogical person like Aunt Cora to understand this. Sherry needed her now, needed to bounce the information off her. To get her perspective on it.

Because the last paranoid building block had finally fallen into place.

The puzzle wasn't a puzzle.

Dennis couldn't be the killer because he couldn't think up the puzzle.

But there was no puzzle.

So Dennis could be the killer after all.

Yes, Sherry knew that made no sense. Yes, Sherry knew intellectually the odds of Dennis actually being a serial killer had to be somewhat less than her chance of winning the lottery. But that made no difference. Her mind wasn't functioning on an intellectual basis now. The fact it was possible was enough. The fact the one obstacle to her logical rejection of Dennis as the killer had now been removed, allowed her to think the thought. Released the adrenaline rush. Brought on the fear.

Sherry's intellect rallied, fought back. So what if the puzzle wasn't a puzzle? Based on an algebra problem or not, the letters still spelled *quit*. And Dennis wouldn't have spelled it. It would never have crossed his mind.

Didn't that exonerate him?

No.

Almost, but not quite.

In the back of Sherry's mind was the thought that if someone else had spelled *quit,* Dennis could have done the killings just fine.

Sherry needed Cora to tell her it wasn't so.

Sherry called information, got the number of the Country Kitchen, punched it in.

The cashier at the front desk sounded young. "Country Kitchen. May I help you?"

"Yes. I'm looking for Cora Felton. I think she may be in the bar."

"I beg your pardon?"

"I need to speak to my aunt. Cora Felton. Could you see if she's there?"

"I'm sorry. This is not a public phone."

"Yes, I know. But this is rather important."

"I'm sure it is. But the customers aren't allowed to use this phone for private phone calls."

"Oh, for goodness sakes. At least can you tell me if she's there?"

"What was her name?"

"Cora Felton?"

"I'm sorry. I have no reservation for a Cora Felton."

"She's not eating dinner. She'd be in the bar."

"Then I can't help you."

"May I speak to the bartender?"

"I'm sorry. He can't come to the phone right now."

"What?"

"It's happy hour. I can't call him away from the bar."

"Oh, for goodness sakes! Don't you have another phone?"

"There's a pay phone for the customers. That's the one you'd have to use anyway. You could try calling that."

"Do you have the number?"

"One moment, please."

Sherry found herself on hold. It was all she could do to avoid biting the woman's head off when she came back on the line. Sherry broke the connection, punched the number in.

The phone rang ten times.

No one answered.

Sherry slammed the phone down in disgust.

There was one other person to call. Sherry didn't want to, but she had no choice. She called information, got the number of the newspaper, and dialed.

A gruff voice barked: *"Gazette."*

"Aaron Grant, please."

"Grant's not in. You got news, let's have it. If not, call back."

Sherry hung up. After a moment she picked up the phone again, called information. "You have a residential listing for an Aaron Grant?"

"I have an Aaron Grant at 325 Maple Street."

"Could I have the number, please?"

Sherry scribbled down the number the operator gave her, broke the connection, punched it in.

A female voice answered on the second ring. "Hello?"

Sherry blinked.

A woman?

That was strange. Had she dialed right?

"Is Aaron Grant there?"

"No, he's not. May I take a message?"

"No," Sherry said.

Sherry Carter hung up the phone. She felt miffed. Wasn't that just like a man? Aaron Grant hadn't mentioned a girlfriend, at least not one of the live-in variety. Surely something like that would be worthy of mention. Unless one were deliberately *not* mentioning it. And wouldn't *that* be just like a man?

Sherry Carter was furious. And not just with Aaron Grant. She was furious with herself. After all, what did it matter if he had a girlfriend?

Aaron Grant meant nothing to her. So his behavior was typically, annoyingly male. So what?

Sherry Carter picked up the phone, called information again, asked for a listing for taxicabs. There were none. There were, however, car services. The information operator suggested one and supplied the number.

Sherry called and asked if she could get a car from her house to the Country Kitchen. The dispatcher took down the address, looked on the map, and gave her a price of nine dollars and seventy-five cents for the trip. He could have a car there in ten minutes.

Sherry was pacing at the foot of the driveway when the cab drove up. She got in, rode in silence to the Country Kitchen, and tipped the young boy driving two dollars, which seemed to make his day.

Sherry went up the steps and in the restaurant door. The cashier, presumably the one she'd talked to, was seated next to the register just inside the door. She was young, with too much makeup and teased hair. She was also chewing gum.

Sherry took one look and was instantly angry. The pay phone was in an alcove just to the right of the front door. The girl had given her that number, heard her call it, and then hadn't answered.

Eyeing her now, the cashier popped her gum, said, "Can I help you?"

"No," Sherry said, and pushed on by into the bar.

It was indeed busy. Even for happy hour, the place was packed. Sherry figured if even half the people in the bar were here for dinner, the place was doing fine.

Sherry looked around, couldn't spot her aunt.

The bartender caught her eye. "Could I get you something?"

"I'm looking for Cora Felton. Have you seen her?"

"I sure have."

"Where is she?"

He jerked his thumb. "Over there."

"Huh?"

"In a booth. She's sulkin' 'cause I cut her off. Nice lady, but she's had enough. Sorry, ma'am, but that's the way it is."

"Uh huh," Sherry said. She turned, headed for the booths.

Cora Felton was in the second one. She was wearing her Wicked Witch of the West dress. She looked a fright. Her elbow was on the table, and her head was propped up in her hand. Her glasses dangled from one ear. Her eyes were slits. They might have been closed—it was impossible to tell.

In her right hand was the soggy remnants of a huge cigar. It had gone out some time ago, but it still stank.

Sherry shuddered. Then she steeled herself, slipped into the seat opposite her. "Aunt Cora," she said. She reached out, shook her arm gently. "Aunt Cora."

An eye opened. The left one. Red and bleary, it looked out with a dull, glassy stare.

"Aunt Cora," Sherry repeated.

The eye fixed on her, seemed to focus. The mouth, which had been turned down, straightened, coming close to a smile. "Sherry," she said. "Sherry, darling. Be an angel, would you, and get me a drink."

"Sure, Aunt Cora. How about a cup of coffee?"

Cora Felton's lips turned back down. "Now, dear, don't be like that."

"Come on, Aunt Cora. We're going home."

Cora Felton set her jaw. "No, I'm not."

"They're not serving you anymore, Aunt Cora. There's no point staying here."

"The bartender and I just had a little disagreement. He'll come around."

Cora Felton stuck the cigar in her mouth. Sucked on it. Seemed puzzled when she didn't get any smoke.

Sherry Carter tried another tack. "Aunt Cora," she said. "I really need your help. There's been a development in the case."

Cora Felton watched her face, as if trying to translate her words. She nodded her head once, then twice. "De . . . vel . . . ?"

"Development. A development in the case. You know, a break in the case."

"Break in the case?"

"Yes. That's it. There's a break in the case, and I need your help. Let's go home." Sherry slid out of the booth, took Cora Felton by the arm. "Come on, now."

Cora Felton pulled away. "Stop. Stop that. Not going home."

"But the case—"

"Tell me."

"Aunt Cora—"

"Tell me."

Sherry slid back into the booth. "Okay," she said. "You stay here if you want, but you're not driving home."

Cora Felton's purse was lying next to her on the table. It was a big, floppy, drawstring affair. Sherry scooped it up, pulled it open, rummaged inside, and came out with a set of keys. "I'm taking your car keys. You wanna get home, you call for a car service."

Cora Felton made a face. "Not very nice."

"No, it isn't. You really should come with me now."

Sherry started to get up again. Cora Felton reached out, grabbed her by the wrist. Her grip was surprisingly strong. Sherry looked at her.

"Break in the case," Cora said.

"All right," Sherry said. "I'll tell you the break in the case. The first girl who was killed. Dana. The girl from Muncie, Indiana. The clue in her pocket. *Four d line five.* Guess what? Dana wrote it herself."

Cora Felton blinked. Her eyes were squinted, her brow was furrowed, as if she were desperately trying to understand. "Wrote it herself?"

"Yes. She wrote it herself. And it isn't a clue, it's the answer to a problem on her algebra test."

"Algebra?"

"Yes, algebra. It's the answer to a math problem. It was never a puzzle clue at all."

Though Sherry would not have thought it possible, the lines on Cora Felton's forehead deepened. Her mouth sagged open, her head twisted in a circle, up and around and down. Her eyes widened, then narrowed again. Her lips formed a perfect O. Then she nodded.

"So," she said. "That's why he took her shoes off."

Sherry Carter looked at her aunt in exasperation. She shook her head. "No, Aunt Cora. We're not talking about her shoes. We're talking about the puzzle clue. Which isn't a puzzle clue. Which doesn't mean anything. We're talking about that."

"Yes, dear," Cora Felton said. She looked up at Sherry Carter, cocked her head. "Could you be an angel and get me a drink?"

"You can't have another drink. Why don't you come home?"

Cora Felton shook her head. "Not going."

"Fine," Sherry said.

She slipped out of the booth, fought her way up to the bar, caught the bartender's attention. "She won't leave. When she sobers up enough to understand, could you call her a car service?"

"She won't try to drive?"

"I took her keys."

"Good. I wish you'd take her cigar too."

As Sherry Carter drove out of the parking lot, Cora Felton was in the process of lighting her cigar. She first found a butane lighter, which she spun several times to no avail. Then she rummaged in her purse, came out with a bedraggled book of matches. She pulled the cover off, discovered three matches. Managed to light the first one without lighting the cigar. Managed to break the second. The third produced a reassuring cloud of smoke.

Cora Felton inhaled deeply, blew the smoke out through her mouth and nose. "That's better," she muttered.

She took another drag, sat there trying to gather her thoughts.

"Puzzle clue," she said. "Puzzle clue."

She braced herself on the table, heaved herself to her feet. Grabbed her purse, lurched toward the front door.

It took her a while to make it. By the time she got there, her car was long gone.

Cora Felton stood on the front steps, looking around the parking lot, peering at every car.

"Not mine. Not mine. Not mine."

Finally resigned to the fact her car was not there, Cora Felton went back in the front door.

The young cashier was not thrilled by her return. "She's back again," she called to the bartender.

Cora Felton fixed her with an evil eye. "Rude," she said.

Cora stood there, looking around. Spotted the pay phone inside the door. Turned, lurched over to the little alcove, slipped inside.

A phone book hung on a cord next to the pay phone. Cora Felton grabbed the phone book, picked it up, turned it around, and looked at it in amazement. Even to a sober New Yorker, it would have seemed incredibly thin. To Cora Felton, it was a marvel indeed.

Cora Felton finally accepted it for what it was, flipped it open, peered inside. All she saw was a blur. She reached up, discovered her glasses dangling from one ear. She grabbed the frames, dragged the wire rim over her other ear, pushed the glasses up on her nose, examined the phone book again.

It was still somewhat blurry, but she could make out the names. She stared, furrowed her brow, tried to reacquaint herself with the workings of the alphabet. After a few moments' contemplation, she began paging through the book.

She smiled in triumph when she finally found the number.

She lost it again getting a quarter out of her purse. By the time she found the quarter, the telephone book was once again dangling from its cord.

This time she was a little quicker looking up the name. When she found it, she clasped the open book to her chest as she reached up and dropped the quarter in. Then she lowered the book, looked at the open page, found the number again. Constantly referring back and forth, she punched the numbers into the phone. Finally, holding the receiver to her ear, she was rewarded in hearing it ring.

It rang three times before she got an answer.

"Hello?"

Cora Felton was startled by the voice. She had forgotten who she was calling. Forgotten she was even on the phone.

Then she remembered.

"I solved your puzzle," she said.

53

SHERRY DIDN'T GO STRAIGHT HOME. ON THE WAY THROUGH TOWN SHE slowed down as she passed the police station. There were no cars out front. That seemed strange. Surely someone would be on duty, and that someone would need a car. Sherry stopped, got out, went up and tried the door. It was locked.

Locked?

That didn't compute.

Sherry banged on the door, got no answer. She looked in the window. The lights were on, but there was no one inside.

Sherry got back in her car, drove on down the street. On an impulse, she hung a left on Center Street, drove by the newspaper. Aaron Grant's car was not there. Sherry wasn't sure what she would have done if it had been, still the fact that it wasn't was frustrating.

Sherry remembered the address the operator had given her. Three twenty-five Maple. Sherry wasn't sure, but she seemed to remember seeing a Maple Street off of Oak. It wasn't more than a mile or two out of town. Of course, there was no real reason to drive by his house. On the other hand, it wasn't often that she had a car. And Sherry wasn't ready to go home now. Not after fighting with her aunt. Not after getting upset over Dennis. She needed to take time out, cool down, clear her head. And what better way than driving around. It really didn't matter where she went, she just needed a destination so she'd have somewhere to drive. Aaron Grant's house was as good as any. Particularly since she knew the address. It couldn't hurt anything to drive on by. To satisfy her curiosity as to where he lived. That was why she was doing it.

It certainly didn't have anything to do with that woman who'd answered his phone.

Sherry turned around, drove out of town, took a left on Oak and went to Maple. The drive was closer to four miles, but that didn't matter, as she was in no real hurry. She drove slowly down the road, looking for street numbers.

The houses here were nicer than on her road. There were stone and brick buildings, two-story colonials, with an occasional contemporary thrown in. Sherry was well aware of what they were worth. She'd priced houses like these before settling on the one she and Aunt Cora had rented.

Sherry spotted a house number. Three twelve. So, pretty near, and on the other side of the street, if odd and even numbers meant anything. Which, Sherry had noticed, in some streets in Bakerhaven they didn't.

On Maple Street, however, they did. Three twenty-five Maple Street was a two-story white house with blue shutters. Aaron Grant's car was not in the driveway. But a blue Subaru station wagon was. So his girlfriend was home. If the woman was indeed his girlfriend, and not actually his wife. Sherry couldn't help noticing the children's swing set in the backyard.

Sherry drove on by. Well, he never said he wasn't. And, anyway, what difference did it make to her?

A few houses down the road Sherry pulled into a driveway and turned around. Yeah, that was enough driving for a while. That had done the trick.

As Sherry drove back through Bakerhaven, a police car passed her going the other way. It was the officer she'd met the other night when they were looking for Vicki Tanner. Sherry considered turning around and catching up with him, asking him where everyone was. But he seemed to be going rather fast. She kept going.

On her way home it got dark enough for her to turn on the headlights. She was reluctant to do so, as it was still light enough it would be easy to forget to turn them off. She shouldn't have worried. When she pulled into the driveway, they shone on the garage. Sherry switched them off and got out.

Sherry locked the car. Cora Felton never locked it, in fact Cora made a big deal of the fact she didn't have to, living in the country. But Sherry wasn't taking any chances. It occurred to her it would be just her luck to have the car stolen when *she* parked it, so Cora could blame it on her. Not that Cora wouldn't be blaming her enough as it was, when she sobered up and realized her car was gone.

The lights were on in the living room. Sherry's first thought was that Aunt Cora was home. Then she realized that couldn't be. There was no way Cora could have sobered up enough to have decided to come home. No, Sherry must have just left the lights on during the day without knowing it.

Sherry went up the front steps, unlocked the door, and let herself in. As she closed the door behind her, she felt a chill. Not from cold, from fear. From the sudden feeling that something was wrong.

She immediately felt foolish. The living room was exactly as she'd left it. Nothing had been disturbed. Not that there was much in the living room to disturb, but still. She was just jumpy. Everything was all right.

Sherry needed a drink. Not necessarily alcoholic. In fact, definitely nonalcoholic. But something to calm her jangled nerves. Maybe a cup of tea.

Sherry went in the kitchen to boil some water. On the shelf next to the wall phone, a light was blinking on the answering machine. She pressed the button, played the message back.

Beep.

"Hi, Sherry. It's Margaret from the nursery school. Adrienne will be out of town, so could you take the four/fives on Monday? I'm going out, so just leave a confirmation on my machine."

Sherry smiled. She most certainly could.

She reached for the phone.

Beep.

The voice leaped from the answering machine. Harsh, guttural, slurred, gloating.

"So. Thought you'd get away from me, did you? Thought I'd never find you? Well, think again. You think you're so smart with your fancy puzzles. Well, guess what. I'm smart too. Real smart. What do you think of that?"

His last words were light, mocking.

Chillingly casual.

"Bye, bye, love."

Sherry backed away from the answering machine as if it were alive. Her eyes were wide with horror.

Dennis.

Good God, it's true.

Dennis.

A floorboard creaked.

Sherry froze at the sound. A thousand thoughts tumbled through her head. There it was, the tired old cliché from book after book, movie after movie. So incredibly trite it couldn't scare anyone.

But in real life . . .

Sherry was suddenly terrified.

He's in the house.

Sherry's eyes darted around the kitchen, anticipating an attack from any side, and looking for a weapon. There was a broom next to the refrigerator, a rolling pin on the counter top, an iron frying pan on the stove.

On the butcher block was a carving knife. Sherry picked it up, held it out in front of her. Tried to control her breathing, which was rapid and shallow. Tried to convince herself there was no one there. *It's an old house, the floorboards creak.*

It's a prefab. Built on a slab. With no basement. The floorboards only creak if you step on them.

Stop thinking so much.

No, keep thinking. No basement means nowhere to hide. Except the garage. Was the garage door locked? Was that how he got in?

Sherry edged her way to the door. She meant to look out, see if the garage door was open. But down the hallway something caught her eye.

The door to her office. Was that a file folder lying in the doorway?

Holding the knife in front of her, Sherry inched her way down the hall. Reached the doorway. Peered around.

This time what she saw chilled her from head to toe.

The office was a wreck. File cabinet drawers were pulled open and emptied. Papers were torn up and strewn on the floor. The desk chair was tipped over, and the top of the desk had been cleared. The computer was smashed and in pieces, the keyboard in one direction, the screen in another, the body of the computer in another. The modem too was smashed, though it was still plugged in, and one of its lights was on. Lucky it hadn't started a fire.

Sherry recoiled as if struck, overwhelmed by the sheer fury of it. The knife in her hand suddenly seemed very inadequate. She backed down the hallway toward the kitchen and the phone.

Not that the phone would do her any good. Not if the police weren't there. Which she knew they weren't. But surely they must have some sort of backup system. Some sort of call forwarding. Someone must be answering their phone.

Sherry reached the kitchen, slipped inside, raced to the wall phone, scooped the receiver up.

Her phone was dead.

Sherry nearly cried out. It was the last straw. More than she could bear. She was suddenly gripped with an overwhelming motivation.

Get out of this house.

Sherry slammed down the receiver, turned to the door.

A man was standing there.

He was holding a gun.

54

"WHO ARE YOU?" SHERRY CRIED.

She had no idea. The man standing in front of her was short, stocky, and balding. Not old, but older than her. He wore a black and white plaid shirt, tucked half in, half out of his gabardine pants.

He was obviously rather drunk. "You're not her," he snarled. "Where is she?"

"Who do you mean?"

He scowled. Waved the question away with his gun. "You know who. The old lady. Where is she?"

"You mean Aunt Cora?"

"Puzzle Lady. Where's the Puzzle Lady?"

"She's not here right now."

"I *know* she's not here right now. Where is she?"

For a second, Sherry debated actually telling him where Cora was. The odds of this man getting to the Country Kitchen seemed slim. But she couldn't bring herself to do it. The thought that stopped her was: *What if he did?*

"She went out for a drink," Sherry said.

"A drink?"

"Yes."

"Where?"

"I don't know."

Sherry held her breath, waiting to see the effect of the lie.

For a second his face looked murderous. Then it contorted, and he looked as if he were about to cry. "Why is she doing this to me?"

"Doing what?" Sherry asked.

"You know."

"No, I don't. I don't even know who you are."

"Sure you do. Everybody knows."

"Everybody?"

"Everybody. Police. Newspaper. Because of *her.*"

"Uh huh," Sherry said. She tried a gamble. "Would you like a drink?"

It didn't pay off. He scowled. "Are you making fun of me?"

"Not at all. Like I said, I don't even know you."

"I'm Kevin Roth."

"Oh."

"Yeah," he said. "You know me now."

It was like juggling hand grenades. Sherry had no idea what might cause him to explode. "Yes. I know you. You're that poor man whose girlfriend got killed."

"Not my fault," Kevin Roth said.

"Yes, I know," Sherry said. "You had a fight. Couples fight. Barbara ran off. There was nothing you could do."

"Nothing I could do," Roth repeated.

"Exactly," Sherry said. She was beginning to sweat. Her hands felt clammy. Particularly her right hand.

The hand holding the knife.

That was what made the scene so bizarre. So far, Kevin Roth hadn't alluded to it. Had given no indication that he'd even noticed it.

Sherry wanted to put it down. She had no desire to fight a man with a gun with a carving knife. But the gesture would call attention to it. And if he saw it, if it registered in his brain for what it was, how would he react?

Would it make him shoot?

Kevin Roth was clearly not doing well. His eyes behind his glasses were bloodshot red. The skin on his face sagged. As she watched, he lurched forward, slumped against the side of the door.

The move startled him awake. He gaped at her, as if seeing her for the first time.

"What are you doing with that knife?" he demanded.

Sherry nearly jumped out of her skin. She controlled herself with an effort. Said calmly, "I was going to put it down."

He considered that. "Where?"

"On the table."

"What table?"

She indicated the butcher block, using only her eyes. He peered at her, first quizzically, then followed where she was looking.

"Okay," he said.

Sherry exhaled. Then slowly, very, very slowly, she moved the hand with the knife. Up. Up. Across. Over. To the butcher block table. And . . . down.

He watched, intently, like a lion watching the movements of a lion tamer.

When she'd set the knife on the table, Sherry moved her hand away slowly and stepped back.

She was now unarmed and totally helpless. Not that the knife would have done her any good. Still, she no longer had even that.

And now he lurched from the doorway into the room, coming straight at her. Was he going to grab her?

No, at the last moment he staggered to the side, veered off to the butcher block, snatched the knife up in his other hand.

His left hand.

His right still holding the gun.

Kevin Roth held the knife up, looked at it, as if observing for the first time the sheer size of it. It made him angry. Sherry could almost see his brain associating the size of the knife with the fact it had been in her hand. With the fact she had intended it for him.

The bloodshot eyes grew murderous again. The left hand raised the knife.

Sherry bit her lip to keep from crying out.

He stabbed the knife down viciously.

Sherry gasped.

He embedded the knife in the butcher block.

Sherry's relief at not being stabbed was short-lived. The violent action had seemed to help focus his thoughts.

He scowled, peered at her quizzically. "Who are you?"

"I'm Sherry Carter."

He scowled again, then pointed his finger.

With his left hand.

The hand not holding the gun.

"You're the one. Billy told me. You're the one. Coming around. Asking questions. Sending the police. Trying to get into my house. Because of you. You and the old lady. Where is she?"

"I told you. I don't know."

"You lied."

He raised the gun, pointed it at her face. "Tell me now."

It was the first menacing gesture he'd made with the gun. And it was very effective. Sherry could see his finger on the trigger. Could feel the tension in his hand. It would not be hard for him to squeeze.

Sherry involuntarily took a step backwards. Her foot caught on the leg of the table. She lost her balance, started to go down.

Falling over backwards, she flailed out with her arms. A reflex action, reaching for support.

Not reaching for the gun.

But that's how it must have looked to him.

Kevin Roth jerked back.

Pulled the trigger.

The explosion echoed through the kitchen. The bullet whizzed over Sherry's head. Sherry went down in a crumpled pile between the sink and the stove.

She looked up, saw Kevin Roth's face.

Firing the shot had transformed him. He was no longer a scared little man, acting out some revenge fantasy. He was the hunter, and she was the prey. She could see this in his eyes, as they bored into her.

Holding the gun in front of him, Kevin Roth crept around the table, stalking her. He stopped, raised the gun.

But Sherry Carter was no pushover. Even when Dennis was in a drunken rage, she always gave as good as she got. No matter how hard he hit her, Sherry never quit.

She didn't now. Before Kevin Roth could fire again, Sherry got her legs under her, and lunged.

It nearly worked. He flinched back in surprise, and she flailed at his gun hand, knocking it down. He staggered, but didn't drop the gun.

Sherry fell to the floor, rolled over, came up in a crouch.

But this time he was wary. He took a step back, out of range of her arms and legs, and raised the gun.

His finger tensed on the trigger.

Sherry balanced on the balls of her feet, prepared to dive out of the way.

To dodge a bullet.

She sucked in her breath, and—

"Hello?"

The voice came from the living room.

Kevin Roth turned.

Aaron Grant came in the door.

Aaron must not have heard the shot, because he stopped short, gawking at the sight of a man with a gun.

Kevin Roth's face registered surprise.

Then recognition.

Then rage.

This was the man who had made all the trouble. The reporter.

Kevin Roth hesitated, not sure where to aim the gun.

It was all the opening Sherry needed. Before Roth could make up his mind who to shoot, she reached behind her, then lunged forward and brought the heavy iron frying pan from the stove down on his head.

55

"SHERRY, I'M SORRY. I COMPLETELY FORGOT."

"Brenda—"

"No, really. It was just so unimportant. They were in town last week, he called up just to take a shower."

"A *shower?*"

"Sherry. I know you always think I have a thing for Dennis. He's very cute, but forget about it. They were passing through, had no place to stay, and I wasn't gonna let 'em. I had a date. I let him take a shower and clean up if he agreed to be gone by the time I got back. And he was, but he must have gone through my address book."

"Brenda—"

"I know, I know. I should have said something. But like I told you, I know their itinerary, and he's not around. I can look up where he is if you want."

"I want."

"Sherry, don't be like that."

"I'm sorry. A lot's happened, and I don't have time to get into it. I'll call you when things calm down. Right now, I need to know where he is."

"Hold on."

Sherry could hear Brenda put down the phone and her footsteps walking away. Moments later she was back.

"They're in Florida."

"Are you sure?"

"They have a gig tonight in Fort Lauderdale. Last night too. Trust me, they're there."

"They're playing tonight?"

"That's right. Two sets. At ten o'clock and midnight. I have it right here."

"Uh huh," Sherry said. "That itinerary list the hotel?"

It did. Sherry got the number, called it, asked the front desk to ring the room.

He answered with a grunt. Slurred, hostile. "Yeah?"

Sherry broke the connection.

So.

That made it official.

Dennis was in Florida.

Dennis wasn't the Graveyard Killer.

Dennis was just Dennis, up to his old tricks again, harassing her with drunken phone calls.

It occurred to Sherry that Dennis was not going to play well tonight. Assuming he managed to make it on stage.

Sherry went back in the kitchen where Aaron Grant was standing guard over Kevin Roth, who was lying facedown on the floor. "Did he move?" she asked.

"No. Did you make your call?"

"Yeah. I called Florida."

"Huh?"

"I called New York and Florida." She handed him the cellular phone. "I'll pay you when you get your bill."

"It's no problem," Aaron Grant said. He was curious, but didn't want to pry. "Is everything okay?"

"Fine," Sherry replied. When Aaron said nothing, she said, "I got a crank phone call. With a killer on the loose, I had to make sure that's all it was."

"And it is?"

"Yeah, it's nothing. I knew it, but I had to make sure." She looked around. "So, where's the police?"

"They're all out."

Sherry frowned. "What?"

"That's what I was trying to tell you when you ran off with my cell phone. They're all out. I left a message."

"They're all out?"

"It's an emergency. Chief Harper's daughter's missing."

"What?"

"She never came home from school. He's worried sick." Aaron jerked his thumb at the body on the floor. "He'll be relieved to know she didn't run into him."

"You spoke to Chief Harper?"

"No. Dan Finley. Why?"

"Then you don't know about the clue."

"The clue? Oh, yeah, Dan told me about it."

"What?"

"Sure. *Four d line five.* The girl wrote it herself. Dan told me."

"Dan Finley knows about it?"

"Sure. Everyone knows about it. He was the first to know. He took the call."

"But . . ."

"But what?"

"That's what I can't understand. This lunatic, this drunken madman, is in my house holding a gun on me. And all the time I know it makes no sense because the clue is not a clue. And if *four d line five* is not a clue, there is no lead to Barbara Burnside at all."

"Then how can he be the Graveyard Killer?"

"He's not. At least, I don't think he is."

"Then what was this all about?"

"I can tell you what I think. I have no proof. But it shouldn't be hard to get. The police will take an interest, now that he's pulled a gun. Basically, the bottom line is this. There was something not kosher about the Barbara Burnside accident years ago. It had nothing to do with the killings, it was something else entirely, but it was there. So when I started probing, I hit a nerve."

"Probing?"

"I spoke to Ed Hodges and Billy Spires."

Aaron Grant's mouth fell open. "Why did you do that?"

"Because you couldn't. Chief Harper ordered you and Aunt Cora to lay off. When the Burnsides came to me, I thought they deserved better." Sherry jerked her thumb at Kevin Roth. "So I asked some questions, and this is the result."

Aaron was incredulous. "Are you saying Kevin Roth *killed* Barbara Burnside?"

"Not exactly. But he lied about what happened, that's for sure. When you wrote the story, he panicked, sent that note telling you to drop the investigation. Then he panicked again—maybe realized the note could be traced to his typewriter—and he came to the paper to try to get his letter back. He bawled you out for writing the story, right? Pretended that was why he came."

"And all the time he's looking around, to see if it's still there, maybe he could steal it off my desk?" Aaron said.

"Exactly. It's already occurred to him what he wrote could get him in trouble. So, when he finds out the cops are trying to get a sample from his typewriter, he freaks out."

Aaron frowned. "And the truth about the accident?"

"I've had a lot of theories. Kevin Roth followed her in Billy Spires' car, then ran her off the road. Or when he found her, she was still alive and he caved her head in with a rock."

"I thought you said he didn't kill her."

"I mean he didn't murder her and try to make it look like an accident. If she *had* an accident, and he added to her injuries, that's a slightly different twist."

"You think he did that?"

"No, I don't. I think the explanation's much simpler. I don't think there ever was an argument. I think Barbara and Kevin got in the car and drove off. Kevin was driving. He was drunk and ran off the road. Barbara was thrown through the windshield and was killed. She hit her head on a rock. Kevin had his seat belt on and survived. That's when he ran back to the house, made up the story about the argument and her taking off in the car."

"And the part about borrowing a car?"

"Never happened. That's what he told the police because he had to account somehow for finding her. That he borrowed the car from Billy Spires. But Billy's the weak link, because Billy doesn't remember it like that. Billy remembers Kevin *telling him* he'd borrowed his car. After the fact. Well, if the keys were in it, Kevin could have taken it, but I don't think they were. So there's no evidence Kevin ever took the car at all."

"But if it was just an accident," Aaron persisted. "I mean, he tried to kill you."

"He was drunk and stressed out. I know it seems out of proportion. But you gotta remember. If he did what I think he did—well, it isn't murder, but it is manslaughter. It's vehicular homicide, it's driving while intoxicated, it's leaving the scene of an accident. It's falsifying a police report, compounding a felony, and conspiring to conceal a crime." Sherry sighed, rubbed the palm of her hand, which was still sore from hitting Kevin with the iron pan. "But it's more than that. It's years and years and years of carrying around this terrible burden. Thinking it's dead and buried, and then having it all blow up in your face. It's enough to push someone over the edge."

"I suppose," Aaron said, dubiously.

There came the screech of tires in the driveway. Moments later, Sam Brogan burst into the house.

"All right, where is he?" He spotted Kevin Roth lying on the floor. "Aha," he said. "Is this our killer?"

"I don't think so," Sherry answered. "But he assaulted me with a gun."

"Why?"

"Guilty conscience," Sherry said.

Sam Brogan looked at her quizzically.

"It's a long story," Aaron told him. "You find Chief Harper's kid?"

"No. Everyone's still out. It'd be a big relief if this was the killer."

"Yeah, I know," Aaron Grant said. He shook his head. "But it isn't."

Sam Brogan frowned. "So who the devil is?"

56

CORA FELTON FINALLY MANAGED TO CALL THE CAR SERVICE. IT WAS hard, largely because she kept forgetting that was what she was trying to do. She'd look up the number, then forget it, wander into the bar or the bathroom, find a quarter, lose a quarter, forget her purse, forget the number, forget she was even looking up a number, forget she was even trying to make a call. But in the end the stars must have aligned just right, because Cora, the quarter, the phone book, the phone number, and the phone all happened to be in the same place at the same time, and she managed to get through to Reynold's Ride, a car service listed in the book.

Of course, the first thing the woman on the phone wanted to know was where she was. That threw her. She knew she was in the restaurant where she played bridge, but the direct question made her blank out the name, and she had to leave the phone booth and ask the girl at the cash register. The fact she was able to get back to the phone and retain the name Country Kitchen was another small miracle, but finally the deed was accomplished and the car was actually on its way. Which, to Cora Felton, meant only one thing.

One for the road.

Cora Felton went back in the bar, petitioned the bartender, but to no avail. It was the fourth or fifth time she'd done so. Still, Cora approached each new inquiry with a drunkard's optimism—perhaps the gentleman had changed his mind.

The bartender had not. Cora lurched dejectedly away to meet the car service, but only got as far as the booth where she'd been sitting before seeming to recognize an old friend. There was something very familiar about that cocktail glass. Could it possibly be full?

Cora padded over, slipped into the booth. Picked up the glass. Frowned at it, raised it to her lips.

It was empty, and familiarly so. Cora had been sipping from that empty glass for the last half hour. Cora looked at the glass in disgust, set it back down, very carefully.

All right, time to do something. What was it that she was supposed to do? Oh, yes. Go meet her ride. Time to get up, get out of the booth, and go meet her ride.

Good. Now that she knew what she had to do, it would be easy. All she had to do was get up.

Cora smiled at the thought. She put her hands on the table to push herself up. Her head slumped down onto her arms, and she was instantly asleep.

In the lobby of the Country Kitchen the young cashier's eyes widened as Rick Reed of Channel 8 News came in the door. The cashier blinked, popped her gum, tried to think of something to say, but he just flashed her a smile and pushed on by in the direction of the bar.

For Rick Reed, it had been a long, hard, unprofitable day, in fact, the worst day yet since Dana Phelps' body had been discovered in the Bakerhaven Cemetery. In terms of the story, the only development had been the finding of the murder weapon. And he hadn't even seen it. He'd learned about it secondhand, after the fact. He didn't even have a picture of it to put on TV. He'd had to send Phil out to a hardware store to buy a hammer for Ernie to shoot. He hoped the irritation hadn't shown in his voice when he'd pointed to it on camera, described the murder weapon as "a hammer *like this one.*" That tape was running on the early news, and barring a miracle, would be running again at eleven.

Rick Reed stepped up to the bar and noted with irritation that the TV over the far end was set to ESPN. Still, he flashed his trademark smile at the bartender and said, "Hi, there, a scotch and soda. And is there any chance of switchin' that to Channel 8?"

"If no one minds," the bartender said.

He turned around to mix the drink, leaving Rick Reed to ask the people at the bar if anybody minded.

Rick Reed frowned. This was not the type of star treatment he worked so hard to cultivate.

Ernie and Phil trailed in from locking up the truck.

"Pair of drafts," Phil said.

"Tall drafts," Ernie amended.

"Is there any other kind?" Phil said.

"Hey, what's with the TV?" Ernie asked. "They don't get Channel 8?"

"Everyone gets Channel 8," Phil said. "Hey, can we change the TV?"

"Get me a draft," Ernie said, "I'm goin' to the can."

The cameraman stalked off in the direction of the men's room, leaving Phil and Rick Reed to order the beers and petition the bartender for Channel 8.

Ernie was back moments later. "Hey, guys, get a load of this."

"What's that?" Rick Reed said.

The cameraman was grinning and pointing his finger. "Here. Take a look."

He led them around the far corner of the bar to where the booths were.

In the center booth, Cora Felton lay with her head on the table, her glasses askew, her mouth open, her hand wrapped around an empty glass. She was snoring loudly and rhythmically, a veritable symphony of sound.

"Well, will you look at that," Phil said.

"Yeah," Rick Reed said. His mouth twisted into a grin. The day wasn't a washout after all.

He nudged Ernie, lowered his voice, and jerked his thumb.

"Go get your camera."

57

"WHERE'S YOUR AUNT?" AARON SAID.

Sam Brogan had just driven off with his prisoner, leaving Aaron and Sherry nothing to talk about. Cora Felton seemed like a safe subject.

Apparently it wasn't. Sherry blushed. "Oh. I'm afraid she's . . . indisposed."

"Indisposed?"

"Aunt Cora sometimes drinks too much."

"She's on a bender?"

"How delicately you put that. She's at the Country Kitchen right now, refuses to go home."

"Her car's in the driveway."

"I went and got it. To keep her out of trouble. You have a problem with that?"

"I find it commendable."

"You do?"

"If she's as out of it as you claim."

"Claim?"

"Some people function better on alcohol than others."

"Are you advocating drunk driving?"

"No. If your aunt's in no shape to drive, I'm happy she isn't."

"You have to argue everything I say?"

"I wasn't aware that I was."

"I'm sure you weren't."

"If your aunt's in such bad shape, why didn't you just bring her home?"

"She wouldn't come."

"Perhaps I'd have more luck. You wanna take a run over there?"

"With you?"

"I won't bite. And I don't like leaving you here alone."

"I can cope."

"I'm sure you can. Kevin Roth was just a nut. Suppose the real killer takes a disliking to your aunt?"

"Let's go get her."

They got in Aaron Grant's car, drove to the Country Kitchen. During the ride Sherry seemed particularly reserved. Aaron put it down to what she'd just been through, tried to draw her out.

"I can't wait to see your aunt," he said.

"Uh huh," Sherry said. If that. She barely made a sound.

"I wanna hear what she says when we tell her the clue wasn't a clue."

"I already told her."

"Oh? When did you do that?"

"When I took her car."

"You told her about it. So what did she say?"

"I'm not sure it even registered."

"Oh?"

"I told you. She's pretty drunk."

"So what did she say?"

"Something like, So that's why he took her shoes off."

"Her shoes?"

"That's what she said."

"So what does that mean?"

"It probably doesn't mean anything. I don't really want to talk about it."

"So I see."

Aaron pulled into the Country Kitchen parking lot. They got out of the car and went inside.

Cora Felton was no longer in the booth.

Sherry looked around. The crowd at the bar had thinned out—apparently most people had either moved into the dining room or finished their drinks and left.

She went up to the bartender. "My aunt's gone. Did you call the car service?"

"No, I didn't."

"Then how did she leave?"

"I have no idea. Frankly, I didn't even notice she was gone. It's been busy."

"When'd she leave?"

"Like I say, I don't know."

"Well, when was the last time you saw her?"

"Actually, not that long ago. Right after I threw out that reporter."

"Reporter?"

"Yeah. What's his name, from Channel 8."

"Rick Reed?" Aaron asked.

"Yeah, that's him. Came in with his crew for a drink. Must have seen her sitting there, 'cause one of them went back to the van for a camera. When I saw what they were up to, I threw them all out."

"They filmed her?" Sherry said. Her voice was dismayed.

"I don't think so. When I saw the camera, I made 'em stop. I don't think he even asked her a question."

"And she left right after that?" Sherry said.

"Not right after. She came up to the bar, tried to get another drink. Of course I wouldn't serve her."

"How long ago was that?"

"Ten, fifteen minutes ago, maybe. I just assumed she went back to her booth."

"Uh huh," Sherry said, distracted. She tugged Aaron away from the bar, said, "You think he filmed her?"

"I *know* he filmed her," Aaron said. "He's really pushing the get-Chief-Harper-off-the-case angle. He'll tie her in with him, use this to make 'em both look bad. You think she left with him?"

"I sure hope not. Let's find out."

Sherry and Aaron went to the cashier, and waited impatiently while the young woman slowly processed a MasterCard.

When the customer moved off, Sherry cleared her throat and said, "Excuse me, but I'm looking for my aunt."

The cashier popped her gum. "Uh huh."

Aaron Grant smiled at her. "You couldn't miss her. White hair, wire-rimmed glasses. She was drinking in the bar."

"Oh, her," the cashier said. She smiled at Aaron Grant. "She just left."

"How?" Sherry said.

The cashier frowned at the interruption, managed to convey the fact that Sherry had just asked the stupidest question in the world. "How?"

"She had no car," Aaron translated. "Did someone pick her up?"

"I don't know. She just went out the door."

"Did she leave with the reporter?"

"You mean the *TV* reporter?" The cashier's eyes were wide. "Isn't that something? You could have knocked me down with a feather. He comes walking in here, large as life."

"Right," Aaron said. "Rick Reed from Channel 8. Did she leave with him?"

The cashier practically guffawed. "Her? Not likely. She could barely walk. Anyway, Charlie threw him out."

"Charlie?"

"The bartender. Can you believe that? They wanted to film right here in the restaurant. And Charlie says no. I gave him a piece of my mind. I could have been on the eleven o'clock news."

"You said she left after that?"

"Sometime after that. I'm not quite sure."

"But you saw her go out the door."

"Yeah, like I say, barely walking."

"And you didn't call a car for her?"

"No, I didn't. But she might have called herself."

"Oh?"

"Yes. She made some calls."

"Calls? You mean more than one?"

"Oh, yeah." The cashier gestured at Sherry, shifted her gum to the left side of her mouth, and spoke to Aaron as if Sherry weren't even there. "She went out right after this woman here. I thought the old lady was gone. Then she came in and used the phone."

"Right after I left?" Sherry said.

The cashier only had eyes for Aaron. "Then later she made another."

"Another phone call?"

"Uh huh."

"Either time she used the phone, did she get through?" Sherry asked.

The cashier shrugged. "I couldn't see."

Aaron Grant smiled at her. "It's important."

The cashier smiled back. "I'm sure it is, but I really couldn't see. But she was certainly in there long enough."

"Which time?"

"Both of 'em."

Sherry left Aaron charming the cashier, and checked out the phone booth. She spotted the phone book hanging from the cord. Sherry scooped it up, turned to the back, looked up car services. There were three listed.

Sherry dug quarters out of her pants pocket, began dropping them in.

She got lucky on the third listing.

"Reynold's Ride," a woman's voice said.

"Yes. I'm calling about a pickup at the Country Kitchen."

"What about it?"

"The call was from my aunt. Cora Felton."

"What's the matter? Didn't it show up?"

"Yes, it did. I'm wondering where it went."

"Where it went?"

"Yes. I'm trying to find my aunt. I understand she took one of your cars. I need to know where she went."

"Oh."

"So can you tell me where she went?"

"I'm sorry. I can't."

"You don't know?"

"Of course I know. You can't hire a car without giving a destination."

"So where did she say she was going?"

"I'm not supposed to give out that information."

"Please. You have to help me." Sherry's voice broke. "Frankly, my aunt's had too much to drink. And I know this is going to sound crazy, but she's got some wild theories about these murders, and I'm afraid she's going to get into trouble. Help me. Please."

After a pause the woman said, "Is your aunt the Puzzle Lady? The woman in the paper?"

"Yeah. That's her."

"I thought I recognized the name. All right, I'm not supposed to tell you this. But, to tell the truth, I wasn't happy dispatching the car to her in the first place."

"Oh? And why is that?"

"Because of where she wanted to go."

"And where is that?"

"The cemetery."

58

CLARA HARPER COULD HARDLY CONTAIN HERSELF. SHE WAS RIGHT. HER father was wrong, and she was right. Just when it looked like tailing Jimmy Potter was a big waste of time, look where he wound up. If this didn't clinch the case, nothing would. It was a classic. The killer returns to the scene of the crime.

While Clara Harper watched from the woods, Jimmy Potter crossed the meadow and climbed over the fence into the cemetery. Clara gave him a couple of seconds' head start, then followed.

Clara wasn't entirely happy crossing the field. The sun had gone down but the moon was full, and the meadow was wide open with no cover. Clara kept low, scuttled across. Moments later she was crouching down behind the fence. She raised her head, peered over. The side of a small, wooden building blocked her view. Jimmy Potter had approached the cemetery from the far side, and gone over the fence in back of the caretaker's shed.

Clara crept to the edge of the shed, peered around.

And saw nothing. Just rows and rows of graves. And the road, twisting away to the right and disappearing into the darkness as it circled down to the gate.

Where was he?

Movement off to the left. She caught it with her peripheral vision. At least she told herself she did. Maybe it was her sixth sense. Maybe it was her intuition. But she knew he was there.

She crept from behind the shed and, keeping low, crossed the road and picked her way through the gravestones.

Five rows in, she stopped and listened. Peered around. Saw nothing. Heard nothing.

It was then that it occurred to her where she was. The fifth row from the road. *Line five.* That's what the old woman had said in the newspaper. And if this was the fifth row from the road, it was just two rows over from the one where the bodies were found.

Clara felt a sudden chill. It was thrilling. She'd wanted her father to take her to the grave, and he'd refused. Although he hadn't actually forbidden her to go, had he? And here she was, just two rows away.

Was that where Jimmy was? If the killer really was returning to the scene of the crime, wouldn't it be that particular grave? The one where the young women were found. Why not? He wasn't anywhere in sight. It was as good a place to start as any.

So where was the grave? If she remembered correctly, it was two rows back from where she was, and closer to the gate. Exactly how close, she wasn't sure. The only thing she knew was it would be four graves higher than the grave of Barbara Burnside. Which would be in this row. So she should stay in this row.

Clara Harper started making her way toward the gate, trying to stay in line five. It was hard, because the row wasn't entirely straight. Sometimes a choice had to be made—was the grave in the row that one or that one? Of course she was distracted by the fact that she was constantly looking around, trying to spot Jimmy Potter. And she had to read all the gravestones, looking for the name Barbara Burnside. She was so wrapped up in what she was doing she almost went by it.

The crime scene ribbon saved her. Once she spotted that, the Barbara Burnside gravestone was no longer an object.

So, this was it.

This was the murder scene.

This was where the two young women had been found.

Clara Harper slipped under the crime scene ribbon, crept up to the grave. Knelt down in front of the headstone.

"Hi."

Clara jumped. Blood drained from her face. The voice had come from behind her. She turned her head. Looked up.

Jimmy Potter towered above her. He looked gigantic, silhouetted in the bright moonlight. He was smiling, a smug, enigmatic smile.

He was holding the knife.

59

THE REYNOLD'S RIDE DRIVER WASN'T CONVINCED. "LADY, YOU SURE this is where you wanna go?"

"Yes, I am," Cora Felton said.

"But the gate's locked. There's no one here."

"I can see that. You think I can't see that?"

"And you don't want me to wait?"

"I don't know how long I'll be."

"I could wait."

"I'm not paying you to wait."

"How are you going to get home?"

Cora Felton ignored the question, rummaged through her purse. "Now, where's my money?"

"If you don't have money, lady, I'll need to take you to someone who does."

"I've got money. Where's my money?" Cora Felton came up with a wallet. "Oh, here we are. Now, how much was the ride?"

"Eight dollars. Don't you remember? You argued about it."

"Well, such a short ride." Cora Felton pulled a ten out of the wallet, thrust it at the driver. "Here you go. Keep the change."

"Eight bucks is too much so you're giving me ten?"

"Not your fault. You gotta eat."

Cora Felton jerked open the door.

"Lady, I don't like leaving you here."

"I'll be fine," Cora Felton said. She climbed out of the car, slammed the door. Took a step and staggered.

The driver, watching through the rearview mirror, frowned, killed the engine, opened his door.

Cora Felton saw him getting out. She waved her finger in his face. "No, no, no. You can't stay here. You have to go." She nodded at him as if he were a small child. "Santa Claus won't come if we stay up and watch."

"Lady—" the driver protested.

"Go on," Cora Felton said. She waved her hand. "Go, go, go."

The driver reluctantly drove off.

Cora Felton watched him go. Then she walked up the road to the front gate and climbed the fence.

She had trouble getting over. Her purse snagged on a nail and held her back. At first she wasn't aware of it, wondered why she was making no progress. When she realized, she had to climb back down to unsnag it, and start all over again.

The second time she made it over but lost her balance, and fell to the other side, landing in an undignified heap. She got up, brushed herself off, straightened her glasses, adjusted her clothes. By the time she finished she'd managed to smear dirt on just about everything.

Cora Felton took no notice. She got her bearings, set off through the cemetery. The cool night air was helping to clear her head. Though she still staggered, it seemed easier now to focus her thoughts.

She knew why she was here.

She knew what she had to do.

If only she had a cigarette.

Cora Felton's sense of purpose wasn't a hundred percent, but she was getting better.

Cora leaned against a tombstone, rummaged through her purse. Came out with a twisted pack of cigarettes. She extracted one, tried to light it, using the matches she'd had the presence of mind to fish out of the cigarette machine when she'd gotten off the phone at the Country Kitchen. Though the cigarette burned, it would not draw. She lit four matches before she noticed the cigarette was broken in the middle. She broke it in half, threw the filtered end away, lit the remaining half and sucked in the smoke.

Okay, where was the grave?

Cora Felton knew approximately. It was just a few rows up and a million rows over. She sure hoped she could find it without starting from the beginning. Surely she didn't need to do that. Surely she'd recognize the gravestone. Surely she could find it in the dark.

Counting was a problem. She thought she was counting, but lost track. She didn't want to start over, didn't have the patience, perhaps realized it wouldn't do much good. She stumbled on, looking for the stone.

Unfortunately, there was no crime scene ribbon to guide her.

Cora Felton wasn't looking for the grave where the young women had lain.

She was looking for the grave where the murder weapon was found.

So she had to look at every stone. At least, when she got near. And how did she know if she was even near when she kept losing count? Was it this one here, or that one there, or—

He appeared in front of her, abruptly, stepping from behind a gravestone into the moonlight. He was not that big, not that tall, not that menacing.

"Well, Miss Felton," he said.

Cora Felton stopped short, swayed for a moment, nearly lost her balance. She steadied herself, looked at the young man standing in front of her. "Hello, Mr. Tanner," she said. "Frankly, I didn't think you'd come."

Stuart Tanner smiled back. "Ah, but you made the invitation so attractive. And so intriguing. On the one hand, it sounded like a trap. On the other hand—and I do beg your pardon—but on the other hand, you sounded somewhat drunk."

Cora Felton's cigarette was almost burning her fingers. She took a last drag, threw it on the grass. "Not drunk enough. The problem is, they shut you off."

"I still don't understand. Would you please tell me why you called me and asked me here?"

"To discuss the crime."

"I don't understand."

"I think you do."

"Well, I don't. You said you'd solved the puzzle. What did you mean by that?"

"Just what I said. I figured it out. I know why you took off their shoes."

"Why *I* took off their shoes?"

"Yes. I know why you did it."

"I didn't do anything."

"Oh, but you did. You killed that poor girl from Muncie, and you killed your wife. You would have killed others if it weren't for the clue."

"What clue?"

"The clue that wasn't a clue," Cora Felton said. *"Four d line five."* She rubbed her forehead, added a smudge of dirt to the one she had on her cheek. "Turns out it had something to do with math. I'm not sure what."

"What are you talking about?"

"I'm not sure." Her eyes glazed slightly, then refocused. "It doesn't matter. Whatever it is, the point is, she wrote it herself."

"She what?"

"She wrote it herself. The girl wrote it herself. So it never was a puzzle clue."

"I'm sorry to say you're not making any sense, Miss Felton."

" 'Course not. Puzzle makes no sense."

Cora Felton dug in her purse, pulled out the cigarette pack. She took a cigarette broken in the middle, ripped the filter off, dug out the matches, and managed to get it lit.

Stuart Tanner watched her patiently. As she blew out a puff of smoke, he said, "Miss Felton, you're not well. Why don't you let me take you home?"

Cora Felton smiled. "You know, that's what Henry said."

"Henry?"

"My fourth husband. I met him at a party. He said, why don't you let me take you home. And I did." She smiled at the remembrance.

Stuart Tanner held out his hand. "Come on. Let's go."

She waved it away. "No. Here. Gotta be here. Where it happened."

"Why?"

"Huh?"

"Why does it have to be here?"

Her face clouded. "Can't remember."

"Uh huh," Stuart Tanner said. "I thought you had something to tell me. Apparently you don't."

Cora Felton put up her hand. "Shoes."

"Huh?"

"It was the shoes. Wanted to tell you about the shoes."

"What about them?"

"I know why you took them off. That's the real puzzle. Why you took off their shoes. The same reason you put their bodies here."

"I tell you, I didn't do anything."

Cora Felton put up both hands. "Okay. Sorry. Let's say *the killer.* We won't say *you're* the killer. We'll just say *the killer.*" She smiled brightly. "How is that?"

"You're trying my patience. Start making sense or I'm going home."

"And leave me here? I don't think so. Don't you want to know what I know?"

"What do you know?"

"I know why you did it. Sorry. I know why *the killer* did it." Cora raised her finger, pursed her lips. "Say the killer was married. And say the killer had outside interests. Perhaps someone he met in the city where he worked. Say the killer loved this woman, but the killer didn't want to leave his wife, because the killer's wife had money. Money and property she'd inherited from her father. Including a valuable inn." Cora crinkled up her nose. "You see the problem? It's *your* wife we're talking about. I can keep saying *the killer,* but it's still *your* wife. You see what I'm saying?"

"You're not saying anything. You're just rambling. I thought you were going to tell me about the shoes."

"Oh, yes. The shoes. I know why you took them off. Very simple. To create the Graveyard Killer."

"To what?"

"To invent a killer of young women. So your wife could be one of them. A victim of the Graveyard Killer." Cora Felton took a deep drag on the cigarette, blew out the smoke. "That was the point of the shoes. The women would be found in the cemetery with their shoes off. The link that ties them together. You took Dana's shoes off so if the cemetery became too dangerous you could dump your wife's body somewhere else. She'd still be a young dead woman with no shoes. And there'd be a connection. You were desperate for a connection. To make your wife part of a series. That's why you would have killed more women, except for the puzzle clue."

Stuart Tanner's face was hard. "What about it?"

Cora Felton took a drag, burned her finger. She yelped and tossed the cigarette butt on the ground. "You don't have a real cigarette, do you? One that isn't broken."

"What about the clue?"

"Oh. You saw it in the paper. Me. On page one. That must have given you a turn. After seeing me at the town meeting. You're about to kill Vicki and here's a friend of hers helping the police." Cora Felton nodded almost approvingly. "Lesser man might have been scared off. But you're a nervy guy. Had to be, chances you took. Typing the clues. Planting the murder weapon. Sticking the letter in my mailbox. Cool as ice."

"You were talking about the clue," Stuart Tanner said patiently.

"Right. That's your link. You saw it in the paper. Crossword puzzle clue. *Four d line five equals queue.* Stupid, stupid, stupid. But if other clues tied in, formed a pattern, there you are. So you made a puzzle. *Queue* is a letter. You took three more words that were letters and spelled *quit.* Sent one to the paper, left one with your wife's body, and another with the murder weapon. Which was very good. It meant you didn't have to kill anybody else."

Cora Felton shook her head. "Only it won't fly." She shrugged. "Not a puzzle clue. And even if it were a puzzle clue, it's different from the rest. One's pen and one's typewriter." She waved her hand. "But that's the least of it. *Four d line five equals queue.* Who says it does? It could mean anything. But the other three clues—they're so simple even I can do 'em. You see what I mean?"

"Interesting theory," Stuart Tanner said. His hand was in his jacket pocket. "Who have you discussed it with?"

"Uh oh." Cora Felton cocked her head. "You bring a hammer just in case?"

"Don't be absurd. It's late, you're rambling, we need to go home."

"No."

"Yes. Come on. Let's go home."

"Need a cigarette," Cora Felton said. She fumbled in her purse.

Stuart Tanner took a step toward her. His hand came out of his jacket pocket. He had something in it. Something small, dark, and hard.

Cora Felton didn't wait to see what it was. She pulled a gun out of her purse, stuck it in his face. "I said *no*. Why is it you men never understand when a woman says no?"

There came a screech of tires from outside the cemetery's front gate. Car doors slammed.

Cora Felton turned her head.

Stuart Tanner lunged. The sap in his hand chopped down on Cora Felton's fingers. Cora cried out, dropped the gun. It fell to the ground in front of her. She dove for it, but Stuart Tanner beat her to it. He scooped it up, scrambled to his feet.

Cora Felton gaped up at him. There was no mistaking his intent, but there was nothing she could do. She raised her hand.

He raised the gun.

"No!"

It came from the darkness. A young girl's voice.

It distracted him. Just for an instant, but that was enough.

Before Stuart Tanner could fire, a shadow shot from the darkness, hurtled through the air. Grabbed Stuart Tanner by the shoulders, and pulled him to the ground.

The gun fell beside the gravestone. Cora Felton pounced on it, picked it up, staggered to her feet.

Chief Harper, Sherry Carter, and Aaron Grant all came rushing up as Cora Felton leveled the gun at Stuart Tanner, struggling in the arms of young Jimmy Potter.

60

CLARA HARPER'S EYES WERE BRIGHT. "DID YOU *SEE* HIM, DADDY? DID you *see* him? He's a hero, Daddy. A real hero. I mean, did you *see* him?"

"I saw him," Chief Harper said. He was somewhat preoccupied by the fact he'd left his handcuffs in the car and had no means to restrain the prisoner as he wrestled him toward the front gate. Fortunately, Stuart Tanner had given up struggling, overwhelmed by the presence of so many people in the moonlit graveyard. Still, Chief Harper was not entirely comfortable holding the prisoner with one hand and his flashlight with the other while being distracted by his ebullient daughter.

"He didn't just knock him down," Clara said, "he held him too. Did you see how he held him?"

"Yes, I did," Chief Harper said. He wished Jimmy Potter were holding him now. Jimmy was helping Aaron Grant and Sherry Carter with Cora Felton. After holding together for her big scene, Cora had collapsed and all but passed out. This had alarmed Jimmy Potter, who thought Stuart Tanner must have hurt her in some way. Sherry and Aaron calmed Jimmy down, and the three of them were now assisting Cora Felton from the graveyard.

"No problem," Cora Felton mumbled. "Can walk. Why you all think I can't walk?"

"Of course you can," Sherry agreed. "It's all right. It's all over, and we're going home."

"Gotta talk to the cop," Cora said. She had not yet spoken to Chief Harper.

"We'll talk to him," Aaron Grant said.

"You don't know."

"Fill us in."

Cora Felton shook her head. "Tell him myself."

They reached the front gate, where Chief Harper was working out the logistics of getting Stuart Tanner over the fence. He couldn't let Stuart go over first—on the other hand, he didn't want to go over first and leave Stuart alone inside.

Fortunately, at that moment a police car pulled into the driveway and Dan Finley got out. He spotted Chief Harper framed in his head-lights, waved his arms. "Hey, Chief. What's up?"

"Got your handcuffs?"

"Sure do."

"Good. I got a prisoner for you."

Chief Harper boosted Stuart Tanner over the fence to Dan Finley, who quickly and efficiently handcuffed him and stuck him in the back of his police car.

Chief Harper helped his daughter over the fence, then helped the others with Cora Felton.

"Can do it myself," Cora said, but it was clear that she couldn't, and they all lent a hand getting her over.

Another car pulled up to the gate, screeched to a stop. This time it was Ellen Harper. She rushed from the car nearly hysterical at the flashing police lights and all the activity.

"Dale! Dale!" she yelled to her husband. "Where is she? What happened?" Then she saw her daughter. "Clara! Oh, my God, Clara!"

"Mom!" Clara yelled. She rushed to her, fell into her arms.

Chief Harper watched and sighed deeply. After holding himself together for so long, he could feel the tension drain out of him.

Someone grabbed him by the arm. He turned to find Cora Felton peering up at him.

"Miss Felton," he said. "Are you all right?"

She waved her hands at Sherry Carter and Aaron Grant, who stood on either side of her. "All anybody asks is if I'm all right."

"I'm sure you are," Chief Harper said. "Well, congratulations. You solved the case."

Cora Felton waggled her finger at him. "No, no, no. *You* solved the case. Arrested the killer at the scene of his crimes."

"Uh huh," Chief Harper said dryly. "And just how did he happen to be here?"

"Called him. Told him to come." She shrugged. "You gotta explain the puzzle clues. Why you withheld them, what they really mean."

"And what is that?"

"Nothing. Tanner made 'em up to invent a Graveyard Killer. When you found out the first clue was phony you knew what he'd done."

"No, I didn't."

"Sure you did. That's why you had me call him and ask him to meet me here. It was a setup. And you wanna know the payoff?" Cora Felton raised her finger and almost lost her balance. But she was so into what she was saying she didn't even notice. "Asked him to meet me where we found the murder weapon. Which proves he did it. Only the murderer knew where that was."

"Right," Chief Harper said. "Why would he ever agree to meet you there?"

"Don't be silly. It's not like I let him argue it. I told him where to meet me and hung up."

"But showing up was an admission of guilt."

"So what? He wasn't going to let me leave alive. And calling him showed him I already knew." Cora Felton looked around. "His car's not here, is it?"

"No."

"Didn't think so. Be on a side road somewhere. Same place he parked when he dumped the two bodies. And planted the murder weapon."

"What about the letters? They weren't typed on his machine."

" 'Course not. Typed them in New York. Probably in a store. Went in, used the demonstration model. Except for the last one. Typed that somewhere else."

"In the library," Chief Harper said.

"Is that right?" Cora Felton nodded. "That fits. Some typewriter everyone had access to. Went in there in broad daylight, typed it up bold as brass. You can ask the librarian. She'll remember him, comin' in with his wife newly dead. Good. All the more reason you figured it out."

Chief Harper scratched his head. "Look, I appreciate what you're trying to do, but there's no way I can tell this story and leave you out."

She waved her hand. "No big deal. Matter of emphasis."

"Huh?"

"It's all right, Chief," Aaron Grant said. "I can handle it. It's all in how I write it up. Yes, she's part of the story. But the story is you solved the case. And the Barbara Burnside accident."

Chief Harper stared at him. "What?"

"Kevin Roth. Vehicular homicide. He was driving Barbara Burnside's car at the time of the crash."

"*Roth* was driving?"

"That's right. Apparently, Kevin Roth wrote that letter to me warning us off, then freaked out when Dan Finley tried to serve a warrant. Sam Brogan has him in custody."

"For the Barbara Burnside accident?" Chief Harper shook his head. "I'm afraid the statute of limitations may have run out on that."

"Well, I wouldn't worry about it." Aaron jerked his thumb at Sherry Carter. "He also tried to assault her."

"He *what?*"

"That's right. He was after her aunt, of course, but she wasn't home. He came at her with a gun. Actually fired it once. You'll have a lot of things to charge him with."

"I'll be damned."

"At any rate," Aaron Grant said. "That arrest is a direct result of a police investigation you authorized, culminating in securing a warrant. Which is how I'll be writing it up."

"Uh huh," Chief Harper said. "Is there anything else I should know?"

"Plenty. Miss Felton can fill you in. Right now I gotta make a phone call." Aaron Grant jerked the cellular phone from his jacket pocket, punched in the number of the paper. It rang six times before Bill Dodsworth came on the line.

"Make it fast. I'm goin' home," the editor growled.

"No, you're not," Aaron Grant said calmly. "I got your lead story. They caught the Graveyard Killer."

"You're kidding!"

"I'm not. Hold the front page, I'll be right there."

"Well, don't kill yourself. We already went to press."

"Then stop the presses."

"Are you kidding me? The paper's bein' run. Now look, you did a good job, this is a big story, you take your time, you write it up for tomorrow."

"No, I don't."

"What did you say?"

"I write it now. And you go down and stop the presses and retool the front page with the headline GRAVEYARD KILLER CAUGHT. Subheadline, CHIEF HARPER NABS KILLER, CRACKS BARBARA BURNSIDE CASE."

"Barbara Burnside? Are you nuts? You can't mention Barbara Burnside. Her father's on the warpath. He'll sue the pants off of us."

"Well, he'll love you for this."

"No, he won't. The paper's goin' to bed and I'm goin' home."

"Suit yourself. I'll be in in fifteen minutes with the story. You can either stop the presses and put it on page one, or you can go home, turn on the TV, and watch Channel 8."

"Channel 8?"

"Yeah. Rick Reed's doing a feature on the eleven o'clock news on how the Puzzle Lady's a lush and Chief Harper should be taken off the case."

"So?"

"So now you got your choice. You let Rick Reed run his feature while you're busy going back to press, then you make him look like a moron tomorrow morning when you undercut him with my story of how Chief Harper and Cora Felton duped everyone including him when they played an act to set a trap for the killer.

"Or you can go home, turn on the eleven o'clock news, and watch Rick Reed interview me. 'Cause I'm breaking this story one way or another."

Aaron Grant slipped the phone back in his pocket, looked around.

At the foot of the driveway, Clara Harper was talking animatedly to her mother, undoubtedly telling her about Jimmy Potter's heroics.

Cora Felton and Chief Harper were huddled together getting their stories straight.

Sherry Carter stood off to one side.

Aaron went up to her. "I gotta get to the paper. I know you need a ride home, but I gotta write this up."

"Go ahead. I'll be fine."

There was something in her tone. He hesitated, then said, "You wanna come with me?"

She looked up. "What?"

"You wanna come with me to the paper? Help me go over this? See if there's anything I missed?"

Sherry Carter looked at him. She squinted her eyes. Opened her mouth. Shook her head. "I don't think so," she told him.

Aaron Grant frowned. "What's the matter?"

Sherry lowered her eyes for a moment, then looked up at him. "I called you tonight. You weren't at the paper, so I called you at home."

"Oh."

"Yeah," Sherry said. "Oh."

"So that was you. I kind of figured it was."

"Yeah, that was me. You never mentioned your living arrangements."

"Yeah, I know. I guess I was embarrassed."

"Embarrassed?"

"Well, sort of. Particularly with you being from New York."

"I beg your pardon?"

"I know you're all sophisticated and all that. If you lived here, it wouldn't seem so bad."

"Oh, is that right?"

"Yeah, that's right. You know what houses go for in this town. Maybe I'm a little old to live with my parents, but in Bakerhaven that is not so unusual."

Sherry gaped at him. "You live with your parents?"

"I'm gonna get my own place, but I'm just starting out. I've only been out of college a year, and— Hey, what's the matter?"

Sherry had gasped and turned away. And everything she'd been holding on to for so long—Dennis, the media, and her aunt—all that tension had suddenly been released in the wave of emotion she felt, the rush of joy in hearing he lived with his parents.

She turned back to him and her eyes glistened. "I'd be glad to come with you to the paper. If you wouldn't mind taking me somewhere when you're done."

"Sure thing. Where do you want to go?"

Sherry glanced across the road where Chief Harper had joined his wife and daughter, was hugging them both in relief.

She looked at Aaron and her smile was wistful. "You happen to know where the Burnsides live?"

SOLUTION

B	O	N	O		A	C	R	E			R	A	N
A	K	I	N		S	H	E	W	S		P	O	L	O
B	A	K	E	R	H	A	V	E	N		R	A	I	D
E	Y	E		E	O	N	S		A	B	O	D	E	S
		H	A	R	T		T	R	E	S			
D	E	C	A	D	E		W	H	I	T	E	C	A	P
E	N	E	M	Y		B	R	A	N		C	O	L	A
A	D	A	M		P	R	O	N	G		U	N	I	T
L	O	S	E		R	I	N	K		S	T	A	V	E
S	W	E	R	V	I	N	G		M	O	O	N	E	D
		H	I	V	E		C	A	R	R			
C	I	N	E	M	A		L	O	N	E		D	I	E
A	R	E	A		T	H	E	H	U	S	B	A	N	D
R	E	A	D		E	A	G	E	R		A	N	T	E
E	S	T		T	O	N	E		N	E	O	N	

About the Author

PARNELL HALL has been nominated for the Edgar, the Shamus, and the Lefty Awards for his mysteries. Bantam will publish his second Puzzle Lady mystery, *Last Puzzle and Testament,* in fall 2000. He lives in New York City.